Y0-ARV-470

A PATHWAY TO HEAVEN

This work was published in French
under the title *Le Fil de la Vierge*,
copyright 1951, Librairie Plon.

A PATHWAY TO HEAVEN

by

HENRY BORDEAUX

Translated by

ANTONIA WHITE

PELLEGRINI & CUDAHY
NEW YORK, NEW YORK

TO

THE ABBÉ CALÈS

CURÉ OF TENCIN

my contemporary and my old friend, for whose first exhibition of pictures, at the Galerie Dewambez in October 1919 I wrote the preface, I dedicate this book. Both as a painter and a priest he has furnished certain traits for my hero who loved the Light . . . hence the Truth . . . hence God.

H. B.

LE MAUPAS. ALL SAINTS' DAY, 1950

LIBRARY OF CONGRESS CATALOG CARD NUMBER: 52-12382

MANUFACTURED IN THE UNITED STATES OF AMERICA
PUBLISHED SIMULTANEOUSLY IN CANADA
BY GEORGE J. MCLEOD, LTD., TORONTO

CONTENTS

There is nothing nobler nor more religious than good painting for nothing stimulates devotion so much as the difficulty of attaining a perfection which, by mirroring the divine, unites man to God.

MICHELANGELO

I

OUR LADY'S TUMBLER

YOU PROBABLY KNOW the story of Our Lady's tumbler. In case you do not know it or have forgotten it, it runs like this. A tumbler became a monk and observed with humble admiration how his brothers in religion consecrated their talents to the glory of the Mother of God. Finding himself too ignorant to produce such work as theirs, he shut himself in the chapel and, as an offering in Our Lady's honour, performed the acrobatics which had once enchanted the crowds in the fair-ground in front of her statue. The prior, spying through a keyhole or a crack in the door, saw him turning his somersaults and thought his novice must suddenly have gone mad. He was about to intervene and put an end to this scandal when he saw the Virgin's statue come to life, descend the altar steps and wipe away the sweat from the tumbler's forehead with a fold of her blue cloak.

This golden legend has inspired poets, novelists and musicians. It has even invaded the realms of Comic Opera. In the seminary at Bellerive it had provided the clerical students with a nickname for one of their colleagues, Calixte Merval. This young Abbé had no aptitude for theological controversies and was as lost in the intricacies of St. Thomas's *Summa* as in the depths of a dark forest. He could only recover his fervour in the presence of the sun rising over the lake or of evening falling in the woods.

There he could see God in the splendour of his creation and, with the brushes and paints he had smuggled in, even attempt to capture that light, along with the landscape it illuminated, on scraps of canvas or cardboard, and bring it back to his cell. Everyone laughed at Calixte Merval's daubs. Even in the kindergarten of his native village, his little companions had already contemptuously christened him the "artist" because, though he sketched them in his exercise books, he preferred to draw hills and trees. Later he was to become known as the "tumbler" and, at the unfortunate outset of his ecclesiastical career, a tumbler whose antics were regarded as the reverse of pious.

Calixte Merval was ordained only after considerable delays and it was some time before he was promoted to the office of assistant priest in the parish of Fontaine-Couverte. During the intervening period he had been drawing-master in a church school. He was withdrawn from this post because his personal popularity was exceeded only by the wild unconventionality of his teaching. The Curé of Fontaine-Couverte, the Abbé Préfixe, regarded his new assistant at first with surprise and soon with hostile suspicion. No heavenly personage, not even the humblest painter ever admitted by St. Peter, ever went out of his way to encourage the efforts of this ecclesiastical art student.

Nevertheless he had speedily acquired one of those reputations for eccentricity whose precious result is to liberate their possessor from professional duties and social routine. He was, however, incessantly hounded down by the remorseless vigilance of his superior and of the latter's sharp-tongued housekeeper. He had vainly attempted to turn the presbytery into an aviary, for he had a passion for birds. He loved goldfinches, chaffinches, canaries and, best of all, those tiny Bengalese birds with feathers bright as flame. He spent most of his time rambling about the country-side and by no means always with the object of visiting the sick or helping the poor. Very often indeed he was content just to worship the Lord in the running water which mirrors the sky, in the movement of clouds and windswept trees, in the solitude of the mountain where His presence seemed so close. Most of all was he aware of that presence in the light which gives new life to tree, sky and water: to all the forms and textures of the natural world. But on his return from these communions with the Creator and His creation he would be heartbroken to find the cages empty and the prisoners flown. However, there were gentle and sentimental creatures among them who had acquired the taste for captivity and returned to it of their own accord.

One day he dared to risk the introduction of a still more unwelcome visitor. This was a charming little marmoset which he smuggled in as a "West Indian squirrel." The result was that all his birds and beasts were ignominiously dismissed from the presbytery and forbidden to set paw or claw in it ever again.

A still more serious disagreement was destined to separate the Abbé Merval from his vicar, now promoted to Archpriest. As a result of some highly successful collections for the purpose, the latter had caused some coloured statues for his church to be sent from one of those flourishing shops which sell pious objects in the neighbourhood of St. Sulpice. The statues, representing St. Joan of Arc, St. Francis of Sales, the Curé d'Ars and St. Thérèse of Lisieux, were typical of that execrable 'repository art' for which the adjective 'Sulpician' was contemptuously coined. Their inauguration was celebrated with much pomp in the parish church of Fontaine-Couverte and the plaster monstrosities were placed on pedestals on both sides of the aisle to right and left of the high altar. The sight of their crude, gaudy colours was a painful affliction to the eyes of the Archpriest's assistant. At the sumptuous meal which followed the ceremony and which was attended by priests from other parishes, he dared to make an open protest. He went so far as to declare that this pious masquerade was an insult to the saints and that he would have preferred plain white statues or, better still, ones with the greenish tinge of old bronze. He told the people sitting near him that he could guarantee to reproduce this with the copper-sulphate they used in the village to spray the vines. This sally was highly appreciated by the lower end of the table to which his humble rank assigned him. The Abbé Rameau, who was Curé of Arvillard, half approving of Merval's revolt against convention, laughingly defied him to go ahead and carry out his audacious suggestion.

"Don't tempt me," implored the Abbé Merval. "I'm capable of taking on the bet."

"I'll take the responsibility," broke in the new assistant at Bellerive. He was promptly scolded by the Abbé Rameau who, on second thoughts, was alarmed by the dangerous suggestion he had just made.

It was, indeed, a most disastrous wager. The next day, the junior parish priest of Fontaine-Couverte rose at crack of dawn, long before his first Mass was due and went off to visit a neighbour who had a vineyard. He borrowed a syringe full of copper sulphate and copiously sprayed the four statues with the wash intended to protect the vines from blackroot and mildew. The strident colours of the statues were replaced by a discreet greenish-grey, strongly reminiscent of a German soldier's uniform. The only drawback was that now they all looked exactly alike and it was difficult to distinguish the Curé d'Ars from St. Francis of Sales or Joan of Arc from the Little Flower. By losing the gaudy colours of their robes they seemed to have lost the only clue to their various identities. When Monsieur Préfixe, the Archpriest, entered his church to celebrate High Mass, he noticed nothing at first, as the statues were invisible from the high altar and he had his back to the congregation. However, when he turned round to bless the faithful, he fancied he noticed on the faces of certain particularly prized sheep of his flock an expression of annoyance or amazement. He did not pay much attention to this at the time, being too deeply absorbed in his Mass. But when he returned to the sacristy, he was besieged by devout ladies and implored to come and see the disaster. What sacrilegious hand had produced this shocking metamorphosis? Flinging up his arms in horror, the Curé swept into the presbytery like a whirlwind, calling on his housekeeper and his assistant to witness this monstrous camouflage which, in his eyes, was nothing less than a four-fold murder.

"Who can the miserable wretch possible be?"

"You won't have to hunt for him, Father. I am the guilty person," said the Abbé Merval, rushing on his fate. "I simply could not tolerate these offences to sculpture."

"To *what*?"

"To art . . . to beauty . . . to God, in fact."

"Monsieur l'Abbé, you have evidently taken leave of your senses. This is the last straw. Kindly pack your belongings and go."

Thus icily dismissed, the poor confused 'tumbler' tied up his clothes in a bundle and thrust his despised daubs and sketches into an old school satchel. Since he was destined always to be misunderstood, he wondered what would happen to him now? No doubt it was possible to serve God without surrounding oneself with birds and squirrels—even "West Indian" ones—and without painting Sulpician statues green. But what could a priest do who felt suffocated in the atmosphere of the sacristy and could only pray wholeheartedly out-of-doors? Only the sight of natural colours inspired him to devotion; travesties which passed for pious art not only offended his eyes but oppressed his spirit.

He decided to go back to Bellerive to ask to be sent to another parish, preferably in the mountains, where his indiscretions at Fontaine-Couverte might be forgotten. But what sort of a reception would he have after the Archpriest's report which was sure to be on its way and would probably arrive before him? His shocking behaviour would be denounced to the authorities in no uncertain terms. Monseigneur Hélouard who had been Bishop of the diocese for many years was an old man and a severe one. He was, moreover, so totally devoid of imagination that he had only to appear in the doorway of his reception room to turn that apartment into a refrigerator. The Abbé Merval felt an icy cloak descend on his shoulders at the mere thought of the interview. How would he ever dare to confront his redoubtable Bishop?

Luckily, he could count on one supporter in the Bishop's camp. He had had one friend at the seminary who had always defended him when the other students were witheringly sarcastic about his theological denseness and his attempts at painting. The Abbé Camille de Servières had been summoned to the Bishop's house and appointed, in spite of his youth, Vicar-General of the diocese. He was the last branch of an ancient family tree whose roots went back to the days when the great cathedrals were built. By the time the sap of that tree had reached his veins, it was almost exhausted. His ascetic leanness made his tall, weak-jointed body seem taller still so that he reminded one of a long stalk, swaying in the lightest breeze and barely able to support the weight of its flower. His pallor was almost transparent, like alabaster, and his spirituality seemed to shine through it. At certain moments, when he was saying Mass or meditating on divine things, this inner light would even warm his hollow cheeks to the faintest rosy glow.

The Abbé de Servières listened to the story of the terrified 'tumbler' and promised to speak to the Prince of the Church in his favour. After he had introduced his friend into the Bishop's waiting-room, he said, in the old familiar tone of their college days:

"Wait there, Calixte. I'll come in person to present you to His Lordship."

"I warn you, Camille, I'm shaking in my shoes. The

mere prospect makes me feel as if I'd been turned into an iceberg."

The waiting seemed endless. The Abbé Merval had soon exhausted any interest offered by the view from the window which consisted in a canal over which drooped a solitary willow. The tree dipped its long green hair in it and dyed the canal to its own colour but the water was too clear to hide the broken bottles and other rubbish in the mud at the bottom. It is nearly always wiser to keep one's attention firmly fixed on the surface of life and not probe too deeply below it.

"My painting is just the reverse," he thought. "Close to, it seems a confused mass of patches of every colour, thick patches that stand out in relief like bits of sealing-wax or the rough icing on a cake. If you stand a few feet away, these dots and splashes of thick paint become trees and mountains, a sunlit pond or the rushes on the bank of a stream. But perhaps I'm the only person who can see them . . ."

Certainly his paintbox must have been one of the oddest in the world. It contained not a single paintbrush but only a mason's trowel and a palette knife with which he worked up his paint and laid it on the canvas as if he were giving an actual material body to his visions. From close to, it appeared a formless chaos. From a distance the chaos broke up and organised itself like the elements in Genesis; the coloured mass no longer seemed heavy but vibrating with light and life. But no one realised this. People invariably insisted on flattening their noses against his pictures with the result that their reactions ranged from a contemptuous smile to a rude guffaw.

Calixte Merval's very appearance invited people to make fun of him. He was tall, thin and angular. His head looked like that of a victim of the revolution; its proper place seemed already to be at the end of a pike. It was deeply tanned by his open air life and scarred and blistered by wind and sun. The eyelids looked as if they had been scorched and his blue eyes, one of which was set higher than the other, were bloodshot as if they had been worsted in a fight with the sun. His gestures were as angular as his body; the gestures one would have expected from the medieval figures sculptured in the doorway of cathedrals. When he spoke, he expressed himself frankly and colourfully. He used language as if it were a more difficult form of painting. He would raise his hand as if trying to catch the elusive word he wanted and seemed to find it harder to pin down than some difficult effect of light or colour.

How long the Abbé de Servières was taking to come and fetch him! His Lordship must have received the letter of dismissal sent by the Archpriest of Fontaine-Couverte. He must be refusing to listen to the pleading of his Vicar-General. He must be positively adamant against giving even the humblest post to this unworthy priest who had dared to despise the chocolate-box masterpieces of the shop near St. Sulpice, those monuments to the glory of unmistakable, correctly dressed saints. He would pack him off to a Trappist or Carthusian monastery. For Calixte, this would be like being buried alive. How could a man who can only exist in space and air and light ever adapt himself to living in a cell? The mere idea of it made him shudder with nervous terror.

The Abbé Merval removed himself from the window and tried to turn his sad thoughts into another channel. He took a book at random from the shelves, a book whose title pleasantly amused him: *Romantic Landscapes.* As if all landscapes, even the humblest—a courtyard, a garden, the midden in front of a farmhouse—were not romantic! He opened it idly and came across this page which ended the description of a pilgrimage to Beethoven's birthplace:

"From the ramparts of Alte-Zoll on the banks of the Rhine one obtains an extensive view of the river in the direction of both Cologne and Coblentz. From here one may count the seven mountains, or, to be precise, six for the Nonnenstromberg masks the Lœvenberg. Their high conical crests are clothed with woods in which one may distinguish, even from afar, the gold and crimson of autumnal tints. My eyes wander through the sparse leaves of the beech trees, seeking the monastery of Heisterbach which is another stage of my pilgrimage. There, the infant Beethoven began to love trees with that veneration which is so typically Germanic. 'I love a tree more than a man,' the Master was to say one day.

"The monastery of Heisterbach is rich in legends. They rise from the banks of that ancient river like morning mist. My own particular preference is for the tale of the monk who, meditating on eternity, listened to a bird's song for three hundred years and returned to his convent a stranger. Standing on this spot, I can imagine that young monk who had strayed beyond the borders of time, forgetting the world in pursuit of his dream. As Shakespeare says of love:

"*Things won are done: joy's soul lies in the doing.*

. . . . .

Men prize the thing ungained more than it is."

A pursuit that endured for three hundred years! What search for happiness could be more blissful!"

The despised young priest closed the book. He had found in it one tenuous thread of a spider's web that was enough to catch him a fly; he forgot everything that he was waiting for in the Bishop's ante-room. "I love a tree more than a man." Are not trees more natural than men and therefore nearer to what their Maker intended? Men dress themselves up in absurd and extravagant clothes whereas trees give themselves up to the seasons who dress them in spring and summer green, then in autumn red and gold and finally strip them altogether to reclothe them in frost or snow. Whenever Merval passed a beautiful tree, he took off his hat as a sign that he recognised its Creator in the beauty of His works. But, most of all, he envied that monk who for three hundred years had pursued the passing reflection of eternity, never attaining to it and never suspecting the length of his pursuit. That man had been lucky enough not to exercise his ministry in a parish presided over by the Abbé Préfixe. Otherwise he would have been sharply called to order by that formidable Archpriest. How could the latter's ignominiously expelled assistant ever forget his own shortcomings and mishaps? One day when he had been trying to transfer the changing light on the water on to his canvas with a palette-knife, he suddenly remembered the dead man at whose funeral he should have been officiating. He had promptly thrust away his painting, leapt on his bicycle and pedalled breathlessly down the road back to Fontaine-Couverte. The coffin had been discreetly deposited in front of the church door. The grave-diggers had taken possession of one of the neighbouring cafés and the relatives of the other. The frantic ringing of his bicycle-bell had wrenched them from funeral libations worthy of pagan antiquity and they had hastily proceeded to the overdue Requiem Mass. While he was apologising for his lateness, one of the undertakers had comforted him.

"Don't worry, Father. At least our clients won't run away."

But he had had another unfortunate lapse of memory, this time in connection with a wedding. Less patient than the corpse, the bride and bridegroom were complaining at the top of their voices. The outcry was such that the Curé was forced to perform the ceremony in person. When his forgetful assistant eventually arrived, the Curé greeted him with blighting words. If only that absence could have lasted three hundred years! Truly, happiness resided in its own pursuit and, for that reason, one must never give up the chase. Even the monk of Heisterbach had returned from his ecstasy, even if only after three centuries of bliss. He wondered whether a painter could ever hope to attain the light.

The Vicar-General appeared at last to fetch the Abbé Merval who was still lost in reverie over the legend of the monk who forgot time. Camille de Servières' cheeks were faintly red as if an invisible lamp were lit inside his thin diaphanous face. Was this a hopeful sign? It must be, for he was not only looking radiant, but smiling as well.

"We've won, Calixte! You're to be given a parish of your own."

"I simply can't believe it! It must be a very remote parish. Probably somewhere right on the very top of a mountain."

"It's one of the prettiest parishes in the diocese. Absolutely perfect for a painter. It's on the edge of a little green lake, at the end of a beautiful wooded valley. It's also at the foot of mountains that always have snow on them. The colours at Saint-Paul-en-Forêt are quite magnificent. It lies beyond Arvillard and La Colombière and it's sheltered by the rocks of Reclus. They're a goodish way off, but they're a great addition to the landscape."

"I've been there before. It's the most exquisite place."

"Don't be too overjoyed at the prospect. You'll run into difficulties, taking it over after the men who have been there before. Your predecessor, who's just died, was an extraordinary man. A kind of saint. But saints aren't always understood."

"Wasn't that the Abbé Sisteron?"

"Actually, he was a Canon. Also he was formerly the permanent secretary of the Academy of Science and Letters of Bellerive. A scholar whom I used to know very well at one time. I had immense respect for him. He specialised in correcting historical errors."

"What on earth was he doing at Saint-Paul-en-Forêt?"

"I'll tell you. One day he realised the vanity of learning because it so often leads to intellectual pride. He renounced all his works and pomps and he burnt all the manuscripts in which he made mincemeat of the ignorant. Then he came and threw himself at the feet of his Lordship to ask him to give him the humblest parish job that was going. The Bishop did his utmost to keep him but it was useless. So, at his urgent request, he sent him to Saint-Paul-en-Forêt."

"But how could I dare come after a man like that?"

"Don't worry. He was anything but a success."

"You said he was a saint."

"Saints are often more remarkable for their virtue than their influence. Moreover, they sometimes happen to be tactless. Ever since the sixteenth century, Saint-Paul-en-Forêt has been extremely ill-disposed towards our religion."

"Since the sixteenth century?"

"Yes. Three hundred years ago, the Bishop of Bellerive claimed his rights to cut wood which were due to him under ecclesiastical law. The inhabitants refused to allow him and they were deprived of their parish priest. For nearly two hundred years, they celebrated their services themselves and baptised themselves, married themselves and buried themselves without the aid of a priest. After the Revolution, they consented to the Concordat and they were allowed to have a priest again. But they kept up their old resentment, as peasants do, and, to this day, they very seldom go to church. Canon Sisteron was, of course, impatient to bring them back to God. He made no concessions to their ignorance or their prejudices but made one last display of his historical erudition to demonstrate the culpable errors of their ancestors. He abused them so much that the result was to alienate them altogether. I advise you to attract them by the picturesque side of your character rather than by fierce sermons and threats of damnation."

"You can put your mind at rest, my dear Camille. There's nothing I like less than appearing in the pulpit."

"Appear in it but stick to the gospel. Keep up all the country ceremonies—rogation days—the altars for Corpus Christi—processions—blessing their houses and their animals. Get together a young girls' choir. Get them to sing first and pray afterwards. Tell them stories."

"The Golden Legend, in fact."

"Precisely. Lastly, I must also warn you against all the pitfalls which await you."

"You terrify me."

"In your parish, you will find the former Curé of Novel."

"Retired?"

"No. Suspended."

"Suspended? Camille, do you mean he's a heretic?"

"Good heavens, no. Only a drunkard. He's a most impressive man. He looks immensely distinguished and he's as strong as Hercules. His Lordship overlooked his failing as long as he could for this Abbé Chavord once saved his life. It was on a Confirmation tour. The Bishop's carriage would have rolled over a precipice if Chavord hadn't held it back with one arm. But he abused his kindness. One day, when he was going through a Protestant village he was followed by a wagon-load of young people yelling after him and pretending to caw like crows. He stopped the wagon with his two hands—it was drawn by two horses—and pushed it over, complete with everyone in it. The passers-by were so impressed by this feat of strength that they cheered him."

"Well, you won't find me picking a quarrel with *him*," declared the Abbé Merval, amused rather than alarmed.

"He's not a bad man," the Vicar-General went on. "Apparently he wanders round the church without daring to go in. You'd better do your best to avoid running into him. The peasants, in any case, have a particularly bad reputation for immorality. But there are one or two other families that you'll have to be rather chary about getting mixed up with. They're supposed to be inclined towards free-thought as well as free-love. One of them is practically ruined and lives in retirement in a little château. The other consists of an illicit couple who live in a new chalet on the edge of the little lake. It's a bad example in a parish where morals are loose enough already."

"You seem to have it all at your finger-tips, Camille. It's amazing how much you know about my future parishioners."

"My informant is the curate-in-charge you'll find there."

"Do you mean to say I'm to have an assistant? Why, it must be quite an impressive community."

"Don't be alarmed. The person who considers herself as the priest's assistant is a widow. A certain Mme Trabichon. She runs everything in Saint-Paul-en-Forêt, particularly the sacristy and the presbytery."

"She sounds a far more alarming prospect than the Abbé Chavord."

"That's you all over, Calixte. I know exactly what you'll do. You'll make friends with all the people I've suggested you should be wary of and you'll send your well-informed benefactress packing. May God preserve you! Now I'm going to take you in to see His Lordship."

"Do I have to see him? I'm shaking at the very thought."

"There's no getting out of it. I didn't think you were such a coward."

The Vicar-General led him away to the Bishop's study. Monseigneur Hélouard received the new incumbent of Saint-Paul-en-Forêt with that icy look which froze every word on his visitor's lips. After a contemptuous allusion to painting as a frivolous and distracting pastime which he strongly advised him to give up, he made a brief allusion to the schoolboy pranks of which the Archpriest of Fontaine-Couverte had so bitterly complained. Having dismissed these as too childish to be taken seriously, the Bishop proceeded to outline, in a few strong, telling strokes, the life of a priest in an indifferent and even hostile parish. He dismissed him with these words which, in his voice, had the ring of a military command:

"As the new parish priest, I count on you, Father."

The Abbé Calixte withdrew. The interview had gone off better than he had hoped. At least, it had taken an entirely different course. Although he had gone in like a whipped dog whose one desire is to be allowed to run away and play in peace, he had come away with a sense of having encountered an unsuspected greatness. A kind of majesty had emanated from that cold, dry little man. How firm and authoritative his tone had been when he had imposed his duties on him! The Abbé Merval suddenly felt himself unworthy of being a parish priest.

"Well?" the Vicar-General asked him as he returned from his audience with the Bishop. Merval shook his head.

"I can't accept it."

He explained his troubles and his scruples to his friend. To his immense surprise, the Abbé de Servières appeared delighted.

"I knew it," he said, with the smile that lit up his pale face.

"Knew what?"

"That you're ten times better than your reputation. Go in peace and be yourself. Don't try to change your character in the slightest degree. Go to Saint-Paul-en-Forêt and keep on searching for the light . . . the true light . . . the only light there is . . ."

II

THE ARRIVAL AT SAINT-PAUL-EN-FORÊT

"WHAT SORT OF Curé have they sent us this time?" the inquisitive postman asked Perpétue, the housekeeper at the presbytery. Perpétue had been installed as priest's housekeeper at Saint-Paul for innumerable years and had passed from one master to another with complete indifference. She ruled the men of God with a rod of iron and allowed them no authority outside the church.

"You can't call *him* a Curé. More like something out of a circus. He ought to have a job in a menagerie."

"You don't say!"

" 'Pon my word, it's true. He arrived with a black dog and a white cat, a parrot all colours of the rainbow, a squirrel, a monkey and a cageful of birds. You don't suppose I'm going to spend my time looking after all those wretched animals, do you? I've handed in my week's notice already."

"Whatever did he say?"

"He just said 'God will provide.' He had the impudence to compare himself to the lilies of the field. Just fancy! Anyway, there aren't any lilies in these fields."

"There are those lilies they call Martagons, Perpétue."

"After that he went out to make some calls and who d'you think he's talking to at this moment?"

"Haven't the least idea. Do tell me."

"That Rosette Billois whose father's just turned her out because she can't hide her shame any longer."

"Rosette! Whose is he?"

"Who?"

"Why, the baby, of course."

"As if one ever knew with these girls!"

Whereupon the postman went off eagerly to the village and carried the news from door to door.

The Abbé Calixte Merval had arrived two days earlier in a van which contained everything he possessed, including his furniture and his livestock. After being sharply put in his place by the housekeeper who had stormily refused him her services, he had gone out to make his first appearance among his flock. It was true that, as soon as he left the presbytery, he had encountered this Rosette Billois. Carrying a heavy bundle, she was crying as she made her way towards the little café where the bus which ran between Saint-Paul and Bellerive stopped to pick up passengers at the terminus on the mountain road.

"Where are you going, young lady?" he had asked her.

She had answered fiercely:

"I haven't the least idea."

Looking at her more closely, the priest was aware of her condition.

"Is it the town you're going to?"

"To the town or to the lake. I'll go wherever I please."

"Why are you running away?"

"The old man's turned me out."

"What old man?"

"My father, of course."

"And your mother?"

"She's frightened of him."

"And the other one?"

"What other one?"

"Well . . . your young man . . ."

"Oh, him! . . . Why d'you keep asking me questions? Can't you leave me in peace?"

"Well, you see . . . I happen to be looking for someone."

"Someone to do what?"

"To run my house. Can you cook, my child."

"Soup and eggs and potatoes. What a question!"

"That's good enough. And can you wash and sew?"

"There's plenty of us at home."

"Very well, then. Come with me."

"Wherever to?"

"To the presbytery."

"The presbytery! What, *me*?"

She could not help laughing through her tears. She was very young and the invitation seemed wildly absurd to her. A bad girl, a lost girl engaged just like that as a priest's housekeeper! It was too absurd to be true. This man in the cassock was just making a cruel joke at her expense.

She asked nervously:

"Are you the new Curé?"

"Yes, my child. What's your name?"

"Rosette. Rosette Billois."

"Rosette, are you fond of animals?"

"Cows or pigs?"

"No. Birds . . . cats . . . dogs . . . squirrels?"

"Why ever do you want to know, Father?"

"Because you'll be living in their company."

"I prefer them to men anyway. Then you're not joking?"

"About what?"

"About taking me back with you."

"I'm taking you here and now."

"Mademoiselle Perpétue won't half make a face!"

"She won't make it for long. She's leaving me."

"Go on. I can't believe it."

"You're taking on her job."

The girl was young enough to pass swiftly from one mood to another. She had been almost gay during this questioning and had even acquired a taste for life again, in spite of her unhappiness. She bent her head, picked up the bundle she had put down, and made as if to go on her way.

"Goodbye, Father. And thanks very much."

"What are you thanking me for?"

"For your kind thought."

"Are you refusing, then?"

"Of course, Father. Can you see me at the presbytery in this state? The whole village would die of laughing."

"Then let them laugh."

"It'd be you they'd make fun of, Monsieur le Curé."

For a moment, he seemed disconcerted.

"No . . . they couldn't think that. I've only just arrived here. When's the baby due."

"Three months. Maybe a bit more."

"Then we've time to see our way. Is there a midwife here?"

"Yes. A witch."

"Does she take patients?"

"She charges a lot."

"Between now and then, I'll have brought your young man back to you."

"He'll run away."

"And I'll have reconciled you with your family."

"You'd better not count on that, either."

"On your way, Rosette! On your way! I'll help you carry your things."

"Oh no, Father. You can't do *that*!"

The odd couple made a sensational entry into the presbytery. Perpétue was guarding the door watched by two or three interested gossips who had just returned from selling their eggs and vegetables in the market at Arvillard.

"Be off with you," shouted the housekeeper in possession when the young girl, following the Curé like a sheep its shepherd, came within earshot. "We don't take in sluts here."

"Gently, gently, my good woman," broke in the Abbé Merval. "Allow me to present your successor."

"My *successor*!"

Perpétue's mouth twisted as if she were going to have a fit. Such a scandal was inconceivable. She tried to bar their road, then fled to the kitchen where she deliberately upset the saucepan of soup which was simmering on the fire. The black dog barked; the white cat mewed; the squirrel frantically turned his wheel; the terrified birds twittered; the many-coloured parrot repeated the key phrase of the limited vocabulary he had learnt from the nuns at Fontaine-Couverte:

"It's the will of God! It's the will of God!"

The deafening din was not perhaps entirely due to the direct intervention of Providence. In the midst of the tumult, Rosette settled to her new duties. She took over the reins of government with the assurance of an elder daughter whom her mother had left in charge of the house while she herself was busy with the poultry and the cows. Already she could breathe more freely now that she had a home and a job; a job, moreover, which she liked. For the moment, at any rate, she no longer felt a creature in disgrace. Only a little while before, she had been thinking of killing herself. Now she felt overflowing with life; conscious, indeed, of a two-fold life as the child in her womb stirred as if it wanted to anticipate the joy of emerging into the light. She stroked the dog and the cat, smiled at the parrot, gave the squirrel a lettuce leaf and sang with the birds. Then she put on the soup again, peeled the potatoes and stoked up the fire. Overhead someone was dragging furniture about and banging tin trunks. In spite of the Curé's admonitions, Perpétue had refused to sleep under the same roof as this tainted creature. She was leaving that very evening with all her savings. Her capital had been augmented by a compensation which the Abbé Merval had paid her out of money he had borrowed to set up his establishment. That loan was to be a grievous burden on his budget and the Mass stipends of a semi-pagan village were hardly likely to lighten it.

However, the postman had already informed Mme Trabichon, who subscribed to the diocesan magazine, of Perpétue's departure. He had told her that the latter was leaving the priest's house, now transformed into a menagerie. He had also mentioned the indiscreet, even improper conversation the newly-arrived Curé had held on the public highway with an erring sheep who had been driven out of the paternal fold.

The lady, whom the Abbé de Servières had described as the self-appointed curate of Saint-Paul, did not hesitate a moment. She flung on her hat and coat and rushed to the rescue. She found young Rosette installed in the kitchen, singing with the birds while she superintended the soup. The parrot was still reiterating that this shocking state of affairs was the will of God. From upstairs came a noise as of an army of occupation engaged in ransacking the premises. Perpétue was moving furniture and emptying cupboards as she packed her trunks. Meanwhile, the Abbé Calixte Merval, either suddenly afflicted with deafness or naturally impervious to noise, was tranquilly saying his breviary in the garden where the pale April sun was trying to coax out the buds on the fruit trees.

Mme Trabichon was accustomed to command. With one glance of her infallible eye, she sized up the situation and decided that it called for a series of attacks and not for a single full-scale operation. The staircase creaked under her swift but heavy footsteps. She entered the servant's room without knocking.

"Perpétue, whatever are you doing, my dear?"

She always used a certain familiarity in addressing this old servant who, for years, had been as much part of the presbytery as the ivy twined round a tree.

"I'm leaving, as Madame can see for herself," muttered Perpétue angrily.

"Put your clothes and dusters away and follow me."

"Wherever to?"

"To your rightful place. The kitchen."

"But I've given notice."

"To whom, may I ask? Certainly not to me."

"To His Reverence, the Curé."

"To the Curé? He hasn't even consulted me. He hasn't even called on me yet! All this means nothing at all. I guarantee that everything will go on exactly as before. I shall make it my business to see that it does."

Perpétue was reassured. She abandoned her packing and followed the irate, majestically corpulent widow downstairs. At the sight of the two women invading her territory, the song died on Rosette's lips. It simply snapped off, as if it were a straw she had bitten through. The frightened birds stopped singing and the cat fled, but the black dog remained and barked threateningly. Undeterred by this hostility, Mme Trabichon advanced on the usurper.

"What are you doing here, Mlle Billois?"

"Peeling potatoes, Madame."

"Then go and peel them in the barn where you receive your young men. Get out of here, you loose girl. And hurry up about it."

"But His Reverence said . . ."

"*I'm* speaking to you now. Be off with you . . . out into the street, where you belong!"

Dropping her vegetables, Rosette stood up and burst into tears. Was it possible that anyone should insult her like that in public? At that moment, the tall thin figure of the Abbé Merval appeared in the doorway, his breviary still open in his hand. Mme Trabichon promptly turned towards him and attempted an affable smile which consorted ill with her thunderous face.

"Oh, Father. I was just waiting for you."

He gave her a ceremonious bow.

"Your Reverence, the senior assistant priest of Saint-Paul-en-Forêt, I have the honour to present my humble compliments. To what may I attribute the privilege of your presence in the presbytery?"

Completely taken aback by this irony, she lost some of her self-confidence. She was one of those people whose excessive activity creates embarrassing situations for themselves as well as for others.

"I came to do you a service, Father. You can't lose Perpétue like this and take on a . . . an untrained girl in her place."

"Thank you, Madame. But Mlle Perpétue has handed in her resignation and I have already engaged Mlle Rosette."

"You don't know either of them. It's my business to enlighten you."

"I have a horror of being 'enlightened', Madame. What people say about each other is always prejudiced and contradictory. I much prefer not to listen to anyone's opinion and to act as I please."

"But, Father, permit me to point out that you've no idea what you're doing."

"So many things happen without our knowing what we are doing, Madame. Please don't interrupt this child in preparing our modest meal. As to Mlle Perpétue, you will, no doubt, invite her to lunch with you. I'm sure she would infinitely prefer that to sitting at the same table as my new housekeeper. Then everyone will be satisfied. Goodbye, Madame."

"It's the will of God; it's the will of God," the parrot confirmed. Every time the priest stopped speaking, the parrot put in his sentence as if to support him with heavenly approbation.

Mme Trabichon was outmanœuvred. For the first time in her life, she had to leave the presbytery against her will. Ever since her widowhood, she had been received there as an invaluable unpaid helper. Did she not devote the greater part of her time to looking after the church and the sacristy, keeping them clean and aired? Did she not provide flowers and candles for the altar and repair the albs and chasubles and surplices? Was she going to stand for such gross ingratitude? Should she not raise the standard of rebellion?

Should she not threaten this indiscreet priest with episcopal thunderbolts? She was known to all the Canons and Vicars-General in Bellerive. Even His Lordship was by no means ignorant of her existence. She sent considerable contributions to the good work which encouraged priestly vocations and which was doing much to overcome the lack of priests in country districts. Yes, there was no doubt that she might well have left the place with a declaration of war and the threat of an immediate offensive. Yet, in spite of everything, her respect for the cloth overcame her furious indignation. All that she did was to say quietly:

"Come along, Perpétue. There is nothing more for us to do here."

The two women retired with dignity. Rosette, who could whistle like a bullfinch, pursed up her lips to accompany their retreat with this life-like and mocking imitation.

"That's enough," said the Abbé, sharply interrupting her mimicry. "Now hurry up and cook the vegetables. I'm hungry."

He was not altogether pleased with himself. Had he not abused that irony which he hated and which often wounded him when it was turned against himself? Had he not been rude and inconsiderate towards that stout, lively lady who, after all, had only been trying to save him a well-trained housekeeper instead of this unknown girl whose work might be as careless as her morals? He had engaged Rosette without taking even the most elementary precautions. And it had only taken him the time to swallow a barely edible and definitely indigestible meal of her cooking to realise that improvisations are not invariably happy and that charity may bring a host of unsuspected evils in its train. Though not a greedy man, he liked decent wholesome food that had not been ruined by the incompetence of the cook. Like most lean people he enjoyed an excellent appetite while fat ones practise self-restraint with no effect. Ah well, every trade needs an apprenticeship! Rosette was inexperienced and no doubt the morning's emotions had upset her; she would improve of her own accord. He gave up the idea of scolding her and began to ask her about her family and her lover.

Her family consisted of seven children of which she was the eldest. Her father was brutal and miserly and exploited them from the moment they left school; her mother lived in terror of him and dared not defend her offspring. They lived on a small farm on a hillside too stony for much to grow, but they had some pasture up in the mountains where they took the cows in summer. There was a chalet up there where the shepherdess slept. Every day she brought the milk down to the dairy to be made into cheese and butter. It was a life of freedom and in the evenings all the young people in the neighbouring chalets met to sing and dance and tell stories. Boys and girls delighted in these parties and understandings grew up between young couples. Sometimes these led to marriage; sometimes they did not get beyond making love.

"I understand, my child. There was no one to keep an eye on you and you went too far. Why doesn't he want to marry you?"

"He's engaged to another girl."

"Did you know that, Rosette?"

"I knew and I was jealous. It was really because of that . . ."

"This other girl . . . had she done the same thing before you?"

"Neither before nor after, Father. She's a good girl. She lives over at Arvillard. She's a Child of Mary and she leads the choir."

"So you know her, then?"

"Yes, Father. I know her."

"Honestly, I believe you think your lover's right in preferring her to you."

This suggestion made Rosette burst into tears.

"Oh, Father, don't you see how awfully miserable I am? Could anyone be more unlucky?"

"Suppose I were to go and see this girl and tell her the truth."

"No, no. Please don't. There's no point in making *her* miserable too. One's enough."

"What's this young man's name?"

"Pierrot."

"Pierrot what?"

"Pierrot Loriot. In the little village up on the mountain. The one perched right on the top, where they shoe their hens."

"Shoe their hens?"

"That's what people say. Because it's so steep."

"Is he well-off?"

"No, Father. He's only got a tiny bit of land. But he's got strong arms and he's a good shot."

"A good shot. How does that help?"

"He shoots chamois. He's a poacher and he does a bit of smuggling too."

"And the young lady over at Arvillard."

"She's got a big farm. But that's not the reason. They're both very nice-looking."

"Aren't you too, Rosette?"

"I'm not any longer now."

"What did this Pierrot say when he knew about your condition?"

"He said: 'What a nuisance.' Then he went back to his home. Now he avoids meeting me and his marriage has been announced."

"Your father is your natural protector, Rosette. Hasn't he done anything to defend you?"

"He thinks I'm a bad girl who goes with anyone and he's thrown me out like a mangy dog."

"What about your mother?"

"She gave me some money she'd kept hidden away.

Not much. Just a bit of money. And she cried . . . oh, a lot. I expect she's still crying. But that won't alter anything."

"Don't be discouraged, my child. God is always there."

"Where is He?"

"Everywhere. And in our own hearts."

"And is He in the water of the lake that's waiting for me to drown myself in it?"

"Soon you'll have the honour of giving life, of creating, like God Himself."

"I'm not going that far, believe me. Who's going to feed a kid without a father?"

The priest, who had got up and was about to go out, replied with a couplet which was rather beyond her grasp:

> "*The bird in the nest on His bounty depends;*
> *Over all nature His goodness extends.*"

He followed this with a more mundane observation:

"Your coffee was very nasty, Rosette. So was your lunch. You must take a little more trouble. Everyone ought to do his job as well as he possibly can."

How well was he doing his own job, he wondered. Was he a priest or a painter or both at once? Since chance or Providence had assigned him a parish where practically no one went to church, had he not the right to spend his time contemplating light as the monk of Heisterbach had contemplated eternity? To salve his conscience, he asked his new cook, as he stood with his hat on his head and his paintbox and drawing-board under his arm:

"Are there any sick people in Saint-Paul?"

"No, Father. We never have any sick people here."

"People die though, I presume."

"Oh yes. But they don't have doctors or medicine. That's our way."

An excellent way, too, he could not help thinking. The peculiar hygienic habits of Saint-Paul-en-Forêt would spare him interminable visits to people afflicted with colds, gout, rheumatism, asthma, bronchitis and tuberculosis. But he would have to keep a look-out for the dying so as to catch them the moment they were ripe, like fruit on the point of falling and rotting.

Thus reassured as to the physical condition of his flock, he went off to roam about the countryside. Soon he came upon a precocious hawthorn bush which had dared to flower in its sheltered spot though the mountain tops were still thick with snow. The advance of spring and the retreat of winter were proceeding in delightful confusion under the April sun.

III

THE CHAMOIS HUNTER

THE VILLAGE OF Saint-Paul-en-Forêt lies some three or four thousand feet above sea-level and extends up the hillside in tiers of little hamlets. It overlooks the valley of the Dranse; *Dranse* being the local name for all the torrents which are produced by the melting snows. Beyond Arvillard, which is not far from the cheerful town of Bellerive on the bank of its blue lake, the high road runs through a wild, narrow wooded gorge. The end of this widens unexpectedly into a valley, hemmed in by the ranges of La Colombière, Reclus and the Dôme. They form a wall of fir-covered rocks, broken at intervals by passes which cross the Italian frontier and provide excellent opportunities for smuggling. A little lake, round as an eye and set in a wide clearing fringed with beeches, oaks and birches, lies behind Saint-Paul. Its water shows green or black according to the season and the time of day. Fish abound in it and it is so sheltered that people come and bathe in it during the hot weather. A small hotel on its bank invites holiday-makers but the sunniest site is occupied by a comfortable chalet of the Scandinavian type. For part of the year, this was the residence of a M. Belarmont, an amateur musician and a slightly eccentric man who was once wellknown in Paris. At great expense, he had had an organ installed in the main hall and was in the habit of playing it, especially at night when silence favoured his inspiration. His audience consisted of a little operetta singer with the stage name of Arlette Jasmin. Presumably she had left her natural haunts—the theatres of the *boulevards*—and followed M. Belarmont for financial reasons. She could often be heard through the open windows, launching trills of protestation against the great voices of Bach or Saint-Saëns, of Widor or César Franck.

The belfry of Saint-Paul is shaped like a pierced ducal coronet; possibly as the architect's tribute to the family which once lorded it in this oasis. The ancient church had been built for a population which must have declined considerably in the course of centuries. No doubt, in former days, it had been sufficient to fill it before those difficulties had arisen about the Bishop's right to cut trees. Nowadays the impiety, or rather the indifference, of the inhabitants painfully accentuated its unnecessary size. Its central arch was Romanesque, but of that elongated type which seems already feeling its way towards the Gothic ogive. The three altars, decorated in the Italian style in now-faded blue and gold, were dedicated to various saints. The high altar was adorned with St. Peter with his keys and St. Paul with his sword. Over the tabernacle hung a gilded crown. The side altars were consecrated to St. Joan of Arc and St. Francis of Sales. But the glory of its interior was the statue of Our Lady, poised on a granite column at the entrance to the transept. It was a stone statue, dimmed and worn by the centuries, with an elegance worthy of the Virgin at the door of the cloister of Notre-Dame or that gilded Virgin in one of the porches of the cathedral of Amiens. Her face, as exquisite in its freshness as a fifteen-year-old girl's, bends tenderly down, with an expression both maidenly and motherly, over the child Jesus who leans back to look up at her and with a natural, almost comic gesture, puts his finger in his mouth. Here was a work of art which had no need of being sprayed with sulphate! Every time he put foot in God's house, the Abbé Merval never failed to stop and pay her homage. Where had she been discovered, this rare pearl hidden in the mountains? What great artist of the thirteenth century had carved her on the spot or what unknown feudal lord had brought her to Saint-Paul? From the moment he set eyes on her he felt bound to her by a subtle bond, as delicate as the silky floating strands of gossamer country people call "Our Lady's threads" because they can only come from Mary's spindle.

The parish church was surrounded, in the old-fashioned way, by a cemetery. The grass grew among the scattered tombs. Once, vanished generations lingered there on their way out from Mass, associating their dead with their own toils and troubles and even asking their advice. Now the dead were no longer consulted. They rested in peace but they no longer conferred that peace on their descendants. Nevertheless, on All Souls' Day, they received their yearly offering of chrysanthemums and autumn leaves. But it was a pagan offering of bright foliage and flowers and seldom accompanied by any prayer.

Separated from this holy ground only by a country lane stood the presbytery. The priest, returning from saying Mass, had only a few steps to walk before arriving at the trellised iron gate of his little garden. The two-storied house was large and square with five windows in its front: it had a high, broad-eaved slate roof, like a hat made of tiles; a roof pitched steep to prevent the snow piling up on it. It had been built in the eighteenth century; in fact, the date 1760 was inscribed on the doorstep. The upper story had been used as a lumber-room. It was too cold to be habitable in winter and no attempt had been made to furnish any room except one which possessed a porcelain stove and could be used to put up occasional visitors. The new Curé, however, took possession of this floor to hang up his pictures. In this improvised gallery he organised an exhibition of his paintings—a one-man show for a one-man public. The ground floor which was a few steps above the level of the soil, amply sufficed for his daily needs. The kitchen was large and the study, with its view over the dark little lake and the lower slopes of the mountains, larger still. With a little ingenuity, the whole floor could be used during the summer months if he shifted some pieces of furniture and was prepared to ignore the shocking state of the wallpaper. The priest's house at Saint-Paul-en-Forêt compared very favourably with most country presbyteries.

On the same level as this principal hamlet of the Commune but at some distance from the church and the town hall stood a small château surrounded by an ill-kept park. The trees in this park, originally laid out in the English style, were never cut or pruned and the château's decrepit air was more due to neglect than to age. Nevertheless it preserved the sober charm of the houses of bygone days, sunned its old walls to their utmost capacity to keep the mildew out of them and kept the dark woods at bay with lawns and a few clumps of rose-bushes. The Baron d'Aimery and his wife had retired there after the blow which had lost them most of their fortune. The Baron, an ex-cavalry officer, had returned from twenty-five years in charge of a garrison at Reichsoffen, an embittered old man. He had remained a fiery and irascible despot. The Baronne put up with him thanks to her faculty for shutting out the external world and occupying herself entirely in botany and the contemplation of nature. But their daughter Béatrice, who was verging on thirty, could ill endure this solitude in the mountains in spite of her remarkable artistic and intellectual gifts; gifts which she must have inherited from some very distant ancestors.

Down in the lower hamlet stood Mme Trabichon's rather pleasant little house with clematis rioting over the porch and climbing right up to the wooden balcony. Mme Trabichon was the widow of a doctor who had died prematurely as the result of going out one winter night to try and save a patient.

Practitioners of his type were suspect in the village. His brief funeral oration consisted simply of the words: "Why ever did he get up out of his warm bed?" He had never been replaced; the inhabitants had decided that, henceforth, they would die by themselves. His widow had mourned him no longer than decency imposed. Too energetic to remain inactive, she had zealously rushed to the aid of the Abbé Merval's predecessors: She organised various ecclesiastical functions and made the sacristy and the upkeep of the church her special charge. Thus, it had been perfectly natural for her to expect to rule even more securely over the new incumbent of Saint-Paul. When the latter had so promptly and pitilessly dethroned her, she had taken the even more shockingly-treated Perpétue under her own roof. There, the two women, having eaten the chicken destined to welcome the new Curé to his parish, were nursing their vengeance over a cup of coffee. They would not be cheated of that vengeance. That slut Rosette, so frivolously engaged, would execute it for them.

"I don't give him a week before he asks you back again," asserted the widow firmly.

"And suppose I refuse, Madame?"

"Don't get on your high horse, Perpétue. Because you're not going to refuse. We're old, both of us. And we're too used to working for priests to change our ways. Do you imagine I'm going to give up making the church look nice on Sundays?"

"You mean to say you're not angry with this Abbé who's treated us so disgracefully?"

"He's a man of God. I can't be angry with God. Goodness, you and I have even forgotten to say Grace."

She stood up and the other promptly followed her example. The two outraged women thanked the Lord whose ways are not our ways and who employs such peculiar representatives. The chicken they had eaten as a result of this unforeseen circumstance had been extremely succulent.

The Abbé Calixte Merval had given up painting the confusion of spring and winter symbolised by the hawthorn in flower at the foot of still snow-laden mountains. He had taken a path which climbed the side of the hill and passed by the last house of the village, the house of that Pierrot Loriot who seduced young girls and deserted them. An elderly woman, gnarled and bent, dragging a bundle of faggots, had seemed disturbed when he asked her Pierrot's whereabouts.

"What do you want with him? He's my son."

"Just to see him and talk to him."

"He's gone off up into the mountains."

"Perhaps I shall come across him."

The mother followed the priest with anxious eyes. But, already, he had forgotten her. He climbed without realising he was climbing and the higher he went the view widened out more and more like music amplifying itself under the echoing vaults of a cathedral. Below him rolled the torrent, swollen by the melted snow of the first spring thaws. Its monotonous voice resounded like a musical accompaniment to the whole valley. On the side of the mountains, the gauzy clouds which still half-veiled them in the morning broke up and dispersed till soon they were no more than a puff of white floating in the blue. Then the whole landscape lay basking in the clear light, revealing all its contours, its pure lines and shifting colours. It was a symphony of green against the brown background of earth; the sombre green of the firs, the bright green of the fields, the pale fresh green of the corn sprouting near the water at the bottom of the valley. And all these greens were contrasted with the dull white of the rocks and the sparkling white of the snow which crackled on the summits and would soon, at sunset, kindle to violet and rose. The sky was of such a strong, even blue that it seemed almost solid; one of those Italian blues which caress and reassure the eyes.

The Abbé hastily set up his easel, put his canvas on it and took his little trowel out of its sheath. He flung himself like a whirlwind on his paint-box and seized the colours he wanted, picking the tubes up carefully and laying them down lovingly. He must hurry, hurry. Soon the light would no longer be the same. The evening would change it all too soon. He must snatch it just as it was, snatch it and imprison it. No, not imprison it. Let it keep its freedom, let it brush the artist for a moment with its wings and fly back to the throne of God, the creator of all this loveliness. How much beauty He had given to men's insatiable eyes! How could he, a poor man and a poor artist, take possession of all this beauty which belonged only to its creator? One fragment was enough for him. He instinctively chose a little pool at the foot of a slender cascade which fell from a rock half-covered with briars, because it reflected the mountain upside down on an azure ground. It was a tiny mirror of water which contained a world. Soon he was so deep in his work that he was no longer conscious of personal life. He did not hear a shot which shattered the silence of space, that silence in which even the eternal music of the river is lost. Yet the valley had resounded with it and the wall of rocks above him had prolonged its echo. All Merval's consciousness was concentrated in his eyes and in the hand they commanded and directed. Suddenly those eyes supposed themselves victims of a hallucination or rather of some special attention on the part of Providence. The limited landscape which held his whole attention had suddenly acquired life. Like a pedestal, it now carried a statue which completed it. What a charming and gracious image was now presented to him . . . a tiny kid. But no ordinary kid! No young goat ever had hair of that brown so dark that it was almost black; no young goat was ever so supple and elegant or had such slim, delicate legs or such a harmonious body. Its perfectly-proportioned neck ended in the charming lines of the lifted head, already about to sprout its horns. It could be nothing else than a chamois, only a few weeks old. Why was it bleating so plaintively, as if it were terrified? Why was it trembling so convulsively that he could see it even from where he stood? At such a tender age, it ought not to be away from its mother. Where was she and why had she abandoned her baby after giving it birth?

Above the waterfall, something parted the bushes with a brutal movement. What new animal was about to appear? A man armed with a gun now occupied the summit of the scene. He carried, or rather dragged a corpse which was too large and heavy for his hunter's sack. Below him, the terrified kid let itself slide off the stone it had been trying to grip with its four barely-formed hooves and fell into the pool. The water spurted up and splashed the Abbé Merval's canvas. In a moment, the unlucky painter, instead of trying to save his picture, had abandoned it and rushed to the help of the drowning animal. Catching it by the neck, he pulled it out and laid it on the grass. Ought he to attempt artificial respiration? He contented himself with rubbing it all over. The tawny, black-irised velvet eyes opened and stared at him in gentle surprise.

While he was rejoicing in this slow, but sure return to life, the man with the gun, who had observed all Merval's movements, had dragged his burden down the slope.

"I'm going to strangle him," he announced calmly. "Not worth the bother of shooting. I've killed the mother."

"Strangle whom?" asked the priest, getting to his feet.

"The kid, of course. It won't take a moment."

The load he was dragging was the mother chamois. She lay there on the grass, stretched out stiff, her eyes turned up, showing only their whites under the beautiful curves of the horns. She still had her splendid winter coat of dark brown, silky fur.

"Look at that fur," he said, pointing to the dead beast. "That'll fetch a lot of money."

The indignant Abbé promptly condemned him:

"Ah! So you're one of those monstrous poachers who go after chamois when the females are breeding and can't defend themselves! It's sheer murder."

This accusation only made the hunter grin derisively.

He had no pity; he was even proud of his shot. He was a magnificent young man, at once slim and muscular, with regular features, bright eyes and hair which curled under his Alpine béret. When he laughed, he displayed splendid, voracious white teeth between his fresh lips.

"Hand me over that kid," he demanded.

"Certainly not. It belongs to me."

"To you?"

"Yes, to me."

"You've no right to it. *I* killed the mother."

"I've the right of having saved it."

The young man was so surprised that he consented to discuss the matter.

"But what will you do with it?"

"I shall give it to a she-goat."

"You don't know these animals. In a month or two it'll run away back to the mountains."

"I shall tame it."

"They can't be tamed."

And he added with his hearty young laugh:

"They're like me."

"Oh, you! Life will make it its job to tame you."

"I suppose you think, because you wear a cassock, that one of these days I'll come and weep for my sins in your sacristy and accuse myself of poaching and smuggling?"

"And of a great many other things as well."

"My poor good Father, you know no more about people like me than you do about chamois."

"I know more than you think, Pierrot Loriot."

The man was startled at hearing himself addressed by name.

"So you know what I'm called? It must be my mother who told you."

"She told me nothing, but I know it all the same. So you kill the mother and you think of getting rid of the child?"

"Of course. Who's going to feed it? It's only able to suck."

"And the father . . . what about him?"

"The male? My poor dear Father, the males are no good. They're unfaithful, for one thing, and cowardly for another."

'My poor good Father'—'My poor dear Father'—what contempt for the man of God! How could he guess that the other was just about to take his revenge?

"In fact, my poor Pierrot, you're deserting Rosette who wanted to throw herself in the lake. And, by killing herself, she'd have relieved you of your unwanted child."

This time, it was the hunter who was touched on the raw. He did not believe in God but he did believe in the devil. This cassock disguised a sorcerer. How could the Abbé, who had only just arrived in the village, know that Rosette Billois was pregnant by him? How was he in a position to tell him that she had wanted to kill herself? But his astonishment was by no means over; further allusions, or rather condemnations, were to follow.

"How could you do such a thing to her, my poor Pierrot, when you were already engaged to that young girl at Arvillard? You can't marry that girl now."

Pierrot Loriot was completely disconcerted. All his secrets were revealed; he felt stripped naked and denounced. What was the use of denying the facts? He had never questioned himself about his right to live as he pleased, about his loves and his lusts. He knew that he was handsome and attractive to women. Why not use them or abuse them according to his fancy? Was it any business of this tall, black fellow who evidently thought he was still in church and in process of hearing his Confession? The only thing was to take a firm line with him.

"I've had enough of all this talk. I'm getting married next month at Arvillard and I'm going to strangle that kid."

"Your fiancée doesn't want to have anything more to do with you and the kid belongs to me."

What assurance and what authority! The chamois hunter had never come up against such resistance. Was it true that his engagement was to be broken off? How could the sorcerer have found it out?

"Shut up, will you? My marriage is all fixed up. We've put up the banns."

"All the same, I assure you it's broken off."

"That Rosette's been talking! I'll strangle that one too."

"Rosette's not the one who's going to talk. You are."

"*Me?* Really, that's the limit!"

He thought for a moment; then, suddenly, his face lit up:

"Ah, so Marie Bernex doesn't know anything yet. You haven't told her and Rosette hasn't either?"

"No. Because you're the one who's going to tell her."

"Honestly, Father, I think you must be out of your mind."

"Just look, my poor boy, instead of talking like an idiot."

Look at what? Pierrot Loriot turned round. The rescued kid had got back the use of its limbs and had discovered its mother's corpse lying on the grass. It sniffed at it, not understanding what death was; intent, like all animals, only on life. It found the empty udder and sucked at it in vain. Grasping the only thing about this abnormality which interested it—the deprivation of food and of the warmth which had already left the body—it began to shiver and to give small, faint bleats. Its eyes were wet. Animals cry like men and can one let a small child go on crying?

"Come now, Pierrot Loriot," said the priest in a friendly voice. "Don't make yourself out worse than you are. Now I can see very well that you've some pity in you, even for a little animal with no mother and no milk. You're not going to leave Rosette to die of misery—you're not going to deny your child. It's spring and nature's coming into flower everywhere. Look, you can see the first buds already. There's nothing so wonderful as all this new life. You're given new life, too, just as God has. You've got to love it in advance, in Rosette's body;—your wife's body. You've got to love it in this child who's coming and who needs a father. You can't reject it and you know you can't. *Now* I defy you to strangle that kid whose mother you've killed."

The hunter did not answer. At last, he muttered.

"What do you want me to do with it?"

"Help me to carry it to the presbytery."

"What about the big one?"

"Leave her where she is. She won't run away. You can come back. I'll leave my painting things here too."

Pierrot Loriot relapsed into silence. He hesitated and the priest was aware that, if he consented, it would be a sign that Rosette's cause was not hopelessly lost. He watched him anxiously when, at last, he opened his mouth to speak:

"It's not very heavy, a kid as young as that. You could carry it yourself."

"I'm not used to them. You'd manage it much better than I would."

"All right, come on then! My mother can come and fetch the chamois. I'll tell her to as we pass the house."

"What about my canvas and my brushes?"

"Take them. It's safer."

Loriot's mother was immensely surprised to see them return together; the painter with his portfolio and her son with the frightened little animal in his arms.

"The big one's up there at the foot of the waterfall, Mother. There's fur and there's meat. Tomorrow I'll go and sell them in Arvillard."

In Arvillard, where his fiancée lived? It was high time to take action. Loriot's mother was still full of vigour. She would take a rope to tie the animal's feet and would carry it on her shoulders after she had gutted it. Not for nothing was she the wife of a smuggler who had died of a stroke up in the mountains, caused by carrying too heavy a load, and the mother of a poacher who specialised in hunting chamois.

The procession arrived at the principal village of Saint-Paul towards six in the evening. The days had been drawing out since January and it was now in the middle of April. The entire population was out in the fields which, at last, were clear of snow. The gate was open and the priest pushed open the door of the presbytery.

"I'll go and call my housekeeper," he said to Pierrot Loriot who stood there holding the kid in his arms. "She'll unlock the wood-shed for you and you can put the animal inside. She'll go and fetch it some milk or find some neighbour with a goat that can act as foster-mother."

The priest then left him, thinking: "Now they can sort things out together. I've managed to bring him here and that was the most difficult feat of all."

The two former lovers found themselves face to face. Rosette, as yet, was hardly disfigured by her pregnancy. Her face was a little drawn but she had kept her fresh, rosy cheeks and her strong, well-knit body which had attracted him so much last autumn at their meetings in the mountain chalet, had not lost its firmness. Though it had not taken him long to seduce her she had not given herself without any resistance. She was a virtuous girl but, as often happens, love had proved stronger than virtue. He had won her heart before he had taken her virginity. When, repentant and tearful, she had hesitantly told him that she was pregnant, he had run away like a coward and given up seeing her. She had searched for him in vain. He escaped on hunting expeditions or went off over the Italian passes with sacks of contraband.

Neither of the two had been prepared for this meeting. Who was the more surprised and the more vexed? Pierrot was the more surprised but, if anyone were vexed, it was certainly not Rosette.

He said to himself: "That devil of a priest has played me a dirty trick."

She thought: "Oh, joy! He's come back."

She smiled at him. He glowered at her furiously. But, after all, he was one of those men who submit to circumstances and have not the strength to resist them. He observed that she was still pretty and it came over him that she was still highly desirable. There was no denying that once he had been in love with her. And, at this moment, his fiancée was far away. Moreover, she was a girl who would keep him waiting till they were married and marriage seemed a long way off.

"It's the Curé's kid," he explained, putting down his burden.

"Where's its mother?" she asked, merely in order to say something.

"I've killed her."

"You ought to have killed the baby too."

"The Curé didn't want me to."

"Why?"

He answered honestly:

"Because of you."

"Because of me?"

"Yes. Because you shouldn't kill children."

She understood and stopped smiling. Her face became grave. Was she going to cry? Men do not like tears, particularly when they are the cause of them. No, she was not going to cry.

A little later, she returned to her kitchen after having gone with him to take the kid to a she-goat belonging to a neighbour, Fanchette Bontemps. The woman only received this gift on condition of being paid for it and the baby chamois began by butting its head against its placid new mother who was astonished at such boorish behaviour. When the Abbé came into the kitchen, Rosette asked him shyly:

"Father, would you mind if Pierrot had supper with me?"

"Is there anything for him to eat?"

"Oh yes. There's soup and eggs and potatoes."

"Very well. He can stay for dinner."

Next morning, Rosette told the Curé that the wild kid had let itself be suckled by the tame goat. It was beginning to get tame itself.

He wondered whether the hunter, too, were beginning to be tamed.

IV

THE CHALET ON THE LAKE

THE ABBÉ MERVAL emerged from the church one day after Mass, not by the sacristy where he had just put away the sacred vessels but by the main door. On his way, he made a quick inspection of the church and noticed that altars, benches, candles and linen were all in perfect order. Some benevolent, unknown hands must therefore be performing this service. They certainly could not belong to Rosette who was rapidly reducing the presbytery to utter disorder and who even forgot to feed the animals. The sacristan spent all his time at the local tavern. But were those hands so completely unknown? At the early Mass there had been only two members of the congregation and he thought he had recognised them as Perpétue and Mme Trabichon. Yes, there was no doubt about it. These female pharisees, as he mentally called them, were playing the self-sacrificing part of Martha who performs all the menial services and without whom people would go dirty and hungry. Perhaps he had judged them too harshly. The judgments of men are frail and uncertain because their heads and their hearts are confused.

On the porch, as he opened the door, he found himself face to face with a very strange beggar who took off his hat as soon as he saw him. He was a man of quite remarkable physique, tall and heavily built. The immense development of his thorax and his limbs made him look fat though he had no trace of a paunch. He had a red face, a long swollen nose, small beady eyes and grey hair retreating from a high forehead. He was warmly and coarsely dressed in brown corduroys such as carters wear in winter. Yet there was something noble, almost majestic in his size and his bearing; something which showed even in the gesture with which he removed his hat. Evidently he was not asking for alms. He looked the kind of man who, if he did beg, would do so by the threat of his Herculean strength which was capable of crushing any recalcitrant donor. Without a moment's hesitation, the priest recognised him. Did he do so by the hidden sign of the priesthood, that ineffaceable seal which preserves human dignity in spite of any vice? He took a step towards his former colleague who promptly fell back to let him pass.

"Why don't you come in, Father Chavord?"

Thus challenged, the other's face was so fiery red already that he could not have blushed. But he could bow and he did so.

"So you know who I am?"

"I guessed who you were."

"Is it so obvious?"

"Yes. *Tu es sacerdos in eternum.*"

"But I am suspended. Why do you speak to me?"

"Because you are a man and all men belong to God. You above all."

"I no longer belong to Him."

"He still belongs to you. Come into His house with me."

"I am no longer fit to enter it."

"I invite you on His behalf."

"His Lordship has driven me out of it."

"You're not forbidden to pray. Come in with me and we'll say an Our Father and a Hail Mary together."

"I've never entered it since I was suspended."

"Why did I find you at the door?"

"They leave it open sometimes, especially on fine days, and I can see the altar at the end."

"God will take the wish for the deed. Come and see the altar from closer to."

"It frightens me."

"We can't be frightened by what we are drawn to. Come along. I implore you to."

"You'll only compromise yourself if you're seen in my company."

"Our Master was always compromising Himself in that sort of way when He lived on earth."

"Well, you're compromised already. Look!"

And, indeed, at that very moment Mme Trabichon and her faithful Perpétue appeared in the doorway, having completed their devotions. They passed the two priests, one good and one bad, deep in unlawful conversation. In their eyes, was even one of them good? However, the two priests went into the church and the Abbé Merval even made the other go ahead of him. Was he going to offer him holy water? He hurried ahead in his turn to give it him. This was too much for the pious ladies. A girl, whose proper place was on the streets, installed in the presbytery and a proscribed priest at the altar! Were such scandals to be allowed to continue?

The suspended priest knelt down right at the back of the church. He had lost the habit of kneeling, for his rheumatic knees cracked. The prie-dieu almost collapsed under his weight. He refused to go any higher than the central aisle. Nevertheless, he meekly imitated the sign of the cross made by his companion and repeated out loud with him the words of the Our Father and Hail Mary. Then, suddenly, he hid his great red face in his hands to hide his tears.

"Come," insisted the Abbé Merval when the other was a little calmer.

"Come where? I can't stand any more. I just can't go any further."

"Ah, but you must. Our Lady is waiting for you. You live in Saint-Paul and you don't even know that heavenly statue which is the glory of my church."

"A statue?"

"Yes. A statue which comes right down from the ages of faith. It shows her as quite a young girl and the Holy Child has one finger in His mouth. She will smile at you."

"No one ever smiles at me now."

"She will. Come."

He persuaded him to follow him. But his companion was not, like himself, sensitive to beauty. He would have admired a gaudy Sulpician statue, one which had not been sprayed with sulphate, just as much. The only thing that impressed him was the mercy of the Mother of God. If he ever repented, perhaps his repentance might one day be accepted through her prayers. He asked nothing better than to repent. But was he still capable of repenting? That was the whole question.

That very question was put to him in the presbytery to which the Abbé Merval had promptly hurried him by way of the sacristy.

"I've only milk and coffee to offer you. I daresay you've had no breakfast."

The former priest became almost angry:

"Can't you smell anything, then?"

"My nose isn't as good as my eyes. What ought I to smell?"

"Alcohol."

His breath positively stank of it.

"It's too late."

"Make an effort every day. An effort, with a Hail Mary."

"I'll try. But don't count on it. And why involve Our Lady with my vice?"

"So that she'll cure you."

After a moment's silence, his host asked him another question:

"Is there anything you need? What do you live on?"

"On a small inheritance which I'm rapidly eating away. Or rather drinking away."

He gave a faint, ironic laugh. Then he added:

"The blacksmith calls me in for heavy jobs. An ox to hold—an anvil to move—iron bars to carry. Because of all this."

He tapped his biceps and his torso. His colossal strength nourished him. Had it not saved the Bishop by holding his carriage back from the precipice and brought confusion on the Protestant crows by overturning their wagon?

"Why shouldn't you go to a Trappist monastery? It's easier to break one's bonds with one blow rather nibble them away bit by bit."

"No, thanks. I should suffocate there."

"But they work out of doors."

"They only drink water."

"Water refreshes one's body and purifies one's heart."

"I'm past being either purified or refreshed."

Nevertheless, to remove any bad impression, the poor man added:

"I'll think it over. I promise you I will."

He was just getting up to take his departure when the Abbé Merval said:

"Come to my presbytery whenever you like."

"Take care or they'll denounce you to the Bishop. But, all the same, you—you, at any rate, are charitable."

On the doorstep, he made that gesture with his hat which suggested a nobleman painted by Van Dyck and which emphasised his oddly aristocratic air. The moment he had gone, his host forgot his existence. The morning light was so beautiful that he must rush out to meet it.

Rush out to meet it! As if he were free to come and go at will! When one juggles with light and wants to catch it on the end of a knife, it is distracting to be the incumbent of a parish, even of a parish of ill-repute and a deserted church. At that very moment Rosette burst out of her kitchen with tears running down her cheeks.

"He's gone, Father. He's gone."

"So I should hope."

"He went away this morning."

"Only this morning?"

"He's gone off to Bellerive."

"And why is he going off to Bellerive?"

"To take his chamois there. He'll sell the meat to the butcher and the skin to the furrier."

"Well, why not? They'll bring him in some money."

"Yes, Father. But Arvillard's on the way. He'll stop there on the way back. He'll see Marie Bernex. Then there'll be no hope for me."

"Hasn't he promised to break off his engagement?"

"He won't break it off. She's got some property and I haven't. She's beautiful and I'm not. I'm hardly even pretty any more."

"She's a good girl. She's the one who'll break it off."

"You can't break love-affairs off like that. You must warn her. You must go over there, Father. Please, please you must."

"But I haven't the right to interfere."

"Not even to stop something dreadful happening?"

How maddening this girl was with her insistence! Why had he ever been such a fool as to take her into the presbytery? She had ruined all his peace. But how perverse men are! That Pierre Loriot, once their night of love was over, was perfectly capable of treachery.

"I'll write to the Abbé Rameau."

"Who's he?"

"The Curé of Arvillard. He's much better than I am at dealing with practical affairs."

"No, no, Father. You must go yourself. You *must*!"

"That's enough, Rosette. I'll take my letter myself down to the bus. It doesn't go till ten o'clock."

Was he going to inform his colleagues of Pierre Loriot's misconduct? Was it not his duty to prevent a marriage which would ruin a girl's life; a marriage which would hardly be conducive to mutual trust between husband and wife? Was even he ingenuous enough to suppose that the fiancé would jilt Marie Bernex of his own accord in order to marry Rosette before their child was born? This Marie Bernex was said to possess a beautiful face and a beautiful voice. But was one not right to be suspicious of these notably pious girls who were often far more passionate and vindictive than the others?

Very slowly, he wrote his letter. How much more difficult he found it to write than to paint! Words have no colour; they look just the same close to or far away. Nothing but invariable black on white; nothing but boring rows of mingled vowels and consonants. The Gospel has its parables. The Gospel speaks in pictures. Why should he not draw a woman expecting a child, slightly over-emphasising the outlines to make the symbol more obvious? But they would only accuse him of impropriety—a Curé glorifying pregnancy! So he toiled on heavily at his explanations with his tongue sticking out of his mouth, like a conscientious child doing its homework.

At last it was finished and he put on his hat to go out to the ticket office of the bus which ran every day from Saint-Paul to the town, passing through Arvillard on its way. The conductor promised to deliver the letter. There was a crowd of passengers; there was a fair that day at Bellerive and the peasant women were going in to sell fowls or buy trinkets. Among the crowd was Pierre Loriot who, like the rest, carried a large mysterious-looking sack. What could be in it? People moved away to make room for him for he did not look a comfortable neighbour. The Abbé Merval spoke to him:

"I'd like a word with you before you leave."

"I can't stand here with this great sack."

"Then put it down on a seat to keep your place."

"Oh, all right then. What is it you want?"

"Just to remind you of your promise."

"I haven't promised anything."

"When you come back from Bellerive with the money you've made out of your poaching . . ."

"For goodness' sake don't talk so loud, Father."

"The entire village heard that shot of yours yesterday. Everyone, that is, except me. Well, on your way back, you're planning to stop at Arvillard."

"How do you know that? It's the first *I*'ve heard of it."

"You'll be tempted to. And you never resist temptation, especially when it happens to come from a woman."

The young man laughed complacently.

"Very well, then," the priest went on. "You mustn't stop at Arvillard on the way back. You mustn't see Marie Bernex."

"But last night, up there by the waterfall, you asked me yourself to tell her the whole thing."

"I know you. You won't tell her a thing. Promise me to come straight back from Bellerive."

"Who *is* going to tell her, then?"

"Her Curé, the Abbé Rameau."

"Everybody wants to poke their nose into this. I never asked anyone's advice. Why can't you mind your own business?"

Really, his insolence was beyond all bounds! The priest grew angry:

"I am minding my own business. My presbytery isn't meant to be a haven for cowardly seducers who abandon their children."

This time he had spoken quite loud. The other was terrified that people might have heard. There was a sudden movement towards the bus. It was beginning to puff smoke from its exhaust for the driver had started the motor and was testing it noisily. To silence the priest, Pierre Loriot promised everything in the world. A moment later he was gone.

The Abbé Calixte Merval was not in the least reassured by this promise flung at him at the last second and obviously only to stop him from bothering him. He reproached himself for his anger. Is not anger a sign of inferiority in life just as much as in art? When it came to art, he could only compose in that calm which alone allows beauty to reveal her secret rhythms. Calm is the first attribute of painting: it inspires painting and painting, in its turn, inspires the same calm in the onlooker. Of course there had been painters and sculptors who introduced storms and violent movement into their works and of course such artists still existed. But what errors the Renaissance had fallen into compared with Greek or medieval art! The angels of Bellini and Boccardi and Fra Angelico were all peace and joy in tranquillity. How often, since he had never had the money to go to Italy, he had admired and copied reproductions of their pictures! It was only humility which had prevented him from trying to paint human beings; they seemed too close to the Creator for him to dare to attempt. The pursuit of light on the things it animates seemed to him miraculous enough, even when that light escaped him as eternity escaped the monk of Heisterbach.

That afternoon, free at last, he went off in search of some landscape of lights and shadows; of something he could circumscribe with his eyes before imprisoning it, still living, on his canvas. Should he go back to the pool formed by water trickling from a long white stone half-hidden by bushes? The kid, as it fell, had ruined his picture but he had saved the kid. Was not life always greater than art which was only its feeble reflection?

Why did the thought of Marie Bernex keep recurring to his mind as his eyes searched the horizon to find some small, chosen space on which they could rest? He only knew her by the reputation of her face and her voice. Had not his friend, the Vicar-General (he was one day to wear a mitre) advised him to make music in this parish where nobody prayed? "Sing first and pray afterwards," he had said. How wonderful it would be if only he could discover in Saint-Paul an enthusiast like this Marie Bernex of Arvillard who was said to be such a marvel. He would announce one Sunday at High Mass—or perhaps it would be safer to put up notices—that the young girls in the village had only to give their names in at the sacristy in order to be taught to sing. He would get together a choir for the Month of Mary. Their parents would come to Church to hear them singing hymns. But who would play the harmonium which replaced the organ, long since mute and quite beyond repair? Who would train these harsh voices?

With such thoughts in his mind, he found himself passing a wooden gate, always open and nearly rotted away by the dampness of the unpruned trees which crowded round it. It was the entrance to the avenue which led to the Aimerys' château. Suddenly he remembered that Mlle Béatrice d'Aimery was said to be very musical and might act as accompanist and singing teacher. He was a man of sudden decisions. Thought is useless unless it leads to action. The next moment he was walking up the avenue which led to the small, dilapidated château. Barely hidden by a beech tree, two young people were kissing each other full on the mouth. A moment later, they said goodbye and parted. The man leapt on to a bicycle and rode past the priest, bowing as he did so. The girl, catching sight of his cassock, remained where she was, waiting for him to come up.

"You're engaged?" asked the Curé, after introducing himself.

"No," she said, looking him defiantly straight in the eyes. "He's my lover."

"I see. But why don't you marry him?"

"Because he's married already. Would you like him to get divorced?"

This village seemed to be decidedly lacking in legitimate couples. Why was she defying the priest? Why was she deliberately putting up this barrier between them from the first moment they had begun to talk?

"My father," she went on, "is old and extremely bad-tempered. He shouts at us all day long. And nothing but death will ever stop him shouting. My mother's the most patient woman in the world. She can manage to forget all her troubles at the sight of the view from our windows or even a pressed flower in her specimen book."

"Fancy, just for a flower!" he said mechanically, trying to sympathise with these domestic difficulties.

"Yes, Father, just for an Alpine rose or a gentian. She's making a little book of botanical specimens for children who come to stay in the mountains—a *flora* of the Alps for people who live in cities. Meanwhile we live on potatoes boiled in their jackets, dried vegetables and polenta."

"Very excellent fare, Mademoiselle. I shall certainly visit your parents some day but, just at this moment, it's you I want to see."

"I suppose you want to preach me a sermon?"

"Sermons aren't at all in my line."

She pointed to the portfolio and the paint-box.

"Perhaps you want to paint my portrait? Like the famous Francisque Beauvais who's painting Arlette's this very moment over in M. Belarmont's chalet."

"I don't know M. Belarmont. Or this young lady called Arlette either."

"They live in the chalet by the lake."

"I'm afraid I only paint the earth and the sky. I find them quite enough."

"I quite agree with you, Father. What do you really want to see me for?"

"To offer you the job of singing teacher in my parish."

Astonished at this proposition, she burst out laughing. She looked younger when she laughed. Did she already need to look younger? Up till now, he had hardly looked at her because he had been distressed by surprising her during that kiss and even more distressed by the insolent avowal which had followed it. Now he looked at her closely.

She had come out without her hat to meet her friend—why gloss it over?—her lover. In the full sunlight her face seemed to melt into the general brightness because of its surrounding mass of fine, fluffy golden hair. She must have been beautiful and was just beginning to fade. Already there were warning signs in the tiny lines just perceptible round her eyes and mouth. Beauty that is threatened is more moving than untouched freshness. Her rounded features had not the faint golden glow which comes from an open-air life. Her skin had remained white and almost pallid, as if she preferred her books and her piano to country walks. Her nose was small and shapely; her delicately-drawn mouth drooped a little at the corners which gave her a sad expression, momentarily banished by her amusement.

"I only like music for my own pleasure, Father."

"You'll learn to like it for other people's. I want to get the whole village to sing."

"You're an odd sort of Curé."

"What's odd about that? Song is a prayer in itself."

"Some songs are obscene. And some music is purely voluptuous."

"Men can always falsify the good things God gives us and turn them to evil. The same applies to love."

"Is that an allusion?"

"If you take it as one. God should never be absent from honest love."

"Perhaps He's not so absent as you think for people like me who don't acknowledge the usual rules. Love is only another aspect of the craving for beauty. But, of course you despise me because of what I said the moment we met."

"Far from despising you, I'm relying on you. I've never despised anyone because I should have to have begun with myself."

"You know—or, if you don't know, I'd better tell you—that I never set foot inside the church?"

"So much the worse for you. But you'll set foot in it for the harmonium."

She let herself be persuaded into accepting the odd and unexpected offer but deplored the fact that the organ was unusable. It was in such a bad state that it was hopeless to attempt to repair it. To buy a new one would cost far too much. What a pity they could not get M. Belarmont's admirable instrument for the church.

"I've played on it sometimes. The fugues of Bach and César Franck and Saint-Saëns. It doesn't do itself justice where it is—the hall is too small and deadens the sound. Your church is big enough to let one hear the full beauty of it. Have you met M. Belarmont?"

"Not yet."

"Then let's go and see him together. I'll play you the Bach Toccata I love so much. But I forgot—you won't want to meet Mlle Arlette de Jasmin."

"I don't particularly want to. But she'll probably be more frightened of me than I of her."

"Then let's go, shall we?"

"What about your parents?"

"Oh, they never count on me."

"Don't you want to put on a hat?"

"I shan't bother to."

They took the path to the little black lake among the pines and oaks and birches which nestled in a hollow of the valley about half a mile beyond the last houses of the village. In the spring, its water looked brighter. The young leaves, reflected in it, gave it a green tinge so that it harmonised with the fields. The sun played on it, striking sparkles from its surface whenever a fish leapt. The sun played too through the branches of the trees whose leaves were still in their first, almost transparent freshness.

"Oh!" said the priest ecstatically, "I'm not going any further."

"Why ever not?"

"God is too good."

"What do you mean?"

"He has made all this splendour. Let me snatch a tiny piece of it."

"What with?"

"With this knife."

He was just opening his paint-box, under the girl's amused, inquisitive stare, when the door of the Swedish chalet opened and the owner appeared. He was a man of about forty, dressed for shooting or mountaineering in leather shorts and gaiters, obviously worn for comfort rather than elegance. He was clean-shaven, with masterful features and a disillusioned, unfriendly expression. He watched the odd couple approaching; the man's long cassock and great hobnailed shoes contrasting strangely with the girl's short frock and pretty legs. Then he saw that the girl was Béatrice d'Aimery. She introduced him to the Curé and, as if to explain an introduction which could have no interest for either of these two sceptics and worshippers of the great god Pan, she added:

"He adores music and, with your permission, I am taking him to hear your organ."

"By all means. I'll come and do the honours."

While he was taking them into the hall, the girl asked him where Arlette was.

"She's shut up with her painter, Francisque Beauvais. She's asked me not to disturb her. The artist's actually finishing her portrait today."

"Is that the M. Beauvais who paints animals?" inquired the Abbé Merval without a trace of malice.

"He paints women as well."

"He also paints flowers," said Béatrice hastily, to smooth the situation. "D'you know him then, Father?"

"Only by reputation. I saw a photograph of a cat curled up between the paws of a sleeping dog. It was in an illustrated paper and his name was underneath."

"A fellow artist," explained Béatrice. "You see, the Abbé paints too."

"Does he paint women or animals?"

"Oh, neither. Nothing but light. To my delight and despair. But I only paint for myself."

Béatrice seated herself at the organ and André Belarmont settled down to blow for her. She began by testing the stops and, when she had satisfied herself, she began to play a Bach prelude. From that she passed to the Fantasia and Fugue in G Minor, then to that Toccata on the airs of old dances which is such a favourite with the virtuoso.

"You ought to play that faster," said M. Belarmont judicially.

For the benefit of her religious audience, she ended her concert with César Franck's *Prayer* which she played slowly, as it should be played.

The priest had folded his hands on his breast as if he were mentally repeating this musical prayer. When the organ was silent, he remained motionless so as to let it go on echoing in his mind.

"*That's* music," said Béatrice, coming down from her pedestal. She was pleased to see him so completely absorbed.

"Yes. You can hear God's voice in it."

"You see God everywhere!"

"Because He *is* everywhere."

"And now, what about some refreshment?" suggested André Belarmont.

"Won't you play something yourself?" Béatrice begged. "Father, you really ought to hear him!"

"No, no. You played the Bach extraordinarily well. Possibly a little too slow and a little too loud."

He did not, however, mention César Franck.

He led them to the drawing-room through an ante-room strewn with chamois-skin rugs which deadened the sound of their footsteps. Going ahead of them and opening the door, he gave an exclamation of fury at the sight revealed to him.

Arlette was in the arms of her painter who was passionately kissing her. Béatrice, who was just behind him, only caught sight of the couple after they had hastily separated but she could not help laughing at what had so obviously been going on. The priest, bringing up the rear, saw nothing but a woman frantically running away and a dishevelled man hastily trying to tidy himself up.

"What's happened?" he innocently asked Béatrice.

"God is not everywhere," she answered.

"You don't know either His ways or His mercy."

Was a thunderbolt going to fall before their eyes? The terrified Francisque Beauvais evidently expected it to. But André Belarmont recovered his self-control as he used to recover it when he directed his battery's fire during the war. He walked up to the culprit, looked at the picture and announced calmly:

"Very good. The portrait is finished. You will take it away tonight and the model as well. I present you with both."

"But . . ." stammered the astonished and disconcerted artist.

"That's settled. This very night. Get your things packed and . . . pleasant journey!"

"But you see . . ."

"I insist."

"But I'm married."

"Then you'll have two women instead of one."

"But I already find it terribly difficult to keep the one I have . . ." protested the unfortunate man. Béatrice was wickedly amused by his horrified expression.

"That will make your disinterestedness even more obvious. Oh . . . I nearly forgot . . . here's the cheque for your picture. I believe this is the amount we agreed?"

As M. Belarmont was pronouncing his verdict, he had taken out his cheque-book. The painter shook his head.

"I couldn't accept it without shame."

"Then accept it with shame."

Then, advancing on him with a threatening expression, he growled:

"And don't let me ever set eyes on you again!"

Turning towards his guests, he added:

"Mademoiselle, Monsieur le Curé, kindly forgive this scene which, I assure you, was entirely impromptu. I hope you will have a pleasant walk home."

On the way back, the girl burst out laughing:

"André Belarmont's quite a wit. He handled that rather neatly. Did you see the painter's face?"

"I'm sorry for him," said the priest simply.

"He's only getting what he deserves."

"What about us, Mademoiselle? Do we get what we deserve?"

If this, too, were an allusion, she could find no retort. She was imagining what would happen to Arlette.

"Mlle Jasmin won't be so easy to get rid of," she asserted. "You'll see that *she* won't go. Men are extraordinarily weak."

As a concession to justice, she added:

"So are women, of course."

"Why ever did he shut that young woman up here?" said the Abbé Merval. "She was bound to be lonely and bored. We are always more or less the cause of our own troubles. Illicit love affairs are invariably unhappy."

"Surely not invariably. What about the other ones?"

"God blesses the other ones as soon as He is invoked. Why don't people invoke Him or only invoke Him too late? Here's your château, Mademoiselle. Bach is a great master and César Franck is a great Christian. Thank you for having let me hear them. They were searching for the light, too. So you'll teach my female parishioners how to sing?"

"If they'll come."

"I guarantee that they'll come."

When he had returned to the presbytery he went out to

say his breviary in the garden. He was by no means free from distractions. Too often, he raised his glance from the book to watch the evening light which spread sweetness and light over everything and invited human eyes to share them. Suddenly he heard Rosette shouting at the top of her voice:

"Father! Father! A gentleman with luggage! He wants to sleep here. Do come and send him away."

Francisque Beauvais, the painter, unable to find any means of transport or any place to stay the night had come to ask him to take him in. This involved shifting various articles of furniture in the room upstairs which the Bishop used on his Confirmation journeys, adding an omelette to their meagre supper and behaving affably to the seducer who had left his conquest behind at the chalet. The presbytery was definitely becoming an asylum for guilty lovers.

V

A SUMMONS FROM PARIS

AFTER HIS MASS, which was attended only by the same two people, the assiduous, zealous and hostile Perpétue and Mme Trabichon, the Abbé Merval hastily swallowed his breakfast. It consisted only of a cup of coffee with a crust of bread dipped in it. Then he hurriedly collected his painting materials so as not to lose a moment of the morning of a fine day. Before leaving the presbytery, he left Rosette her instructions:

"When the gentleman wakes up, give him some breakfast. He'll be taking the ten o'clock bus to Bellerive. I'll be back in time to say goodbye to him."

But at ten o'clock the Curé had not returned. He had gone off to the banks of the green lake to capture the light on the water. Once there, time ceased to exist for him. The monk of Heisterbach's three centuries had passed oblivious of the church bell which strikes not merely the hours but the halves and the quarters and without the tedious interruption of day by night. It was not till just on noon that he returned to his house, apologising for his lateness and inquiring what had happened to his guest.

"He's a nice one!" said Rosette indignantly. "He nearly missed the bus. And he's robbed you, Father."

"Robbed me? But I've nothing for him to steal."

"He just said: 'Tell your master that I'm taking away two pictures and he'll soon be hearing from me.' I couldn't make him give them back. But I thought there were so many of them up there that it wasn't worth the trouble of fussing about those two. It's not as if they were worth anything!"

This contemptuous estimate of his work made the Abbé laugh.

"You were perfectly right, Rosette. It's nothing serious and I gladly give him those daubs he carried off. Whichever ones could he have chosen? But however did he discover them?"

"He went poking all through the rooms upstairs. I could hear him from down here, swearing like anything. He was shouting: 'Good God! Good God!' "

"There's no need for you to repeat it, Rosette."

"He said: 'God Almighty!' too."

"That's enough."

"And he said 'God's truth!' He just kept swearing like that over and over again. In the end I went upstairs to see whether he had gone out of his mind. He was poking his nose into everything in your—what d'you call it?—your exhibition. There's something else you call it—your gallery. Fancy calling it a gallery! Just two or three rooms where you've covered all the furniture with bits of cardboard and canvas that you won't let me sweep away. They look to me as if a kid had been making mud-pies with a paintbox! Well, he took them one by one, sniffed at them as if they were something to eat and then held them out at arm's length. Sometimes he even put them down so that he could see them from a bit farther off. Then he'd rush forward and clutch them to his chest to try and smash them. He was so furious, he just couldn't stop himself from swearing. When he saw me, he shooed me out like a dog. 'Get out, will you? Artists mustn't be disturbed!' Then he looked at the time and said: 'I'll miss my bus.' He took two of them, not just any two, but choosing ever so carefully. He wrapped them up ever so carefully and then he rushed off after he'd threatened you: 'He'll be hearing from me! He'll be hearing from me!' Not even so much as a thank you! Not even five francs! That's your *gentleman*!"

"Artists aren't like other men," explained the Abbé,

highly intrigued. "One doesn't understand them till after they've gone."

He added to himself:

"Possibly only after they've gone forever."

Without realising it, he was echoing Balzac's thought that glory only illuminates the dead. Nevertheless, he was extremely interested in this report of Francisque Beauvais' behaviour. He might be an unscrupulous guest as regarded his models, but he was an excellent and original painter of animals and flowers and even of women, who have something in common with both. There was no doubt that his one-night guest had discovered the picture gallery upstairs which the cook regarded with such open contempt. He had flung himself into it like a boar charging into the undergrowth; he had gone from one picture to the other and had grasped the painter's method. He had realised that paintings done with a trowel or a knife have to be looked at from a distance for the mass of colours to assume their true contours. But what exactly did his blasphemous exclamations signify? Were they to be interpreted as signs of approval or of revolt against an art unlike his own? But, if he were indignant, he would hardly have removed the two pictures. What was he going to do with the stolen canvases? Was he going to show them in the Paris studios as a real discovery or to make the painter a laughing-stock? "He'll be hearing from me!"—that was what he had said as he left. Rosette had judged his tone to be angry or threatening. Yet it might, on the contrary, indicate publicity. For the first time, the works of the Abbé Calixte Merval would be seen by unknown and competent judges. He took fright at once at the thought of what their verdict might be. Then he realised that he was lucky to have this chance.

He believed that he only painted for his own pleasure; from a compulsive personal need to express his love of nature and his preoccupation with light. Now his eyes—those eyes which brought him such joy in seeing things that, the moment he woke up, he rushed to the window to look out—were suddenly blinded by a discovery which altered his whole conception of art. No painter, musician or writer works only for his private delight. He must communicate with other men, with as many of them as possible, and convey to them his vision, his music or his thought. He himself, therefore, must unconsciously have been seeking the approbation and flattery of the public. He had never been disinterested. He had run after fame, perhaps even after glory; he had entered on the path which led to vanity and pride; he was no longer himself. He felt so deeply ashamed that, alone there with his cook who could not possibly sympathise with anything so intimate and mysterious, he suddenly felt his eyes fill with tears as if he were mourning the loss of his virginity as an artist.

Had he not been warned that the road he was taking would arrive at a crossroads where he would have to choose his direction? Mgr Hélouard, the Bishop of Bellerive, had dismissed him with the words: "As the new parish priest of Saint-Paul, I count on you." Had not his friend the Vicar-General, Camille de Servières, urged him to pursue the light there? Had he meant spiritual light or material light? But did they not interpenetrate each other? Surely the light which transfigured nature, the light whose play on cloud or water he tried to capture was none other than that which penetrated the human heart and illuminated the human mind? Ought he not, therefore, to bear witness to it by transcribing it on his canvas? Was not this witness a hymn of praise in honour of the Creator as revealed in His creation? He called to mind all his predecessors who had worked in stone and paint; the statues on the doors of cathedrals and the pictures in their sanctuaries. Many, even most of them were by unknown artists. He would like to be one of those unknown ones whose works turned men's eyes towards the beauty of the universe and from thence towards its Author.

Thus reassured, he went up to the first floor and carefully inspected his collection of pictures. He searched through them, looking to find which two had disappeared. He was curious to know which ones Francisque Beauvais had chosen and whether the judgment of his first critic coincided with his own. It was not long before he identified the ones which were missing. This painter's choice—he could think of Beauvais now as a brother-artist—proved to be admirable; he could not have chosen better himself. One was a picture of some golden rushes on the bank of the Dranse, with the river reflecting the clear morning light against a background of sparkling snow. The other showed a little wood with russet autumn leaves at the moment evening was falling. It was the time he called the mauve or violet hour because the mists which herald the fading light take on these delicate, fugitive tints which one has to hurry to catch.

Now he could dismiss the idea that the whole thing had been nothing but an amateur's whim and understand what the despoiler of his gallery had meant by 'You'll be hearing from me.' It must mean that he had been delighted by his discovery and wanted to share his pleasure. As soon as he arrived in Paris, this Francisque Beauvais would forget the capriciousness of Mlle Jasmin and the insolence of M. Belarmont. He would show the two landscapes to his painter friends, possibly to art critics, possibly even to picture dealers. He might even sell them at a good price and let the author know. The Abbé Merval had never even thought of selling his pictures. Now and then he had offered one to charity bazaars and it had been accepted out of pity, so as not to upset him. Occasionally some kindly old lady or some contemptuous young woman had bought one for next to nothing and hung it up in some dark passage. He had never heard it mentioned again. And now, in Paris of all places, he might be going to find a buyer. It was an exciting idea. Had it ever occurred to him that he might make a profit out of his art? It seemed to him dangerous that it should be involved with money. A little while ago he had been nervous of fame; ought he to be nervous of fortune as well?

Fame and fortune! What absurd imaginings for a poor Curé. He stopped taking himself seriously and, coming back to reality, began to laugh. Rosette was not merely mystified by this laughter but thought it extremely ill-timed. Pierre Loriot was probably at this very moment with Marie Bernex, not in order to break off his engagement but in order to kiss her and talk of love.

A few days later, when he returned from his painting expedition, she brought her master a telegram concerning which the postman had said: "They're all off their heads in Paris. The whole post office has been splitting its sides about this here." The entire post office consisted of the postmistress, a clerk and the two postmen. This bench of judges had minutely examined the despatch which the Abbé Merval was now hastily studying. When he had finished he was even more surprised than the post office had been. It surpassed his wildest imagination. The news the blue slip of paper brought him was as follows:

Please send Paris fifty or even sixty pictures if possible stop packing agent Bellerive arranging prompt despatch stop will fix exhibition date later letter follows stop you are staggering stop Francisque Beauvais.

What struck Merval most at the first reading was the inordinate length of the telegram. No one would spend so much, thought the economical Abbé, except for some very important object. But this consideration soon gave place to another. What excited him most of all was the final compliment. Though he was not used to slang, he knew very well that 'staggering' was being used in anything but an unflattering way; it obviously meant that the other thought his work astonishingly good. Was pride going to get him in its grip by one of those wiles in which the Evil One is so adept? Without a moment's delay, he went upstairs and walked through his 'gallery'. Yesterday he had called it a gallery merely as a joke; today he felt justified in calling it so in reality. He made the round of his pictures and counted them. They were not large, but there were a great many of them. Some were in the form of a rectangle, greatly elongated so as to contain more space; the others were almost square. He counted them and found there were well over a hundred. That was too many: which ones should he eliminate? Some were only unfinished sketches yet these were not without merit. Indeed, their spontaneity had caught certain effects of light more boldly than the finished ones. They showed more verve, more daring, more audacity. In Paris, people would probably like this daring which carried the artist beyond the beaten path into a mysterious world. Should he send them? He would send some of them, at least; those which seemed the strangest and boldest and most significant. He could not bring himself to decide to leave out any of them. He became aware that he loved all his works, like pieces of himself. Taken as a whole, they represented certain moments of his life, the most beautiful of them. They were a record of his joys and his enthusiasms, of his communions with nature and, beyond nature, with his Creator. Why choose? Why show any preference? Why despise any one part of his existence as an artist? But was not that, too, a temptation to pride?

No, he would show himself a severe, implacable judge. He would not let any error of composition or style or drawing or colour escape his critical eye. Now, he could discover nothing but faults in his pictures; clumsiness, impurities, incoherencies, tricks which were next door to lies. Was he capable, then, of lying? If so, how could he see clearly enough to accuse himself of it? In one picture, had he not tried to camouflage lack of drawing by specious charm of colour? In another, had he not replaced a tone which he could not reproduce by one which was merely approximate? But is it possible to put down, in all its truth, that light which is always changing and escaping before one's eyes? He was so haunted and tormented by this question of light that sometimes he had forgotten everything else. It had swallowed up objects, destroyed perspective, confused plains and mountains, sky and earth, until it became like a firework, a devouring flame, an apotheosis of the divine splendour. Should he send the pictures in which he represented it like this? His friend Camille de Servières, who was extremely intelligent, even about art, had seemed interested in his attempts when they left the seminary. Had he not spoken to him one day about an English painter who had a whole room to himself at the National Gallery in London and who had ended by abandoning all vanishing lines so as not to hinder the diffusion of this light he so much loved? He thought his name was Turner or something of the kind. If another had made the attempt why should not he, in his humble way, have tried to do the same?

In his humble measure;—but was he so sure of his humility? Why, after having rejected half his paintings, did he surreptitiously take them one by one to add to the pile he had just chosen? Why could he not make up his mind to leave them out? There was no fixed number. According to the telegram, it could be anything from fifty to a hundred. Finally, the vacillating artist stopped at seventy-five to which he added, not without hesitations and scruples, five sketches to which he accorded a satisfied smile. Eighty was a round figure which would honourably fill a catalogue. For the exhibition would be accompanied by a catalogue, with a list of the pictures and possibly even a preface. It would be necessary to find titles for that list. What a bore to have to give definite titles stating the subject. What could one call a subject? Three trees and a pool; a river and some rushes; a waterfall among some bushes; a hovel at the edge of a wood; a path covered with dead leaves; —what could he call such vague landscapes? What made them charming and sometimes touching to look at was nothing more than a momentary sense of poignant awareness of light. However, since they would insist on it, he would have to find them. They ought to be titles which would attract attention. Was he already becoming a showman? And who would edit the catalogue? Would a great critic lower himself so far as to introduce this unknown man? Robert de la Sizeranne, whose *Religion of Beauty* he had read and Louis Gillet whose *Raphael* he knew, came to his mind. But great critics do not disdain to pose as discoverers of new talent. Perhaps he might be lucky enough to interest one or other of them.

"Take care, Calixte Merval; you're listening to the voice of the Evil One. He's tempting you to put yourself on a level with the master painters of the great days. And though you may shrug your shoulders and refuse his offers, you're listening to him with decided interest. My poor friend, you've taken the wrong turning. Why couldn't you stay that obscure artist who rushed all over the countryside in a kind of ecstasy to catch the sunbeams as they fell? . . ." Such was the lecture which he kept giving himself from time to time but at longer and longer intervals. This exhibition preoccupied him, tormented and excited him till it gradually become the accompaniment of all his thoughts.

A few days later, a second telegram arrived announcing the visit of the agent from Bellerive who was to arrange the packing of the pictures and their transport by lorry. It contained a final postscript after one of those mysterious interpolations 'stop'. The Abbé was so unused to receiving telegrams that he still presumed 'stop' represented some word which the local post office had been unable to decipher. The postscript warned him: *Beware of flatterers and refuse their offers.* What could this possibly mean? He had never met any flatterers nor had he ever received any offer to buy his pictures. Had his name already been publicised? Was it already known in the art market, if such a thing existed? He wanted to remain anonymous. Could he not exhibit in Paris without signing his work? So many Italian and Flemish painters had never been identified; was there not still time for him to imitate their example? Ought he not immediately to inform his protector, Francisque Beauvais, of this wish—or rather of this decision?

The packer and carrier had already invaded the presbytery and was in process of dismantling the gallery when a car drew up at the door. It was a luxurious car which excited the curiosity of the entire village and out of it stepped a stout, glossy, important-looking person who, without so much as a word to the priest, suspended the packing operations.

"Stop! Stop! I want to see."

"We're in a hurry," the agent answered.

"Just one moment—one glance, one word!"

He rummaged through the canvases, put now one, now another on one side and then, for the first time, addressed the Abbé Merval. The latter, utterly disconcerted by this onslaught, stared at him in bewilderment.

"Are you the painter?"

"Certainly, Monsieur."

"I've heard about you in Paris. I should like to be useful to you. Your exhibition may be a success or it may be a failure. That depends to a considerable extent on me. I am a picture dealer. Everyone agrees that my taste is infallible. You have talent. An original talent about which there is going to be considerable discussion. That's exactly what we want. These colours laid on with some flat instrument—a knife, possibly . . ."

"Quite right. A knife or sometimes a trowel."

"That's interesting. A new form of Impressionism. Nature

caught in the raw. Now I can definitely assure you that you're going to be a success."

"Thank you very much."

"Who's your publicity agent?"

"I haven't got one."

"What, no publicity agent? Surely there's someone in Paris who's dealing with your exhibition?"

"Certainly there's someone."

"Very well then, he must put a label 'sold' on the five pictures I've just picked. As soon as the public sees those labels, they'll buy the rest. The public is nothing but a flock of silly sheep."

"But sold to whom, Monsieur?"

"Why, to me of course. I'm buying them here and now. How much do you want for them?"

"But they're not for sale."

"You mean they're not for sale any longer. I've come all this way expressly to see them and buy them."

"I'm sorry, but I'm afraid that you've made the journey for nothing."

The dealer was surprised at this resistance but thought he could guess what lay behind it.

"Oho, Father, you want to make me pay through the nose, do you? Well, I'm not mean, you know. I'm willing to pay for what I fancy. I offer you a thousand francs apiece for them. That's a very good price. And I'll throw in a donation to your church."

"It's extremely obliging of you, Monsieur. Thank you very much indeed for your kind offer. But I'm afraid I can't accept it."

A thousand francs was a considerable sum; an unhoped-for sum. It was beyond anything he had imagined and seemed a positively extravagant figure for a poor country priest. Had it not been for those warning words: *Beware of flatterers and refuse their offers*, whose meaning he had suddenly perceived, he might have yielded to such a dazzling offer. But he stuck to his refusal in spite of his visitor's insistence. Furious at being dismissed, the picture dealer at last took his leave, uttering repeated threats:

"So you're going to be stubborn, are you? All right, then! You'll be hearing from me."

The Abbé Merval had heard those words on another occasion. He wondered whether they would have a similar sequel. But the speaker hastened to make his meaning perfectly plain.

"I'm in a position to blow your exhibition sky-high. That business of yours of painting with a knife! No difficulty in making you look a complete fool. Everyone in Paris will be laughing at you—it'll be a godsend to the caricaturists. Goodbye, Your Reverence. We shall meet again in Paris. I shall get there first and I shan't let the grass grow under my feet."

Red in the face and still gesticulating, the dealer climbed back into his limousine and drove off.

"Dear Lord," prayed the Abbé, "confound this wicked man and preserve your servant."

As soon as he was out of doors he forgot all about the dealer's invectives and only remembered the price he had refused. At such a rate, he would have been suddenly transformed into a rich man. Eighty pictures at that price, plus the ones he had kept, what a fortune! Whatever should he do with it? His imagination began to work furiously. He would exchange his bicycle which had only one speed and, in any case, was nearly worn out. Why shouldn't he replace it by one of those motor bicycles which demand no effort from the rider and to which distance means nothing? They climbed hills at full speed and he lived in an extremely hilly district. They could cross the mountain passes into Italy in a few hours. To think that Italy, the land of beauty, would be within easy reach! All the same, a car, a little 5CV, would be more comfortable and convenient. It would enable him to carry his luggage, his canvases and all his painter's equipment. But why a little 5 CV? Why not a 10 or 12? It would be a more solid affair and much faster. If necessary, he could add a trailer or even a caravan so that he would have somewhere to spend the night during his long drives to Florence or to Rome.

La Fontaine's fable about Perrette and the jug of milk, which he had learned at his first school, recurred to his mind as he imagined more and more ambitious modes of transport till he had substituted a kind of motor train for a modest bicycle. He promptly began to laugh at himself and to repudiate the selfishness which proposed to use these riches entirely for his personal pleasure. Could he not use them in some less personal and more disinterested way? The church of Saint-Paul-en-Forêt needed a new window and its organ was unusable. Suppose he acquired an organ with multiple stops, now powerful as a trumpet, now soothing as a cello, which would attract his recalcitrant and indifferent flock to the services? Would not that be a pious, apostolic work which would bring a blessing on the giver? He was filled with excited pleasure at the thought of his generosity. Already he could see the crowd filling the aisles; a crowd of villagers who had come out of curiosity, swelled by various music lovers from Bellerive who wanted to hear the concert given by Mlle Béatrice d'Aimery on this marvellous instrument. Her agile fingers would also accompany the choir formed in Saint-Paul with the assistance of this Marie Bernex, the angel of Arvillard. He seemed to float on waves of music and light, seeing himself spreading joy and faith all round him.

But was not this too a purely artistic pleasure and therefore a personal one? Was not charity more important than art? Would he not be more pleasing to God if he distributed this wealth to the poor? Saint-Paul-en-Forêt was far from being a rich parish but every family and even every unmarried person in it possessed a little property. Material poverty was unknown there even if moral poverty was only too obviously widespread. But that very moral poverty would be an excellent reason for founding a rest-home for unmarried mothers. There should be a nursery for the dirty, abandoned children who ran wild about the village. There should be a clinic for teaching mothers how to look after their babies. There should be a home for old people, since old age was inevitable and the old were harshly and contemptuously treated. He could spend his entire fortune on all this and, in so doing, contribute to the public good.

His fortune—his reputation—why not his fame? 'My poor man, beyond all doubt you're going out of your mind. Go and throw yourself at the feet of Our Lady and ask her to protect you against temptations to pride. Ask her to give you the strength to renounce this journey to Paris.' Having thus admonished himself, he went straight into his empty church and flung himself on his knees in front of the old stone statue of a fifteen-year-old mother smiling at a child with its finger in its mouth. Had he not been her 'tumbler' since his seminary days? He had dedicated all his acrobatic tricks to her—tricks which, in his case, were those pictures in which he juggled with rays of light. She had been indulgent to him. Had she not even encouraged him since now he was known or, at least, he soon would be known if he went to Paris? Her protection was so evident that the least he could do was to thank her for it. He prayed that this protection might shield him against the caresses of fame; that it might nerve him to this difficult renunciation which would be the supreme sacrifice of his vanity. He invoked her fervently and, when he got up from his knees, he felt calm and serene.

But human beings, even when they are priests, are weak. His exhibition was announced and he was urgently invited to be present. Between Sundays, his time was his own. A few days later, he left for Paris.

VI

THE MONTH OF MARY

WHILE PARIS WAS sending the Abbé Merval those urgent telegrams which so disturbed his imagination and which finally ended, in spite of his belated scruples, in his accepting their invitation, the daily life and daily misfortunes of Saint-Paul went on as usual. He had to buy Fanchon's she-goat because the little chamois had killed her legitimate kid by butting it and trampling on it. Rosette Billois had arranged a stable in a corner of the big woodshed, large enough for this wild creature to gambol in. Marie Bernex had come in person to break off her engagement. The old Baron d'Aimery, Béatrice's father, had died suddenly. M. Belarmont had gone off in his car in pursuit of Arlette Jasmin. By one of those contradictions typical of men in the grip of passion, he had no sooner driven her away than he wanted to get her back and shut her up again. The suspended priest, the Abbé Chavord, after having broken a bottle of brandy (an empty one), had asked to be admitted by the Trappists. A number of things had, in fact, happened. Each of these requires further comment, except the case of the young murderer whose horns were just beginning to grow and whose behaviour requires no explanation.

The Abbé Rameau, Curé of Arvillard, had answered the letter of his colleague of Saint-Paul by return of motor-bus and through the good offices of the conductor. A wise and discreet priest, he had not told Marie Bernex that he knew all about Pierre Loriot's behaviour. He had merely warned Marie Bernex in a general way that it would be a good idea if she made certain enquiries before her marriage. Her fiancé did not live in her own parish and his was too far away for her to be thoroughly acquainted with its families, its customs and its attitude to religion.

"Marie Bernex," he wrote to his brother priest, "is a pious but very independent young girl. She lost her parents when she was hardly more than a child (they died in a typhoid epidemic which ravaged the village ten years ago) and she has always managed her own affairs. The uncle and aunt who brought her up very soon left her in complete charge of her property which is quite a large one for these parts. She knows all about running a farm and gives her labourers their orders kindly, but very firmly. In a word, she has one of those very rare natures which Providence watches over with special care. For her thorough grasp of practical affairs is not the least hindrance to her spirituality. Her face, which one cannot help noticing, has an almost supernatural charm. You, who are a painter, would be particularly aware of this almost angelic appearance. She is extremely musical and her pure voice, which seems so soft, fills the church as the nightingale fills our woods in the spring. Thanks to her, I have been able to get together a Children of Mary's choir which is a great addition to our services. It is a great stimulus to the young girls in the congregation and a great attraction to their parents. Perhaps she will be able to help you too to start a choir at Saint-Paul-en-Forêt. She will shortly be coming to see you. She turned her fiancé away when he came to see her on his way back from Bellerive where he had sold—and sold extremely well—that chamois he poached out of season. She told him that she would see him later and that *she* would go and see *him*. She is determined to make her enquiries on her own and she wants Pierre Loriot to confess of his own accord. I am not sending her to you without considerable apprehension. She has been quite frank with me about her feeling for this hunter—or rather this adventurer. This feeling surprises me in a girl so well-balanced and religious. But we know from the Confessional (I am not her confessor) what secret passions can hide under the shyest and most reserved appearances. I think this feeling has a double origin. Partly, no doubt, it comes from the physical good looks with which your young parishioner appears, from all reports, to be liberally endowed. But I believe it also comes from the desire to save a soul in danger; to convert it and bring it back to God. A generous idea, of course, but one which needs to be regarded with caution and which can even be very dangerous. Did not our dear Saint François de Sales strongly discourage Mme Brulart when she was thinking of marrying her daughter to a handsome but very dissipated young man? The mother thought he would mend his ways under the influence of his wife but the saint wrote that it was tempting God to trust the fate of a young girl to such an unreliable suitor. I advise you therefore—if you don't mind an older man offering you advice—to have Marie Bernex to stay at the presbytery when she comes to Saint-Paul and to confine yourself to helping her in her enquiries. Don't try to direct her; that might only annoy her and give her the idea that there was a kind of organised conspiracy against her marriage . . ."

The Curé of Arvillard could not have foreseen the embarrassment this letter would cause the Abbé Merval since he had no idea that Marie Bernex's rival, Rosette Billois, lived at the presbytery. The most admirable plans are occasionally upset by circumstances. How could the Abbé Merval let these two young girls, the fiancée and the mother-to-be, come face to face as soon as the bus arrived in Saint-Paul? At all costs, he must prevent this meeting. The unhappy priest went over to ask Béatrice d'Aimery to come to his aid, using her love of music as his excuse. Would she not consent to offer a day or two's hospitality in the château to the girl who was coming over to discuss the question of forming a choir?

"Gladly," said Béatrice. "That is, if my father will allow it. He's stiff with prejudice and he would think a village girl ought to stay down at the farm. Actually, he's crippled with rheumatism at the moment and doesn't leave his room. So he needn't know anything about it. Mother hasn't any of his absurd ideas and invites anyone and everyone straight into the drawing-room. Yes, send me your Marie Bernex."

"Couldn't you possibly wait for her at the bus stop and bring her back with you? She'll be coming from the direction of Bellerive."

"But how shall I recognise her?"

"By her face."

"By her face? What is there special about her face?"

"It seems she has a face like an angel."

"Have you seen angels already, Father?"

"In reproductions of pictures."

"But in real life?"

"I've seen some children with absolutely frank, innocent eyes. Mlle Marie Bernex has this rare quality. I imagine her rather like those Virgins by Perugino or Raphael which I so much want to see in Florence and Perugia. I don't suppose I ever shall see them but they must make us praise God in his most perfect work. There is no need to know her in order to recognise her."

"Then I shall just have to go by your description."

When it came to the point, she found his description quite sufficient. She saw a young peasant girl getting out of the bus; a girl very simply dressed and wearing the local head-dress of a little winged bonnet. Her beauty was so pure and so unexpected that Béatrice stood for a moment nailed to the spot. She would have let the girl pass by had not the latter stood looking this way and that, uncertain which way to take. She went up to her quickly and asked:

"Mademoiselle Marie Bernex?"

"Yes."

"I am taking you along with me."

When she wanted to be charming, no one could be more so than Béatrice. But she needed all her charm to overcome the surprise and suspicion of the unknown girl.

"But I'm going to the presbytery and M. le Curé is expecting me."

"It's he who sent me. You're to lunch at the château and the Abbé Merval will come over to see you there."

"Then I'll leave my luggage at the presbytery."

"It isn't heavy and the château isn't far."

"But where am I going to sleep?"

"At our house, of course."

Marie Bernex began to laugh gently.

"I am not used to staying in big houses."

"Oh, ours is only a ramshackle old place. You won't be any more uncomfortable there for a night or two than you would be at the presbytery."

The young girl was too intuitive not to sense at once that there must be some obstacle to her marriage. Almost at once Béatrice raised the subject of forming a choir at Saint-Paul.

"I do wish you would sing me a hymn or a song before lunch. I'll accompany you on the piano."

She yielded simply and naturally to the request. She was willing to fall in with her hostess's wishes and she was completely charmed and reassured by this young woman who had treated her from the first as an equal and a friend.

"Gounod's *Ave Maria*, if you'd like that. Or the hymn that I always sing when the children make their First Communion."

They walked together up the neglected avenue whose borders, between the trees, were overgrown with bracken and briars. There was grass growing between the stones under their feet. Mme d'Aimery, invariably kindly but indifferent to everything but her dreams and her Alpine flowers, had suddenly developed a new mania. She had taken to pursuing butterflies, with a long-handled net. Elderly as she was, she suddenly came running towards them, dressed in girlish white, and flung herself on an innocent victim.

"A swallowtail!" she cried triumphantly. She seized the blue, black and gold insect and held it out to the unknown visitor.

"Oh Madame," Marie implored her, "please do give it back its freedom. Don't stick a pin through it. Look, its little body is quivering in your fingers."

"You're perfectly right," said the lady, promptly opening her hand and letting it go. As the three of them went into the château together, loud cries were heard coming from a room next to the drawing-room.

"Take no notice," said the Baronne. "My husband has a bad attack of rheumatism in his knees. I'll give him an injection in a moment to quiet him down."

"Let me see him. I am supposed to be good with sick people."

"Certainly, if you like. But you won't be able to put up with him long."

Marie Bernex went into the invalid's room. At the sight of her, he stopped shouting.

"Oh sir, it is a rare privilege to suffer so much!"

"Hmm, you think so, do you?" he answered indignantly.

"God must be thinking of you very specially at this moment."

"Well, I'm certainly not thinking of Him. I wish He'd leave me in peace."

"Don't drive Him away like that. Your daughter and I are going to amuse you with our singing. We'll leave the door open."

Béatrice was astonished at the immediate ascendancy this little peasant had established over him. She sat down at the piano and played the accompaniment of the *Ave Maria* and the First Communion hymn. To her astonishment the old man, whose temper was always intolerable during his rheumatic attacks, called out to them:

"Ah Mademoiselle, that absent God of yours must have sent me that heavenly voice."

Marie's voice had the crystal purity of a woodland spring bubbling over moss, yet its tone was rich and full. She took her high notes with the utmost ease; she had no need of any forcing to give them resonance. When she had finished singing, Béatrice was so delighted that she threw her arms round her.

In the afternoon, the Abbé Merval came to see her. He had asked in vain to be allowed to visit M. d'Aimery at the same time. The old gentleman had declared that he was not going to see a loathsome black cassock after having had a glimpse of heaven. How was he going to persuade Marie Bernex to break off her engagement when her marriage was already announced? The Curé of Arvillard, the Abbé Rameau, had warned him against direct intervention. Marie was sensitive and no doubt very much in love with this handsome, untamed boy. Moreover, in her religious fervour, she was ready to sacrifice her own happiness to bring him back to God. But, while he was searching for a tactful opening, the girl herself took the initiative.

"I am very happy here, Father, but why aren't you putting me up at the presbytery? Perpétue would have got a room ready for me."

"Perpétue is no longer my housekeeper."

"Well, then, whoever is working for you now. I can guess . . . I can feel it from the way dear Father Rameau spoke and because you seem so embarrassed . . . that my marriage displeases you but you daren't say so. Don't you think I have the right to ask you for the truth? I've thought a very great deal about the importance of marriage which is an eternal promise before God. How could I give it if something is being hidden from me?"

"Very well then. You have a right to know the truth. But you must ask your fiancé to tell it you in person."

"That is what I came for."

"And if he refuses to tell you, you'll learn it for yourself at the presbytery. I shall expect you there tomorrow."

The next morning, the Abbé Merval found her in the church for his first Mass at which she received Communion. She remained for a long time with her head buried in her hands and, when he went to fetch her, she lifted up a face wet with tears. But she smiled at the priest and said simply:

"God is good. Now let us go and see Rosette Billois."

They went out together towards the presbytery. Mme Trabichon and Perpétue followed them with interested eyes. So the Curé was in the toils of another pretty girl!

What had happened between Marie and Pierre Loriot? The afternoon of the day before, she had gone up to the last house of the village where she had found the young man and his mother. Had she spoken to him alone or in the presence of the old woman? No, she had taken him up to the little pool under the stone slab where, knowing his power, he had wanted to kiss her. But she had kept him at arm's length until he had told her the whole truth. He had not been able to hide this truth or even to gloss it over. Marie herself was as transparent as one of those still pools which reflect things without the slightest distortion. Her straightforwardness banished lies as morning dissipates shadows. When he had admitted that he had seduced Rosette, she would have forgiven him for the sake of redeeming him. But when he had had to confess that she was with child by him, she had no longer hesitated about the necessity of breaking off their engagement.

"You must marry her and recognise the child."

At first his answer had been:

"I am quite willing to recognise the child but I don't want to marry the mother."

"Why?"

"Because there's only one woman for me. You."

"But it's impossible now. You're responsible for this other girl."

"No!"

"You can't separate her from the child."

At that, he had once more become the lawless hunter and poacher and had threatened her roughly:

"I forbid you to marry any man but me."

"My poor Pierre, you've no rights over me any longer."

"Get this into your head. If you marry anyone else, I'll shoot him."

"Why not shoot me?"

"You? Never."

She had laughed at his threat, partly because she did not believe it, partly because she was in no danger, since she had no thought of ever marrying anyone else. Then suddenly she had begun to weep.

"Why are you crying, Marie?"

"Because I'm unhappy."

"Then you *do* care for me?"

"I always shall."

He had held out his arms:

"Come here."

"No. Never again. I shall love you from a distance, my darling Pierre. And I shall pray for you."

"To hell with praying. Come here."

He had tried to fling himself on her but she ran away. He had caught up with her and seized her by the arm. She said gently:

"No, Pierre, let me go."

Her face must have worn that strange, supernatural look for, in spite of his fierce desire and his physical strength, her lover dropped her arm as suddenly as he had seized it.

"Go then, and I wish to hell I'd never set eyes on you."

"Not like that. Say goodbye to me kindly."

"No."

"But I shall always love you."

"Love me? How?"

"In God."

"I don't want that kind of love. . . . All right then, goodbye, Marie."

"Goodbye, Pierre. I'll be godmother to your child."

He did not answer and she walked slowly away. When she returned to the château she said nothing to her new friends but Béatrice guessed what had happened. She had been tempted to confide her own guilty love affair but what was the good of disturbing this utterly innocent creature? She sensed vaguely that Marie Bernex belonged to that rare type almost incomprehensible to ordinary mortals; the type of Bernadette of Lourdes and Thérèse of Lisieux. All that evening, the two of them charmed the bad-tempered old man with their music. When they parted for the night, Béatrice kissed her and, unbeliever as she was, asked her to pray for her.

The priest went ahead of Marie down the passage which led to the presbytery kitchen.

"Here it is. Rosette doesn't know that you're here. Would you like me to come in with you?"

"Just as you like, Father, but I don't need anyone. It's all quite simple and women find it easier to talk if they're alone."

She did not knock at the door but walked straight into the kitchen which opened on to the garden down two or three steps. As soon as Rosette had seen her and recognised her, she turned very pale, gave a gasp of surprise and stepped back as if in terror.

"Take care, Rosette. The steps are just behind you. You mustn't fall with the baby."

With the baby! The intruder knew everything then and had come to torment the victim. But Marie did not leave her a moment longer in doubt. She even forced herself to laugh as she said:

"You'll be the bride. And I shall be the godmother."

How right she had been to assure the Abbé Merval that it would all be very simple. In less than a minute, in a couple of sentences, she had cleared up the whole situation. Rosette could not believe her ears. She looked as stunned and stupefied as if someone had just beaten her. It was hardly the expression of someone who has just been granted happiness and release. At last she said:

"Do you really mean that, Marie?"

"Kiss me, Rosette."

Should she resist this kiss of peace? But who had ever resisted Marie Bernex?

"No, no, it's *you* he loves. You're saying this just because you're good. *He* won't want it."

"I saw him yesterday. He does want it. Tell the Curé to publish the banns and have the wedding as soon as possible because of the baby."

Seeking for a final proof, Rosette asked shyly:

"Will you come?"

"Yes, I'll come."

She promised it just to reassure her rival, but she told herself she would not keep her promise. What was the point of making a spectacle of herself before the entire village who would only be maliciously amused at her presence? What was the good of reminding him of a past which she knew he would not have forgotten? Already, Rosette was thinking along the same lines.

"No, no. If he sees you again, he won't want to any more."

"All right then. I'll go off into the mountains that day and I'll think of the two of you . . . of the three of you. Goodbye, Rosette."

"Goodbye, Marie. Forgive me."

"Forgive you?"

"I've loathed and detested you, I was so jealous."

"You must love me, Rosette."

"Oh, I will! Everyone loves you."

But Marie wondered whether she herself had lost the right to love. A little while later, she left the presbytery. Like Béatrice, the Abbé also asked for her prayers.

"It's I who need yours, Father. Especially today."

Wounds which bleed inwardly are the most painful. She would not refer to her own but the priest divined it.

"I am only a poor creature, Mademoiselle Marie. I can only see God's light reflected on earthly things and you can already see it as it is."

It was after the young girl's departure that he had given up the idea of his journey and renounced the lure of Paris. But in the end the artist was to yield to the temptation after all.

One evening Béatrice d'Aimery arrived at the presbytery; she had been running.

"Come at once, Father. My father's had an attack. He's dying."

"Ought I to bring the Holy Oils?"

"No, no, it would be too late."

Would this old miscreant, in any case, consent to receive the last Sacraments? He had always lived outside the Church but he had never hurt a fly. He had never hurt a fly but he had never made anyone happy; he had, in fact, incessantly made his presence trying, even odious, to his family by the bad temper which broke out in daily rows. Happy are those who have a pleasant disposition and happier still those who have the good fortune to live with them!

They hurried up the avenue as fast as they could. But the old man had already expelled his last breath and that breath had been a loud cry. He had died as he had lived: shouting. His wife was still supporting the body which was stiffening fast and swathed in fold after fold of an immense shawl.

"I had to wrap him up tight like this," Mme d'Aimery explained, "because he complained that he suddenly felt cold all over. He was groaning so terribly that I knew the end must be near so I tried to find his hand to hold it. He was so huddled up in all his coverings that at first I couldn't find it. When I did find his hand, it clutched mine till it nearly crushed it, then suddenly it relaxed. His head fell back and he was dead."

With the fidelity of women who are used to suffering and find nothing strange in a lifelong slavery, she wept for this man who had never given her any happiness. But Béatrice remained dry-eyed. Her father's hypochondria had driven away many suitors who had been attracted by her smooth freshness and her musical talent when she was between twenty and twenty-five. Tired of waiting, she had let herself be tempted by love for its own sake. Did she feel a certain remorse in the presence of this priest whom she had so cynically affronted at their first meeting? As she walked back with him, she confided to him a hope which compensated and more than compensated her for the loss of her father.

"I think, Father, that things are going to come right."

What things? He guessed what she was alluding to and realised that her thoughts were already far from the dead.

"Oh," he said. "So you have listened to Marie Bernex."

"Marie Bernex? My father's last pleasure. Don't you know that she has broken off her engagement?"

"And you have broken your . . . your ties."

"On the contrary, Father. On the contrary."

"What do you mean?"

"I am going to make them closer. My . . . friend has lost his wife. Quite suddenly."

"And you are going to marry him?"

"I hope so."

"That's a good thing, Mademoiselle. But now you must go and help your mother."

"Soon you'll be blessing us."

"Whenever you're ready."

"You certainly bring us luck, Father. After the marriage of Rosette, your housekeeper, it will be my turn. No more guilty passions . . . only loves which are pleasing to God after having been pleasing to the devil. Everyone has his turn. Isn't that true?"

She had not lost her taste for mocking law and order even if they were divine.

"Oh!" said the Abbé Merval carelessly. "God always has the last word."

At M. d'Aimery's funeral, André Belarmont followed at a little distance from the family, behind the weeping widow and the calm, indifferent Béatrice. Later on he came to the presbytery and explained that, after going a few miles, he had given up the pursuit of his unfaithful mistress.

"So you're leaving for Paris, Father."

"Who told you that?"

"M. Francisque Beauvais. He sent me back my cheque and told me about your exhibition. What a triumph!"

"Ah! So he's sent you back your cheque."

"Yes. I'd sent him the portrait of Arlette Jasmin whom I had turned out of my house and he was trying to behave like a gentleman. Didn't like to keep the picture and the price as well. He'll find a buyer for Arlette—both the original and the copy. And he'll get his money back over your pictures. Apparently you're going to have a fantastic success."

"You surprise me. Only by the grace of God."

"What are you going to do with this fortune?"

"However should I know? Ah, I *do* know though. I shall buy your organ for my church."

"It's not for sale."

"It will be. That will save me the cost of transport."

M. Belarmont was amused at this offhand assurance.

"An organ is not so easily replaced as a woman."

"You're not going to replace this singer?"

"I don't like living alone. *Vae soli.*"

"Then get married. I can quite see children playing by the water in front of your chalet."

"It's a pretty picture. But I'm past the age."

"You're past the age of folly. When one builds a house, one builds it to make a home, not to keep a series of mistresses in."

"You're severe, Father."

"So is truth."

"What is truth? Wasn't it Pilate who asked that?"

"He didn't find out what it was."

"And who taught you the truth?"

"The light I never stop pursuing."

"In painting! Take care, it will destroy you in the end."

It will destroy you in the end. He had touched on the raw spot and, once again, the priest asked himself whether he had the right to go to Paris. He asked himself but, in the end, he went.

There was yet another visitor to the presbytery: the suspended priest, Father Chavord. Little by little, the Abbé Merval had persuaded him not to be content just with looking at the tabernacle through the open door but to go into the church and say his rosary in the kindly shadow of a dark corner. One evening, just when night was falling, he came and rang at the door. It got dark so late at the end of May that Rosette was already asleep and the Curé was on the point of going to bed. He opened the door himself to his visitor, whose face was flaming red. It was soon obvious that he was extremely drunk though he still preserved his oddly aristocratic manner.

"I've come to say goodbye, Father, for I'm going away."

"Where are you going to?"

"To the Trappists. That's what you wanted, isn't it?"

"To the Trappists? You can't think how happy and relieved I feel, Father. It's just what I hoped you would do."

"Good advice. I'm taking it. I'm breaking off. I have broken off. Not just broken. Smashed. Smashed everything."

"Smashed everything!"

"Mustn't exaggerate. Only a bottle. Symbolic bottle. Bottle of brandy. Naturally emptied it first."

"You've drunk a whole bottle of brandy?"

"It was only half full. Now I've got the strength."

"Strength?"

"Strength to go away. Where was I to get strength? In the only possible place, of course."

"Oh yes, do go there. Go as soon as you possibly can."

"Tomorrow morning."

"Would you like me to come with you? I'll gladly take you over to the Trappist monastery at Tamier. That's the nearest one."

"That's where I'm going."

"I'll go with you."

But the other sneered:

"I don't need a nurse."

His eyes were glittering but his voice was thick. He kept his balance only by that habit of holding himself well which was second nature to him and was proof even against drunkenness. Nevertheless the Abbé Merval walked back with him to his home, as tactfully as possible so as not to wound his self-esteem. He was afraid that, if he let him go alone, he might have some mishap.

As he returned under the starry sky, he hummed the old hymn which Béatrice d'Aimery had taught the choir of Saint-Paul, now reduced to two or three of the village girls.

C'est le mois de Marie
C'est le mois le plus beau . . .

He broke off his humming to laugh. He had suddenly remembered something which had happened when he had been Assistant Priest at Fontaine-Couverte. This episode had brought about his final rupture with his Curé's housekeeper. In the aviary which he had introduced into the presbytery, his favourite bird had been a hoopoe. It had been a magnificent hoopoe, as big as a blackbird, with a long, curved beak and a tuft with a double row of black-edged feathers which looked like a provincial lady's Sunday hat. The cook had spitefully opened the cage at the very moment when he had to go to the church to celebrate the Month of Mary with hymns and the rosary. Torn between the religious service and the desire to recapture the fugitive, he had suddenly decided to combine the two. He had taken his girls' choir out into the woods to look for the hoopoe and made them pray and sing hymns as they did so. But this ingenious arrangement had only got him into severe trouble.

The next day he went over and made sure that the suspended priest really had gone off to the Trappists. What a relief for the parish and what a hope of rescue for the man of God who had fallen so low!

VII

TEMPTATION IN PARIS

WERE FAME AND fortune awaiting the Abbé Merval in Paris? The enterprising picture-dealer, who had tried to get in first as his impresario, had carried out his threats of trying to ruin his exhibition but in vain. His colleagues and rivals, only too delighted to put a spoke in his wheel, had banded together to launch this new type of painting with a knife or trowel. They had done everything they could to provoke public curiosity and to put their own price on the pictures. On his side, Francisque Beauvais, who was genuinely delighted with his discovery and who also wanted to turn it to his own profit and prestige, had managed to get a good art critic to edit the catalogue. Charles Dagnaux was neither a Robert de la Sizeranne or a Louis Gillet but he exercised undoubted authority and had a fruity style. Knowing his job and being perfectly aware that snobs are far more attracted by the personal touch than the profound study, he had begun his preface by a character sketch of the Abbé. He had padded this out with picturesque anecdotes provided by the man who had painted Arlette Jasmin. Nothing which might amuse or attract the public had been left out. It was all there—the late arrival at marriages and funerals due to the priest's preoccupation with catching effects of light; the marmoset introduced into the presbytery as a 'West Indian squirrel'; the spraying of the saints with copper sulphate; the Month of Mary procession in search of the escaped hoopoe. But after these whimsical stories which led one to conclude that a poor curate gets into trouble with his superior when he leaves the church to go off into the country armed with a palette, the celebrated critic took another tone:

"Nevertheless," he wrote, "he honours God with a passionate enthusiasm. He honours Him in all the wonders of creation, in the running water which reflects the sky, in the moving clouds and in the trees. He honours Him in the solitude of the mountain where His presence seems so near; in the wholesome vivifying air of the peaks and, most of all, in the light which gives life to water, sky, cloud and all the myriad forms of the universe. He is incapable of working shut up in a room. All his pictures have been painted on the spot. He has never been content to make rough sketches or to jot down hasty notes of changes of light and colour to be worked up and amplified later in the calm of the studio. He sees his picture instantly as a whole. One may meet him now on the bank of the Dranse, pushing aside the reeds ruffled by the wind; now up on a mountain; sometimes even on the glaciers, studying the blue reflections so that he may capture their jewelled glow. His paint-box is the oddest in the world. It does not contain a single paintbrush but only a trowel and a knife with which he works up his paint and lays it on the canvas as if he were giving a material body to his vision. Seen close to, it appears a formless chaos; at a distance the chaos breaks up and organises itself like the elements in Genesis; the coloured mass no longer seems heavy but vibrates with light and life.

"In the days when he was an Assistant Priest, he occasionally gave Latin lessons. One night he suddenly broke off the lesson, clambered out of the window and ran off in pursuit of the sunset. In winter, he has been known to take a couple of hot water bottles on his expeditions to keep out the cold, for winter skies have a special luminous quality which he well knows how to catch. One night, when he was camping on the shores of the little lake of Rozet which lies in the mountains, a storm caught him and ripped up his tent. The poor Abbé's only thought was to save, not his tent, but his pictures. He clutched them with both hands and, though the wind tore one away, he saved the rest. That is how we must think of him, fighting storm, cold and weariness to catch some effect of light which to him is a reflected gleam of the glory which radiates from the throne of God. He counts it no hardship but a privilege to toil to exhaustion to capture its beauty. He paints in the spirit of that medieval tumbler who performed his difficult tricks in front of the Virgin's statue as a humble offering in honour of herself and her divine Son.

"Painters know the secrets of light. Each part of a country has its own peculiar light which is almost like its soul. It does not merely affect the character of the soil and all that grows in it; it affects the very blood and thoughts and habits of the people who live on and by it. It affects their appearance; their voices; their whole attitude to life. Let us be grateful therefore to our painters since they help us to understand our familiar landscapes with a new intimacy; since they know how to bring out the peculiar quality of the light of our own countryside. Light, more light, light abundant and overflowing . . . that is the whole work of the Abbé Calixte Merval. That is its entire significance, the only criterion by which it should be judged."

A final paragraph emphasised the extraordinary, possibly unique case of an artist who saw his work as a vocation which was the complement of his religious life. It explained that he had never considered the possibility of showing his work or seeking public approval for it. Instead of wishing to turn his talent to his own profit, he had sought only to record his visions as acts of adoration for the Author of all created things.

The Abbé Merval found this catalogue at his hotel when he arrived in Paris after a sleepless night in a third-class carriage. He was horrified. Was it really permissible to undress him like that in public, to use his inmost thoughts as a publicity stunt? The whole preface affected him like a personal outrage. All he had wanted was to pass unnoticed; to remain anonymous. How would he ever bear being stared at by the people who came to it? They would regard him as some curious beast, some wild animal on show in a menagerie. In his innocence and ignorance, he did not realise that all these stories about him would contribute more to his success than his works themselves; that they were the best possible propaganda and would assure him the maximum publicity. On the contrary, the section devoted to his pictures and to his eternal pursuit of light enchanted him; it even revealed to him his own technique to which he had never given a conscious thought. As to the last paragraph, he saw in it a menace to that artist's solitude in which he had lived so peacefully and happily. He sighed when he thought that he might have gone on living in it but for the treachery of Francisque Beauvais. Why had this man taken it into his head to draw him out of his obscurity just because he had rummaged about on the uninhabited floor of the presbytery. It was true that all he had sought in his pictures was to record his ecstasy when confronted with the divine beauty. Now, at the price of humility and peace of mind, he had consented to be delivered up to the crowd for their approval or contempt. Already he trembled inwardly as he waited for the verdict that crowd would give on the merits of these eighty pictures now hanging in a fashionable Paris art gallery. Already he was wondering whether they had been arranged with due care for balance and contrast so as to display them to their best advantage.

After the turmoil of conflicting emotions aroused by reading the catalogue, he recovered his spirits. He left the little hotel on the Left Bank, highly recommended to the clergy, and made his way to the gallery. He arrived too early and, not knowing the ropes, tried to force open the door. A watchful official intercepted him.

"We don't open for another ten minutes."

"I'm in a hurry. Please let me in."

"Orders are orders."

When the ten minutes had elapsed, he tried again. The man enquired:

"Have you a card of admission?"

"No, I haven't."

"You'll have to pay, then."

Were they going to make him pay to see his own work? He muttered shyly:

"I am the painter."

"Ah, so *you're* the painter, are you? They told me it was a priest. All right, go in and make yourself at home."

He did not even know that the private view had been held the day before in his absence. They had deliberately not invited him because they wished to confront him with an accomplished fact and they had been afraid of some outburst on his part, some bucking in the shafts cunningly arranged to restrain him. The private view had itself been preceded by a confabulation of picture dealers and art critics which had produced a mutually satisfactory arrangement. The success necessary to the sales was a foregone conclusion. The morning papers which he had not read, or even thought of reading, were definitely favourable. There were even allusions to him in the Paris gossip columns whose paragraphs are far more effective than long articles. Without knowing it, the poor priest had become a star overnight.

Unconscious that he was now a fashionable personage, he stood there all alone in the room whose walls were hung with his pictures. He was alone with himself, or rather with his two selves, for was not the real Merval in these records of his passionate pursuit of light? He discovered himself and he was as surprised, and as ready to admire what he saw, as if he were looking at some other unknown person. His pictures had not been hung just anyhow. They were grouped with an intelligence which astonished him. For now he was able to follow his own instinctive and unconscious development. He could perceive a definite direction in it which came as a revelation.

He saw himself at first as the young priest who had just arrived at Fontaine-Couverte. Down in the valley, by the the river in flood, he had wanted to express the transparency of the atmosphere. He wanted to transpose the very movement of the sunlit stream on to his canvas; to make it actually flow before one's eyes. That was the first time he had glimpsed his own particular path as an artist. Hitherto he had wandered in the track inspired by the one or two Impressionists he had seen in Bellerive. Then he had followed at a distance; now he had gone on ahead. The water and the leaves pulsed with life. Yes, certainly, he had more or less caught their colour and movement; what he lacked was a true sense of values.

It was the mountains which had attracted him next. During his short holidays on the rocks of Colombière and Reclus and on the steep slopes of the Dôme, he had found new inspiration. When he had returned to the valley, it was autumn, the most luminous of all seasons. Drunk with this light, so much more varied and transparent than that of summer, he made his new canvases blaze with fire. A ruddy glow suffused water, sky and cloud; willows, reeds and osiers flamed like torches on the river bank. The golden clouds still reflected the brilliance of the vanished sun. Then he became fascinated by another aspect of light. This was the 'violet hour', the mysterious twilight that he loved. The purple water flowed, more slowly as it seemed, between purple banks and under purple trees at the foot of the purple Alps. But all these mauves and purples and violets were subtly differentiated and made up an ethereal harmony of softly graduated tones. All the works of those years of his youth, the years which had followed the first World War, had a boldness, a violence, almost a frenzy in which he could rediscover the ecstasy of his first intoxication with light.

Later, the paint became thicker; the style broader and more emphatic; the values more assured. Perhaps his youthful fervour was passing into a deeper, more contemplative phase. He found himself laughing aloud with pleasure at those haystacks in a meadow at the foot of the mountain, at those trees whose leaves positively quivered, at that troubled water under a sulphurous sky. The spangled, ever-changing water had been a constant torment to him. Often, in desperation, he had scooped up handfuls of it as if, by doing so, he could force it to give up its elusive secret. That low house on the river bank was the last house he had painted. Why remind himself of human beings? Nature more than sufficed him: the river with its reeds; the valley with its trees; the mountain with its glaciers. Once upon a time he had consented to paint a shed, a barn or a mill. Now he was so completely preoccupied with light and the movement of wind and water that he cared for nothing else.

Then, to his surprise, he realised that he must have gone through a period of that anxiety which attacks the creative artist like a disease and makes him lose confidence in his work. For a time he had suppressed colour altogether and worked only in tones of grey. It seemed to him that the atmosphere had become oppressive; that the light had lost its warmth and no longer enveloped things with its former love. He was frightened and constrained; he had lost his old daring and begun to doubt. At the time, he had been unconscious of this doubt but he perceived it plainly now that he saw his pictures hung in chronological order as his patrons had been intelligent enough to do. This clouded state corresponded with his expulsion from Fontaine-Couverte after the episode of spraying the statues.

Then the nightmare lifted. Now he was in full possession of himself. There was more space in his pictures and that space was more luminous than ever. There was less mass and the colours had grown quieter and more delicate; the values were true, the tones no longer in harsh opposition. All sense of tension and effort had vanished. The landscapes, though firmer and more static, gave, nevertheless, a clearer image of the changing face of nature and of the transparency of the air. They conveyed the sense of the invisible, eternal presence of the divine splendour.

He could hardly believe that it was really he who had painted these wonderful things. It gave him immense pleasure to see them all collected together. Huddled together on the empty floor of the presbytery, they were barely distinguishable one from another. He honestly could not have believed he had such a talent. Was it pride he was feeling now or simply the pleasure of an artist satisfied with his work? Pride is satanic but his pleasure was so frank and ingenuous that he truly thought it could not be pride.

But now, little by little, the gallery was filling up. The loyal public—the paying public—was arriving. Suppose he hid himself in a corner to overhear the talk and the critical appreciations? Would that be indiscreet? But was it not, after all, the only means of knowing the unvarnished truth? An elderly couple came up, standing too near the pictures. The woman made no secret of her disgust.

"Look at this mass of colours. A blob here and a blob there. You can't tell what it's meant to be."

"It's modern painting, dear."

A group of young girls had placed themselves at the right distance.

"Oh, isn't it queer? The water's moving and you can see the wind blowing through the rushes."

The lady who accompanied them congratulated them.

"The wind . . . and the light too, if you look."

"I like this one even better," declared a middle-aged man who knew the lady but who was far more interested in the young girls and wanted to make them notice him.

He was pointing at a picture of the 'violet hour'—the hour when it is just getting dusk, when the daylight dims and softens. He added:

"Unfortunately, it's sold."

There was indeed a ticket stuck on the frame bearing the word *sold.* And this label was also affixed to other pictures. The Abbé Merval had not noticed them and was astonished. His exhibition was hardly opened and already people were flocking to buy them. Who were these already numerous buyers and what prices had they paid? Would this money come to him and make him rich? He was smitten with shame and blushed. Up to that day he had never marketed his pictures and if he had presented one or another to charity sales, the organisers had received them grudgingly and had attached no importance whatever to such curious gifts. What a revenge for all that contempt! He forgot his shame and began to rejoice in the material advantages which would be the undoubted proof of his fame.

He had no more time to listen to the visitors' remarks. His brother-artist—he had the right to call him that now—Francisque Beauvais pounced on him in his dark corner with a troop of painters. He pointed him out to this crowd, urging them on as if they were a pack of hounds and the unfortunate Abbé the prey they had brought down at last.

"Here's our man! Here's the hero of the day!" he cried, embracing him in order to make it quite clear that he was the person who had discovered him. Promptly the rest surrounded him and congratulated him; some in all sincerity, others with barely suppressed resentment and jealousy. The poor priest was incapable of distinguishing the real admiration from the false. The public had observed this scene and hurried to join the circle.

"There he is," the middle-aged man said to the young girls who hastily attached themselves to the group, anxious to be in on a new sensation.

"What an odd-looking priest!" muttered the old couple.

He soon felt himself being stripped, searched and pierced by all these prying eyes. In an instant, he had become the fashion, like an actress or a film-star. His ingenuousness protected him like a shield. He hardly noticed the interest which was focussed on him and, for a little while, wondered why all these people were standing round them. A much befeathered young woman whose face was a whole palette of colours came up to him:

"Don't you recognise me, Father?"

"I'm afraid I don't, Madame."

"Arlette Jasmin."

How could he have recognised her? He had only seen her back view, flying from the arms of Francisque Beauvais to escape the wrath of M. Belarmont. Although he felt the awkwardness of this intrusion, he bore it with a slightly forced smile. Why spoil this wonderful day by giving good conduct lessons? In any case, Mlle Jasmin was promptly annexed by the troops of painters to whom her former lover resigned her without any obvious reluctance. He seemed, indeed, rather relieved to get rid of her since he was interested in something more immediate. The almost triumphal success of Calixte Merval, increased by the fact that he wore the cassock, was his work and he wanted to make sure everyone knew it. As a result, his own painting must take on a new lease of life and share in the sudden munificence of the picture-dealers who had fixed the prices by mutual agreement. He appointed himself the keeper of this new prodigy, this man in black whom all the snobs in Paris would be running after, and organised the way he should spend his time.

"In a moment you must receive the journalists."

"Me? Where?" asked the Abbé in alarm.

"In the little room opening out of this big one."

"Whatever shall I say to them?"

"Anything that comes into your head. This afternoon, you'll be free. Go and see the Impressionists' exhibition and, if you've got time, the Italian landscapes. Those will interest you. But don't let them spoil your originality. The Impressionists are already back numbers and for goodness' sake don't start bursting into Mignon's song which won't suit your voice at all."

"Mignon's song?"

"Yes, of course. 'Knowest thou the land where the lemon trees bloom?' . . . You know . . . golden oranges glowing under dark leaves . . . all that stuff. After that, you're dining with us at the Brasserie Royale. Everyone will be there. I warn you, it'll be very gay. I hope you're not easily shocked."

"I don't think so. But ought I to accept?"

"Naturally, since you're giving the dinner and paying for it."

"Me? But what with?"

The painter made a vast, sweeping gesture.

"With *that*. Don't worry. Your fortune is being well administered. You'll go back to your hole covered with laurels and with your purse full."

"I'd like to go back there at once," muttered the priest. The fear of the world . . . of what the *Imitation* calls the world . . . was beginning to take possession of him.

"Not to be thought of," insisted his guide. "Tomorrow night we're dining with the Comtesse Joëlle de Bréhat-Latour, our national muse. Her salon ought to launch you on the absolute crest of Paris society."

"No, no, *no*. I prefer my village."

"Too late, Father, too late. When the wine's poured out, one must drink it. You're famous . . . or you will be tomorrow. That involves certain obligations you can't possibly slip out of. For the moment, you're our prisoner."

"But the only thing I like is freedom."

"Ah, here are our journalists. Come and receive them with me."

They both retired into the small room where they were promptly besieged by reporters. A painter-priest, what a scoop! A Fra Angelico of landscape; what a chance of embroidering on an old yet up-to-date theme! They began at once plying him with questions on his origin, his early work and his vocation (not, of course, his priestly vocation but his artistic one). He began mumbling wretchedly, rather like Alphonse Daudet's drummer, Valmajour: *It came to me by night hearing the nightingale sing; it came to me by day watching nature wake to the sun.* Little by little his sincerity found the answers for him; answers that were lucid, simple, disarming in their frankness. They were to serve to compose picturesque portraits of his personality in which mockery would be cunningly disguised under false rhetoric. In the anti-clerical papers, he would be an excuse for lightly bantering religion.

One of the journalists brought up the question of other painters who had been preoccupied with light, notably Ravier who had recently emerged from obscurity and the celebrated Turner, suggesting that he must necessarily be their disciple.

"Ravier? Yes, I've heard of him. I know that he lives at Morestel in Dauphiné."

"He's dead."

"Ah, what a pity! He was passionately interested in sunsets."

"Have you seen any of his pictures?"

"One or two at Bellerive, yes."

"What about Turner?"

"One of my friends has talked to me about him."

"You've been to London, to the National Gallery?"

"Never, I'm only an ordinary village priest."

The journalist shook his head and whispered to his neighbour:

"He's pulling our leg, pretending to be as simple as all that. He's a knowing one."

"Obviously," the other answered. "But the whole thing's in the bag. It's a hot line and it'll go over big. Why spoil a good story?"

After this carefully arranged interview, Francisque Beauvais took the Abbé Calixte Merval home to lunch with him. This man with a weakness for models lived in a thoroughly bourgeois way. He had a wife, who must have been very beautiful but who had grown fat and ceased to take any trouble about herself, and two children; a boy and a girl. These two, ten and twelve respectively, were untidy, ill-behaved and badly brought up. But the priest was soon on easy terms with them as he was with all instinctive creatures whether animals or men. That evening, he had been cast for the part of Maecenas at the Brasserie Royale: he supposed he had better employ his afternoon in the way his mentor had suggested.

The Impressionists were exhibiting at the Jeu de Paume in the garden of the Tuileries. But the painter found himself stopping by a basin where children were sailing their little boats. A faint wind which barely ruffled the water lazily puffed the white sails. His eyes rested on the clear water which reflected the little boats and, round the stone edge, the happy, absorbed faces of the children. That picture by any Impressionist could equal this! It struck him how different this civilised aspect of nature was from the wild one which, hitherto, he had preferred. It added human pleasure, human choice, to the elements furnished by God—trees, water, stone and sky.

No, he would not go and see the pictures in the Jeu de Paume. But he made his way quickly via the Rue Royale and the Faubourg Saint Honoré to the Galerie Charpentier where the Italian landscapes were being exhibited. It was only an hour before closing time. Would these pictures cure his vague sense of disillusion? But the moment he entered, he was utterly dazzled. Time suspended its flight, and, when closing time came, he had to be positively driven out. He had fallen into a kind of ecstasy before Nicolas Poussin and Claude Lorrain. He was ravished by Poussin's *Apollo and Daphne* and even more by *Orpheus and Eurydice* where the two lovers meet again in the dark wood by the water and the château of Saint-Ange appears in the background under a halo of clouds. He loved, too, Claude Lorrain's *Village Fête*, where people danced under the trees in front of pillared arcades and his *Mysterious Castle* reflected in a clear lake which the light breeze ruffled no more than the keels of the children's boats in the Tuileries. At first he felt oppressed and discouraged as if he were completely out of his depth. He was discovering an art utterly different from his own simple imagination which was concerned only with the play of light in all its aspects. This art interpreted nature; it was superior to nature by its deliberate composition, by its perfection of line and drawing, by a kind of transposition in which the artist's feeling and intelligence permeated the things he saw and gave them human significance. Poussin fixed the perspectives, ordered the planes, arranged his figures and his landscapes with infallible skill. But the colouring that Claude Lorrain gave to the atmosphere made it vibrate with life; one could breathe the soft air, one could feel the warmth or coolness as if one were actually in it. He took one by the hand to draw you in under those trees or to lead one into the mysterious castle. Was it the light of the Roman Campagna or some dreamy, magic world or a true intuition of the secret of divine creation? As he looked, the Abbé forgot everything. He was only aware that he belonged to this magic world: this world of God seen through the vision of man.

He had no idea that his eyes were full of tears or that he was all alone in the empty room. He did not hear the doorkeeper shouting 'We're closing now.' He was reeling from the impact of genius. Driven out at last, he muttered out loud to himself in the street:

"I'm nothing. Nothing. Nothing."

But those other painters who had just acclaimed him, what were they?

VIII

MORE TEMPTATIONS IN PARIS

THE EVENING AT the Brasserie Royale restored the Abbé Merval to normal after he had been so shaken by coming face to face with genius. Conducted by their self-appointed leader, Francisque Beauvais, the chorus of his brother painters loudly attacked the Old Masters as they ate and drank copiously at the expense of the exhibition he had organised. They accused them of classicism and conformism and pointed out the independence, the audacity and disorder of nature itself. The next day the Abbé returned to the gallery to look at his own pictures again. At first he felt like repudiating them. Then, persuaded by all the eulogies he had heard, he smiled on them once again.

Who could this Comtesse Joëlle de Bréhat-Latour be who had invited him to dinner and who was to launch him in Parisian society? The idea of being launched like an aeroplane taking off from the ground amused him. He had brought his sound peasant commonsense with him to the capital. Francisque Beauvais, his mentor, had described this lady as a national muse and he did not know a single one of her poems. However, total ignorance was better than those abortive attempts at partial understanding. They would simply take it for granted that he was a backwoodsman. Was there no way of getting out of this invitation? He felt shattered at the mere thought of it, so alarming was the thought of this unknown world to a shy man like himself. But the unavoidable Francisque Beauvais arrived to fetch him at his hotel. He was in tails and a white waistcoat. There were even decorations pinned to his coat. He explained these by saying:

"Apparently some Minister's going to be there."

A taxi, which he left the priest to pay for, put them down in the Rue Murillo in front of a large house beside the Parc Monceau. A footman in knee-breeches ushered them in and announced them. The room was crowded and all the women wore low-necked dresses and were plastered with pearls and diamonds. The Abbé Merval felt ill-at-ease among all these bare shoulders and naked backs. He longed to run away and even made some tentative steps towards the door, as if he had forgotten something in the outer room. But the mistress of the house, whether because she guessed his embarrassment or whether simply because she was an expert hostess who was used to receiving all kinds of guests and being amiable to all of them, cut off his retreat. She introduced him all round with compliments so cleverly devised to please him and enhance his reputation that he could not be upset by them.

He promptly became the lion of the party. Each of the ladies praised his painting to him as if it had been her own personal discovery. He was questioned about the trowel and the knife. Fortunately for him, the arrival of the Minister created a diversion and saved him from being suffocated with praise.

At dinner, he was put on the left of the Comtesse de Bréhat-Latour, only second in place of honour to the Minister on her right. This underlined both the homage which was being accorded him and the importance of his exhibition. It could also be interpreted as a sign of that respect for the cloth which social etiquette still demanded. On his left sat a certain Mme Raynouard, the wife of an industrial magnate, who was said to be the Minister's mistress. Though she had passed her first youth, which means that she was forty if not more, her exaggerated décolletage proved that she was successfully holding her own against the menace of age. Her dress, which exposed not only her shoulders but the hollow between her breasts, aroused in the priest a kind of repulsion which he found it hard to conquer. Round her neck she wore several rows of pearls and on her bosom was a huge diamond brooch. He could not think how to begin a conversation with her when the mistress of the house abandoned him to turn to the Minister. As she bent her head to admire her rings, he asked her awkwardly:

"Do you love your jewels, Madame?"

It was an excellent opening, for he received the gratified answer:

"Ah, so you've noticed them? Doesn't the green of the emeralds set off the fire of the rubies marvellously?"

"You certainly do love them."

"I'm crazy about them."

What idea had suddenly passed through the mind of this poor country priest, launched against his will into Paris society through the machinations of Francisque Beauvais. Was he going to evang lise his neighbour?

"What about your soul? Do you love that?"

Astonished and dumbfounded, she repeated:

"My *soul*?"

"Yes, Madame, your soul. What are your jewels compared to your soul? Goat's dung in comparison with a rose?"

Still more startled, she could only echo him again:

"Goat's dung?"

People who overheard this remark could only suppose they were having a scatological conversation.

"Precisely," went on the Abbé. "Nothing more or less than goat's dung. You ought to love your soul, Madame. But first, you'll have to discover it."

"I've got one just as everyone else has."

"But you don't know how to use it."

"What do you want me to do with it?"

"Lead it to God by the way of charity. Or beauty . . . which comes to the same thing."

"I prefer beauty."

The Comtesse de Bréhat-Latour was getting tired of the Minister's political harangues which she found unendurable since they gave her no chance to talk. She leant over to her left, and having caught one or two words from their last exchange, she murmured, or rather chanted in her tenderest, most expressive voice:

> "*Never, ah never to find*
> *The soul that is ours tonight.*"

She was convinced that someone or other would be sure to recognise one of her best lines and thus arouse the general enthusiasm. But the number of the illiterate increases year by year. Should she humiliate them by quoting the entire poem? She contented herself with improvising a couplet on genius and beauty.

"Isn't it so, Father?" she said at the end. "Isn't beauty superior to virtue?"

But Calixte Merval was beginning to find his way among these lyrical paradoxes.

"Oh, Madame, it is only virtue that maintains the purity of art. There is no art among degenerates."

The national muse hastily returned to inspiring the Government. Mme Raynouard, who had not forgiven her neighbour for his remark about goat's dung, decided to put him on the rack.

"You were talking just now about beauty. But you miss all the beauty of women because of your vow of chastity. Don't you suffer terribly on account of that vow?"

He thought to himself:

"Very well. If you want war, you shall have war."

Aloud, he answered:

"No, Madame. It would be the opposite that would make me suffer."

"Do you hate women?"

"Not in the least. They interest me extremely . . . if only as workers in the same field."

"In what field?"

"Painting. They do quite a lot, nowadays, don't they? They seem to specialise in various shades of red. And then, it was a woman who inspired so many masterpieces."

"Which woman?"

"Why, the Virgin Mary, of course. No woman in the world can stand comparison with her. She is the tower of ivory, the house of gold."

His hostess once more turned her attention to him. Her expert ear had caught the religious topic and she saw a good opening. This was a chance to demonstrate her erudition and her broadmindedness in defiance of the critics who wanted to label her only as a pantheist and a worshipper of the eternal forces of nature.

"How right you are, Father, to glorify the Virgin as the inspirer of art. I don't know which I prefer—the gilded Virgin of Amiens, smiling at the child sitting on her left hand or the crowned Virgin of St. Denis with the veil down her back and that cunningly pleated dress. Or possibly the marble Virgin that came originally from Sens that I've seen in the Cluny museum. Do you know her? She's letting the precious little hands of the Child stroke her. Oh . . . but then there's that amazing Virgin suckling the Child in one of the windows at Chartres, all transfigured in light! Oh . . . and wait . . . don't you know that miniature in the Hours of the Duc de Berry at Chantilly, where she's in ecstasy over the newborn child?"

The Abbé Merval listened, at first with deference, then with a kind of beatitude which made him clasp his hands above his plate as if he wanted to pray.

"In my little church at Saint-Paul-en-Forêt," he said simply, unaware of the sound of his voice, for he had forgotten his surroundings and was talking to himself, "there is an old stone statue which shows the Virgin as a very young girl . . . fifteen perhaps . . . bending her face down, with such a delicate movement, over the Child Jesus. He's looking up at her, with one finger in His mouth. It's the work of a completely unknown artist. Real artists ought to be anonymous. They are only the servants of the divine beauty."

But the Comtesse de Bréhat-Latour was listening only to herself. She had already switched over to her right-hand neighbour and was launched on a new discourse—this time a purely social one.

The dinner ended in a general babble of conversation, in which all the latest gossip about Paris celebrities, statesmen, ballet-dancers, singers and academicians was eagerly recounted. The Abbé found it all quite meaningless since the names conveyed nothing to him. But, during the dessert, he had a chance to put a word in. A wonderful dish of fruit was presented to the guests: fruit that seemed to him as if it must have come from the Promised Land. Apart from the peaches and apricots that were in season, those apples and pears must have been grown in hothouses or brought from some exotic country. Mme Raynouard had selected one of these miraculous apples when, just as she was about to cut and peel it, the priest stopped her:

"No, Madame. Don't eat that fruit."

"And why shouldn't I eat it?"

"Because it was after she had eaten the apple that Eve realised she was naked."

She found this warning so amusing that she repeated it to the whole of one side of the table. Francisque Beauvais overheard it where he sat at the end and envied from afar the honour paid to this painter-priest whom he had discovered. The priest himself, who had only meant to teach the lady a lesson and was rather surprised at his own daring, found himself suddenly considered a wit. Such a reputation, which snobs will go to any length to acquire, is usually hard enough to make yet sometimes a single repartee is enough. The Abbé himself had only one desire: to get away. He longed to escape from all these fine ladies; from the aggressive Mme Raynouard and the eloquent and lyrical Mme de Bréhat-Latour. He had no idea how one could take French leave on such an occasion. The company left the table and reassembled in the drawing-room where trays of coffee and liqueurs were handed round. At last a door opened and he made a bee-line for it. Other guests who had been invited to the party made a noisy entrance. In the general commotion, no one would notice his flight. A moment later, he was outside the door and able to breathe again.

He had hardly collected his hat and his umbrella and disappeared before his hostess noticed his absence. This surreptitious departure was a decided disappointment to her. She had counted on having a reputation to make, on a Fra Angelico from the mountains whom she could exhibit to her set, always greedy for any new sensation. All round her there arose a buzz of praise and recrimination.

"Do you mean he's actually run away?"

"Mme Raynouard terrified him."

"What nonsense! He admired my rings and then he gave me a scolding."

"Gave you a scolding?"

"Yes, about my décolletage."

"He must have admired you then. He's got taste."

"He's a saint."

"He's an artist."

"And a wit. Did you hear the story of the apple?"

"Another Abbé Mugnier."

"Not so subtle, but more colourful."

"Give me his address, darling. I simply must ask him to something."

"I haven't got it. Ask Francisque Beauvais—he brought him."

"Monsieur Beauvais, do come along and bring your Abbé. What night are you free?"

"Ah, Madame, he's a savage."
"We'll civilise him."
"Have you seen his landscapes?"
"Not yet."
"But you talked about them with the greatest admiration."
"Really! If one had to read someone's book or see someone's picture before congratulating them!"
"How right you are! Actually, it makes it so much easier to be polite about them."
"Shall we arrange to go to this gallery the same day, at the same time, just before tea? There are still some pictures unsold."
"Are they expensive?"
"Fairly."
"Is he out to make money?"
"Good heavens no, poor chap. It's all for his church."
"Heaven defend us from people collecting for good works. They hold a pistol to your head."
"Especially if they happen to be priests. Pay up or go straight to hell."
"Do reserve a picture for me, M. Beauvais. I don't mind what I pay."
"With pleasure."
"Is it a good investment?"
"Oh, definitely. Everyone in Paris is going to talk about—in fact they're talking already, as we are tonight—this Curé who paints with a knife, like a murderer."
"You're perfectly right. Very well, I'll have two then. But make sure they're good ones."
"I want two as well."
"So do I."
"Let me just make a note in my little book. There! When will you come and see them?"
"Tomorrow, of course."
"No, tomorrow's impossible. There's the dress rehearsal at the Comédie Française in the afternoon."

"The day after tomorrow?"

"No, that's the garden party at the British Embassy."

"Very well. We'd better telephone each other."

"Yes, that would be best."

One of these ladies was suddenly struck by a brilliant and unexpected idea.

"Suppose we got him decorated?"

"Decorated?"

"My dear, we're in luck. We've got a Minister here in this very room. The most influential of the lot. Absolutely *the* man of the moment. Let's go and ask him."

"Darling, what a marvellous idea! It would be immensely useful to the Government. He's supposed to be anticlerical and he decorates a village priest. The Right will swing back to him again like one man."

The politician was promptly surrounded, solicited and practically blackmailed. The Honours List for the Fourteenth of July was not yet closed. What could one name more or less matter? Yes, but what would the Academy of Fine Arts say if they had not been consulted?

"The Academy of Fine Arts? They're completely conventional and utterly out of date. You must look towards the younger school."

"You'll have all the modern art enthusiasts on your side."

"And all the others against me."

"They don't count any more."

"Are you quite sure of that?"

"Of course they don't count. One must move with the times."

"Very well, I ask nothing better. The moment Mme de Bréhat-Latour adds her vote to yours, your request is granted."

"Bravo, Monsieur. It'll be immensely to your credit."

The next day, the Abbé Calixte Merval, who was far from proud of his evening in the great world, returned to his exhibition rather like a whipped dog slinking back to its kennel. He found Francisque Beauvais there waiting for him.

"My dear Curé, your ears must have been burning last night. Why did you run off like that? All those ladies were asking for you and buying you. They were even arranging to decorate your buttonhole or rather your cassock."

"I'm not for sale. And I don't want to be decorated."

"Nonsense. You'll be quite pleased when you've made a fortune and been given the Legion of Honour."

"Don't laugh at me. I've definitely come to say goodbye and to thank you for everything, although you've led me into temptation."

"Goodbye? I say, you can't do that. It's absolutely essential that you should stay. Haven't you read the morning papers? The Montrouge murder and your exhibition are on the front page. A rich woman strangled and a Fra Angelico in society . . . what a field-day for the journalists! The Comtesse de Bréhat-Latour is the finest publicity agent in Paris. No, no, your going away simply isn't to be thought of. You'll need another week to accept all your invitations and sell the rest of your pictures."

"My invitations?"

"Yes, of course. I've been told to pass them on to you by your female admirers of last night. There are at least three of them. I've written them down and we'll choose the nights together."

"Honestly, it's no good. I won't accept any of them. Last night was more than enough for me. Those parties are no place for a priest."

"I didn't think you were so narrow-minded. We've heard rumours that you're particularly kind to unmarried mothers and guilty couples out there at Saint-Paul."

"Jesus did not despise anyone."

"He let Himself be perfumed by Mary Magdalen."

"And He answered 'She hath done it for my burial.' I can only repeat . . . goodbye."

"You've positively decided?"

"Positively."

"Then I must call a meeting with the organiser of the exhibition and your dealers for them to show you your accounts."

"My accounts? My dealers?"

"Of course. Naturally, the accounts will go on but the picture dealers will keep in touch with you."

The meeting could not be held till the morning of the next day. Four majestic personages appeared. Two of them were stout and had large beards; one white, the other pepper and salt. The other two were lean, distinguished and clean-shaven, with noses like scimitars. A Rembrandt or a Franz Hals would have used them as merchants round a coveted treasure or relatives assisting at a death-bed. The Abbé Merval appeared before this august assembly like a schoolboy before his examiners. Some money was about to be ceremoniously bestowed on him.

"Excuse me," put in Francisque Beauvais, when the priest was just about to sign, without question, all the figures proposed to him. "The minimum price for every picture in the gallery has been fixed."

"Certainly. That is exactly what is shown in our accounts."

"But this price has frequently been exceeded. Particularly in the orders I brought in yesterday after the Comtesse de Bréhat-Latour's party."

"Our agreement did not foresee such a contingency."

"On the contrary, it foresaw it so clearly that it allows you thirty per cent on every sale."

One of the bearded old gentlemen took the offensive in turn. He had a nose like an eagle's beak. He looked furious and his eyes flashed:

"But what about you, Monsieur? Didn't you begin by helping yourself first? How much are you handing over to the painter for those two pictures you sold to us?"

"They were a present," declared the Abbé Merval.

"As a reward for his services?"

"No, for his discovery."

The painter had, in fact, helped himself. Had he not a perfect right to? If he had not rummaged about on the empty floor of the presbytery, the Curé's pictures would still be lying about there. It was he who had given the signal. All the success was due to him and the dealers were forced to admit it.

Finally they reached agreement on a figure which stupefied the Abbé and which left more to come in the future. A positive Pactolus was going to flow into the presbytery of Saint-Paul-en-Forêt.

"How would you like to be paid, Father—by cheque or in notes?"

"Half one, half the other," insisted his mentor, Francisque Beauvais. "Do you know, my dear Abbé, what to do with a crossed cheque?"

"I'm rather vague about it."

"Have you a banker at Bellerive?"

"A banker? Me? Good heavens, no."

The idea was so absurd that he laughed.

"That's a nuisance. But, with your cloth, you won't have any trouble with the bank. At the worst, a slight delay."

The painter could hardly have been more obliging. He was practical and had not let himself be done down by the picture dealers. He had protected his discovery against the sharks of the art world.

"Then you insist, Father, on leaving tonight?"

"This very night. I've booked my seat already."

"How are you going to spend your last afternoon?"

The great critic, Charles Dagnaux, who had written such a picturesque preface to the catalogue, said:

"You can't leave Paris without having seen the Impressionist exhibition."

"Perfect," declared Francisque Beauvais. "Then I'll

leave you in the hands of your apologist. When you get back to Saint-Paul, tell M. Belarmont that I have sold the portrait very satisfactorily to his successor."

"His successor?"

"Yes, the present proprietor of Arlette Jasmin. He'll never guess who it is. Actually it's the State itself. It's been bought for the Luxembourg."

"Ah!" said the priest. "I always thought that you hadn't deceived M. Belarmont."

"You're a lucky man, Father. You've pursued the light so zealously that you've lost the notion of evil. And you'll leave Paris just the same as when you arrived."

Just the same as when he arrived? The Abbé wished that he could be quite certain that this were true.

IX

THE LAST DAY IN PARIS

THE ABBÉ CALIXTE MERVAL could hardly have refused to accompany the great art critic, who had launched his exhibition, to the Jeu de Paume. The Impressionists did not really attract him and, left to himself, his only wish would have been to go back to the "Italian landscapes" and look once again at the Poussins and the Claudes. What was the point of filling his eyes with other visions and overloading himself with things he did not want to see? Nevertheless, he gave in to his self-appointed companion's wish. His peasant's shrewdness told him that the famous journalist was setting a trap for him; that he meant to collect material for an amusing, colourful article in which he would comment on the reactions of the hermit of Saint-Paul when brought face to face with the modern masters. However, at the last moment, he made a tentative bid to escape.

"Doesn't it seem a pity to leave the banks of the Seine to go and shut ourselves up in that square stone building? What lovelier pictures could we see than the ones in front of our eyes? Look at this rippling water, reflecting the trees on its banks. And, over there, look how the Île de la Cité plunges into the river like the prow of a boat. Look at those willows on it, with their long green hair. Let's go and glance at the façade of the Tuileries again. Or the pure line of the Louvre and the sculptured mass of Notre Dame. I've heard about the roses at the Bagatelle in the Bois de Boulogne. Couldn't we go and smell them?"

But his guide was ruthless.

"No, no, Father. You've got to come and judge the masters of painting."

"Oh, the masters of painting aren't in *there*. They're outside and their names are the Earth and the Sky. In fact, of course, there's only one."

He seemed about to pronounce the name of God but instead added hastily:

"I'm incapable of judging anyone, anyway."

Nevertheless he followed Charles Dagnaux into the Jeu de Paume. It was badly lit and ill-suited to an art exhibition. A large canvas near the entrance showed a boy playing on a flute.

"Oh!" he exclaimed in spite of himself. "That child's much too big."

"Too big?"

"Obviously. A painter begins by choosing the size of his canvas. It's the first sign of his taste. Why make that boy as large as life? It only needed a small picture. A small picture like one by those Dutch masters that I've only known and admired from photographs."

"Do you know who painted it?"

"However should I know?"

"Manet."

"Manet?" the Abbé echoed blankly. The name meant nothing at all to him.

Charles Dagnaux did not take him up on his criticism but led him on through the exhibition. It was a very incomplete one, representing hardly more than a duel between the two great painters Degas and Manet.

"Which do you prefer, Father?"

"Oh, undoubtedly, your M. Degas. I'm not a good judge of his café scenes and his bathers and his ballet dancers. But his self-portrait seems to me to belong to the great school—the Flemish or rather the Italian. Forgive my ignorance. I've only seen reproductions. And above all *The Misfortunes of Orleans* and his *Semiramis* don't belong to any time, any age. They're true, like the primitives."

"Ah, you've a taste for the primitives?"

"Certainly I have. They had faith."

"If you'd care to, let's go on after this to the Orangerie. There's an exhibition of Flemish painting that you'd enjoy more than this. And the Manets, what do you think of them?"

"I think that M. Manet isn't an Impressionist. In fact, he seems to me quite the reverse."

"The reverse?"

"Definitely. I thought that the Impressionist school had tried to bring a new expression into painting because it had realised that the air vibrated. They saw that, because of this, objects swam in a living halo in which their contours were etherealised . . . sometimes almost vanishing, sometimes melting into a kind of continuous movement. Didn't they observe on the banks of the Seine or the Marne—I forget which—the moving reflections of the sun on the water? Didn't they try and fix that continuous dance of light by means of flickering colours? Miles away, up there in my mountain, that was how I used to explain to myself the art of these people—Manet, Pissaro, Renoir, Sisley—whose works you've just been showing me. When I saw those water-lilies of Monet's and Sisley's acacias and those flowering trees of Pissaro's and Renoir's *Banks of the Seine at Champrosay* I felt I hadn't been off the track when I'd imagined them for myself. They were after just what I was after myself."

"It was obvious that you really did like *them*."

"I like them because there's something sincere about them. Something touching . . . and incomplete."

"Incomplete?"

"Yes. They've searched for something with their eyes and they haven't found it."

"But what were they searching *for*?"

"The meaning of light."

"Well, what does it mean?"

"Why, God, of course. He is everywhere."

The critic smiled. This answer would make others smile too when it appeared in his article.

"Just now, Father," he went on, "you were saying that Manet couldn't be classed among the Impressionists—that his art was even the very opposite of Impressionism."

"Undoubtedly. Just look at his pictures. He puts a black line round objects to enclose them in a definite shape instead of surrounding them with air. His *Picnic on the Grass* is even comic with his chilly naked woman among all those heavily dressed men. Degas would never have made that mistake or got up to such antics. But I feel as if I wanted to clear my eyes. Can't we get out of this sarcophagus?"

Charles Dagnaux was getting too much good copy out of his victim's perfectly sincere observations to abandon him when they left the Jeu de Paume. He suggested a visit to the Orangerie nearby where a rather hastily-assembled and badly-arranged exhibition of Flemish masters was being shown.

"I'm sure they will interest you considerably more than the Impressionists. You can't go back to your mountains without having finished your education."

"I'm afraid my education didn't go very far."

"I'm talking of your artistic education."

"I never had any."

"Then you need models to study."

"They'd only put me off the track."

"On the contrary, they'd excite you to emulation."

"I'm not jealous of anyone."

"You won't risk losing your originality by looking at these old painters of centuries ago."

"My originality, no. But my self-confidence, yes."

"On the contrary, they'll reinforce it."

Charles Dagnaux's insistence won the day and the Abbé consented to visit the Orangerie. He calculated that there would still be a little time before his train for a last look at the Poussins and the Claudes. They passed by the basin in the Tuileries where, the day before, the priest had stopped to follow the tracks of the children's sailing boats on the sunlit water. Delighted, he stopped to look again and noticed with astonishment that his companion could no more spare a glance for this living picture than he could for the Seine broken by the prow of the Cité or the long green hair of the willows. Do art critics live sealed up in museums and literary critics in libraries? Do they never confront pictures and books with the reality of nature and that of living, changeable human beings? This particular critic, however, was possessed of inexhaustible erudition. He indicated, with copious and well-informed eloquence, the gaps in the Flemish exhibition.

"Oh, Father, it isn't enough to dispense you from a visit to Belgium and Holland. You'll really have to go and see them on the spot."

"But a poor village priest simply isn't in a position to travel."

"But you're no longer a poor village priest. You're a wellknown artist—a painter who's arrived."

"Arrived at what?"

"At celebrity."

"Today, perhaps. Tomorrow I'll be forgotten."

"That depends entirely on you. You need to renew yourself and, to do that, you need to acquire the experience you lack. With the money that's going to shower on you, begin by visiting the picture galleries in Brussels, Bruges, Antwerp, Amsterdam, the Hague . . ."

"Good heavens, what a programme!"

"After that, it should be Italy. Why, it's next door to your own province."

The Abbé remained sceptical. Nature had sufficed him in the past and would suffice him in the future. In order not to annoy his guide, he agreed with him whole heartedly.

"Your Orangerie will have to take the place of all these

galleries in Belgium and Holland. What a wonderful piece of luck for me."

"No, my dear Father, no. The exhibition we're going to see is quite lamentably incomplete. The finest Memlings, the best Gérard Davids have been left in Bruges. You won't find Van Eycks from Brussels nor the Breughels with their *Nativity in the Snow* or their *Massacre of the Innocents*. You won't see that marvellous *Burial of Christ* by Quentin Metsys which is in the Antwerp museum. It's a tremendous picture ... the Virgin doesn't even need to lift her eyelids to express all the mother's suffering. It's as if her tears had completely dried up her eyes. And you'll miss heaven knows how many other masterpieces of the fourteenth, fifteenth and early sixteenth century. Still there'll be enough to enchant you and even to inspire you."

They entertained themselves for a few moments—only a very few—before Jerome Bosch's *Conjuror* and his *Madmen*. But the Abbé Merval was a landscape painter and promptly set off in pursuit of the landscapes of his predecessors. His eye dwelt tenderly and avidly on the twisting road, the black trees and the scattered castles of Pierre Christus's *Pieta*. In a Jean Van Eyck, the painter had imprisoned the twisting river with its bridges and boats and its flowery, sunbathed banks between two colonnades. Joachim de Portenier enchanted him with the backgrounds of the *Flight into Egypt* and *St. Jerome in the Desert*: enormous rocks, black spinneys, friendly-looking little Flemish houses. But he stayed much longer before a mysterious *Landscape* by Gérard David. Here, closely-growing trees with thick foliage dipped their roots in a dark pool where heavy oxen were drinking. The animals were almost invisible under the thick vault of leaves through which only a faint ray of sunlight pierced uncertainly, as if terrified by so many shadows. It was the first time that nature was treated by the painter for herself alone and not subordinated to some scene or person or reduced to a mere accessory or decoration. The Abbé

Merval stared, ravished, at those dark greens, at the vague yet detailed mass; at those grey or brown trunks standing out against the background of leaves. He admired the work of art yet it aroused his indignation.

"I should suffocate in there. I need more space and more light."

Charles Dagnaux interrupted this inspection of landscapes.

"My dear Abbé, aren't you attracted by the innumerable Virgins of these Flemings?"

"Indeed I am. But I hardly dare to look at them."

"Why ever not?"

"Their faces are supernatural. I'm not worthy to rise to their heights."

"Who's suggesting that you should? All you need to do is compare them with one another. Then you can tell me your preferences."

Once again, the Abbé Merval hesitated. What was the reason for these childish hesitations? Now he had paused in front of *The Girl and the Dead Bird* by Juan de Flandes: a little girl in a tight bodice, her hair hidden in a bonnet which let no rebel curl escape, holding the stiffened feathers in her hands. Her eyes were fixed in an indescribable terror that she could not analyse: she had discovered an extraordinary and terrible secret—the secret of death. Her face had ceased to be a child's and taken on the gravity of a woman's.

"Yes," observed Charles Dagnaux, seeing the other's absorption. "The painting is rather flat. His *Christ and the Woman of Samaria* has considerably more colour. Though the Christ in his long robe looks like an undertaker's mute and the Samaritan woman—far too well-dressed, incidentally—is curtseying to her pitcher. But you've got all these Virgins to choose between."

The Abbé Merval, thus forced to choose, went from one to the other. Which did he really prefer? Jerome Bosch's with her long curling hair, very shy in the presence of the

Three Kings, especially of the negro dressed in white who seemed so proud and stately? Thierry Bouts', with her hair parted on her forehead and almost hidden under her veil, looking gravely down at the Child Jesus as if she knew His cruel destiny? Then there was Jean Van Eyck's *Virgin at the Fountain*, hardly more than a girl and pressing the baby so tenderly against her cheek, while the angels seemed already to be crowning her. There was the Virgin of the Master of Flemalle, overwhelmed by the mystery of the Annunciation; troubled by the presence of the too handsome angel who seems troubled himself by the strange, divine message he brings. Was there not also the Virgin of the unknown Master of the Legend of St. Magdalen whose eyelids droop as if dazzled by too bright a light and who looks at the smiling Child with over-grave sweetness? Then there was Roger Van der Weyden's with her long oval face, clasping her tapering hands round the Child to whom she offers her virginal breast. But there were two which made him forget all the rest. One was Gérard David's exquisite *Virgin of the Milk Soup* who holds the Infant Jesus with her left hand as she dips the spoon in the basin with her right. This one was Martha and Mary in one, the good housewife and the contemplative. The other seemed even more marvellous. It was Quentin Metsys' Virgin with the long silky fair hair, gazing at her Son with an expression of ineffable ecstasy. One felt that she knew that this Son was to cause her Seven Sorrows; over that pure face, the face of a girl of fifteen, passed the shadow of the Cross.

"Well, my dear Abbé, have you chosen?"

With a feeling too strong to hide, Calixte Merval indicated his favourite ones in order of preference.

"Why . . . how passionately you love them! I've never heard you talk with so much feeling. Why don't you proceed now from landscape to the human face and figure. All you need is a few drawing lessons to perfect your technique."

"No, no. I remain fixed at the fourth day of Creation."

"The fourth day?"

"My learned friend, don't you know your Genesis?"

"I've forgotten it if I ever did. Nobody in Paris thinks about Genesis."

"So much the worse for Paris. In the country we think about it a great deal."

"All right, Father, tell me about it."

"Well, on the first day God created heaven and earth."

"All at once? A pretty good day's work!"

"The earth was shapeless and the darkness covered the face of the abyss but the Spirit of God moved over the waters. Then God said: 'Let there be light' and light was separated from darkness. That was the work of the first day and I might have stopped there."

"What do you mean, stopped there?"

"Why . . . because light was created and light is what I pursue."

"But your God did not stop there."

"Ah, no, indeed. The second day He divided the waters and separated the firmament, the earth and the seas. On the third, He ordered the earth to produce grass and fruits. On the fourth, He created the sun, the moon and the stars to light the earth day and night. And that is enough for my painting."

"It wasn't enough for the Flemish masters or even for the Impressionists."

"They have the other days."

"How many days do you leave to them?"

"Two. The fifth and the sixth. Because, on the seventh, God rested."

"And what did He do on the fifth and sixth? You must forgive my ignorance."

"Shouldn't we say your lack of imagination or your desire to mystify me? Can you see the earth without a living creature? *I* can . . . very well. I find it so bright and beautiful that it would be all I needed to make me worship God. On the fifth day, God created the animals, the fishes in the water, the birds in the sky and the beasts on the earth. And on the sixth, there came the supreme creation . . . Man in God's image and likeness to command the fishes, the birds, the animals and the whole earth. Now are you satisfied?"

"Not quite. What about Woman?"

"The Lord God formed Man from the slime of the earth and breathed the breath of life into him. He called him Adam and put him into the Earthly Paradise. Then, while he was asleep, He formed the companion He gave him out of man's own flesh."

"Ah, I was waiting for Eve to appear, Father. She corrupted the first man. No wonder you are reluctant to paint her."

"Don't condemn her, for the pride was in man. And here we are surrounded with pictures of the Virgin who redeemed that first fault. How could I feel worthy to approach her and paint her in my turn? The human being is beyond me and I am content with the earth. Even these hands are enough to overwhelm me completely."

Still talking, they had halted in front of the joined hands of Laurent Froimont, eternally fixed in prayer by Roger Van der Weyden.

"They're neither beautiful nor finely-shaped. The palms are heavy and the knuckles are all wrinkled. The ring on the index finger of the right hand . . . see how it's caused a swelling. Yet, how they speak! Can't you almost hear the prayer that's passing through them? I've got a photograph of my mother . . . she was a poor washerwoman . . . in which her two hands stand out on their own, all covered with cracks. I can't look at it without tears coming into my eyes. They're like a poem of work . . . work for *me*, her son who's a priest. One day, I tried to make a sketch of them. But I couldn't get their expression. I burnt it and never started again. So how can I ever attempt the human face? It is a reflection of God."

"A reflection of God! You're joking. Look at that fat woman with the round eyes who's just put up her lorgnette to stare at you. Or that little man with the pointed nose who's sniffing at Laurent Froimont's hands and sneering at their gesture. They're hideous enough to give one the creeps. Your God has been much more lavish in the infinite variety of ugliness than in the matter of beauty. Beauty is rare and it obeys strict laws."

"What does all that multitude matter? Twice I've seen God distinctly manifest Himself in His creatures. I don't know whether they were beautiful or ugly. Such judgments aren't within my scope. But the reflection was enough to transfigure them."

"A reflection of God? Hmm. In two men or two women?"

"In one man and one women."

"Aha! So one *was* a woman?"

"Her name is Marie Bernex. She's a peasant girl. She is radiant . . . and she diffuses peace. She has a voice like a woodland spring: absolutely limpid and pure. She's only got to appear for evil to vanish."

"A young girl? She'll get married and the charm will evaporate."

"She was engaged. She broke off her engagement to restore her fiancé to another young girl whom he had seduced and who was going to have a child by him. I don't believe she will ever marry. God has probably other ideas for her."

"Who's the other?"

"The other, Monsieur, is a priest. One of my companions in the seminary who does me the honour to be my friend. At the moment he is Vicar-General at Bellerive. One day, he'll be a bishop. He has an emaciated face that's as transparent as alabaster. He's like the sanctuary lamp that shows the flame through it."

After these verbal portraits, the Abbé made a gesture of discouragement.

"How could one ever put impressions like that on canvas? One would need all the innocence and sincerity of the Primitives."

"Qualities you share with them, my dear Abbé."

"I certainly don't share their genius. I can only do my little conjuring tricks with light. Besides, you can't separate the face from the body."

"And that's what worries you most, eh? The body whose anatomy one's got to know like a surgeon . . . whose nakedness one's got to know like a sculptor."

"But couldn't one do without it?"

"Now you're trying to be funny."

"I haven't travelled much. Still, one day, I did go to Beaune. I went there for the first Mass of a friend of mine. In the sacristy of the cathedral, I saw the famous tapestries of the life of Our Lady. In one of them, Mary, as a young girl is being led to the Temple by two angels. Her hair is unbound and so light that the air lifts it and plays with it. Now one of those angels is descending from heaven but the other is walking up the steps of the altar with her. And through that one's robe—it's pale green if I remember right—you can see the step distorted, just as it would be if you saw it through water. So the body is fluid and transparent."

"Angels aren't men, Father. Still less are they women."

Charles Dagnaux was immensely satisfied. He had collected enough remarks from his victim to furnish him with an original and picturesque article for some illustrated art review. As he took leave of the Abbé Merval, he repeated, almost word for word, Francisque's Beauvais' farewell observations.

"Goodbye, my dear hermit of Saint-Paul-en-Forêt. You are the last of the Primitives. So go on ignoring the idea of evil as you pursue the light . . . the light of the fourth day of Genesis. That delicious day before the creation of the carnivorous wild animals; before the creation of man with his vanity and woman with her perverseness."

Pursue the light! Others had pursued it before him and, happier than he, had caught and fixed it. He had one hour of freedom before he left Paris. Should he return to the "Italian landscapes"? He did so and recovered his ecstasy before the Poussins and the Claude Lorrains. Had not painting regressed since the days of those masters? The Hubert Roberts, the Guardis and Canalettos presented too civilised a charm for his taste. In them, the splendour of the daylight served only to enhance the houses and churches and ruins which caught or reflected it. It stopped at the façade of things and never penetrated within. Then suddenly, he discovered a fresh source at which to quench his thirst for beauty. Who was this Camille Corot whose *Fountain of the Villa Medici* and *Rome, seen from the Pincio* he was contemplating when suddenly the *Goatherd* caught his eye? He was transfixed, as he had been by *Orpheus and Eurydice* and the *Mysterious Castle*. This goatherd, seated in the foreground, was charming his goat as he played on his flute. Beyond the bushes which encircled him, stood trees, one of which had its trunk twisted by the wind. It was the edge of a wood on a plain which spread like a peaceful lake at the foot of a hill crowned with a few houses. The sky was of an indescribable purity . . . an azure as fluid as water and as delicate as the breath of spring. Why was this simple landscape so adorable? Because it was no longer a piece of nature but something spiritualised by love. As opposed to the mother whose face is transfigured when she looks at her child, it was the man's look which had transfigured nature. The artist had given himself to it so that his work had become a gesture of pure love. He had made the landscape so lovable that one wanted to hug it to one's heart.

It was this supreme vision that the Abbé Calixte Merval carried away with him. In his humility, he declined the challenge of a virginal or angelic face, feeling himself both unworthy and incapable of expressing it on canvas. But Poussin, Claude and Corot had revealed to him the truth of the art of landscape. This truth was neither imitation nor pursuit but the very respiration of the world. No corner of the earth was without its poetry, not the smallest weed or humblest pebble—provided the artist gave his whole self to it. That giving was the homage of the human heart and spirit to the splendour of created forms; to the eternal search for the living God. It was as if the world were a system of invisible things manifested visibly—and was not that precisely what St. Paul had said? Was not art even a province of theology in which he had been so sadly inexpert at the seminary? The sensible presence of the invisible God . . . was not that just what he was pursuing in light? Henceforth he would pursue it with a new fervour.

X

THE RETURN TO THE PRESBYTERY

THE ABBÉ CALIXTE MERVAL got out of the noisy and uncomfortable motor bus which had brought him from Bellerive to Saint-Paul on the last stage of his journey from Paris. He was somewhat exhausted by his night on the train and the jolting of the bus when at last he reached his presbytery. No sooner had he opened the garden gate than he saw before him one of Francisque Beauvais' pictures: his black dog was lying on his side with his paws encircling the white cat Mireille who nestled in the hollow of his body. The dog recognised his master and half-opened his eyes but contented himself with barking softly. He deliberately did not move so as not to disturb the sleeping cat.

"Ah," thought the priest. "That's what the painter forgot . . . the look and the charming way he's considering the cat's comfort. However would one express all that?"

While the parrot kept repeating his "It's the will of God" and the birds were singing in their cages Rosette heard his step and appeared from the kitchen. Her stomach seemed to have grown larger during his short absence and she looked as if she must be near her time. She gave a cry of surprise, burst into tears and sank into the nearest chair.

"What's the matter, my child? What are you crying about."

"He's gone off again!"

"Again? Where's he gone to?"

He had a shrewd idea where Pierre Loriot had gone. He ought to have guessed this would happen.

"To Italy."

"He'll come back with his contraband."

"He doesn't want to marry me any more. He still loves Marie Bernex."

"Has he seen her again?"

"No, no, she's shut her door to him. But how can one forget Marie Bernex?"

"He's got to forget her."

"I've asked the midwife . . . she's a witch . . . for a potion. She's promised me one."

"Heartaches can't be cured with drugs."

"Well, what can they be cured with?"

"With prayer."

"I don't pray nowadays and he never does."

"With time then."

"Time! But what about the baby?"

Shamelessly, she pointed to her stomach. It was evident that she had not much time left.

"Very well, very well, Rosette. I'll go and look for him. I'll bring him back. No other news to give me? No one ill in the village? No deaths . . . no marriages . . . no baptisms? The Curé of Arvillard promised to take my place."

"Oh yes, Father. Lots of things have happened."

"Then tell me as quickly as you can."

"The squirrel died from eating too much salad and the little chamois has run away. He's run away into the mountains. I looked for him and called for him the whole of one day. I took the goat with me on a string. She bleated and I shouted. We went by Pierrot's house. I thought he might help me. His mother gave me such a nasty look. She wasn't a bit sorry for me, seeing me pregnant and sweating all over."

"She doesn't know you, Rosette. Perhaps she knows nothing about all this. Your Pierre keeps things to himself."

"Oh, yes, she does, Father; she knows everything. If I'd been a stranger, she'd have offered me a glass of brandy to pull me together. She didn't even offer me a glass of water. When I got home, I was dead tired and aching all over. I thought I was going to have the baby then and there."

"Oh no . . . that would have been really too much . . ." the unfortunate priest exclaimed in spite of himself.

He could not help a horrified glimpse of the scandal that would ensue if she had her baby in the presbytery itself. The entire village would roar with laughter. What a triumph for Mme Trabichon and her confidante Perpétue! What justified rage on the part of the Bishop! There might even be some malicious allusion in the local papers which might possibly find its way into the gutter press of Paris which would be only too delighted to have a joke at the expense of the painter-priest. But he scolded himself for his vanity in caring about such possibilities. After all, the essential thing was to help the unfortunate, whoever they were and whatever the consequences might be. What did it matter if the help given was maliciously misinterpreted? It was God who saw and judged the truth. Recovering his calm, he comforted the frightened girl.

"Don't worry any more, Rosette. We can do without the wild chamois."

"You can't tame those wild creatures, Father. Animals and people, they're all the same."

She was right, he thought. Chamois and poachers inevitably went back to the mountains and to freedom.

"And then you know," she went on, "it's not only *them*."

"Well, what other news?"

"There's that unfrocked priest, that Chavord you used to have in the house."

"He went away to the Trappist monastery."

"He didn't stay there. He's back already."

"He can't have stayed long."

"He's like the others. He follows his instincts and *his* is drink."

"Did he come here to see me?"

"He certainly did come. He didn't only come but he carried off some of the altar wine."

"And you let him take it?"

"I'd like to see anyone try to stop that giant from stealing and getting drunk! You might as well stick a straw into a waterfall."

Nevertheless that giant had once been consecrated and consecration is for eternity. The Abbé Merval took up the defence of his fallen brother-priest.

"You did quite right, Rosette. I've still got some altar wine in a locked cellar. M. Chavord doesn't steal, he only borrows. He's unhappy. . . . that's why he wants to make himself forget."

"I'm unhappy. But *I* don't get drunk."

"You're not as unhappy as he is."

"I'm quite unhappy enough."

People always think of their own miseries and ignore those of others.

"I assure you that Pierre Loriot will come back."

"He won't. No more than the little chamois will."

"Well, is that the last of your list of bad news?"

"Oh no. The young lady from the château . . . she's been here too."

"Mlle Béatrice d'Aimery?"

"She seemed to be in an awful state about something."

"When did she come?"

"Yesterday evening, just as it was getting dark. She wants to talk to you."

"Very well. I'll go over."

His few days' absence had been enough for all sorts of troubles to pile up in them. But, when one returns home, delighted to be back in one's own rooms and to pick up one's old occupations, doesn't one usually find that all sorts of worries and troubles have accumulated in one's absence? If one is a landlord, there are inevitable complaints from one's tenants and urgent demands for repairs.

Tenants, too, find themselves faced with mysterious obligations and alarming threats if these are not fulfilled. In any case, there is nearly always the menace of unpaid bills. The return to which one had so pleasantly looked forward is usually poisoned in some way or other. Men are not always so charmingly considerate as dogs; they have no compunction in disturbing the repose of their fellows.

The Abbé Merval really did not know where to begin. Should he go to Pierre Loriot's hostile, sullen mother and try to get some information about her son's journey over the frontier? Should he visit the suspended priest who had not been able to stay even one week with the Trappists? What trouble could have brought the unbelieving Béatrice d'Aimery to a priest's house? He decided to go first to the Abbé Chavord. In the afternoon he would visit the château. He thought he could safely wait till the smuggler had had time to return over the pass from his expedition into Italy.

He found the unhappy Chavord in his shack, which had not been swept for days, sitting in front of a still full bottle of brandy. The drunkard stood up as he entered and made his oddly aristocratic gesture of greeting.

"Aha!" he mocked after this demonstration of politeness. "So you've come back too. Paris couldn't keep you. I hear you've made a lot of money out of your little sketches. Well, I haven't a bean. The blacksmith chucked me out yesterday because I gave him a tap. He made a joke that didn't strike me as funny. It's true that I knocked him flat. Well, that's how it is. I've nothing left. Nothing except *that*. I bought it with my last note."

He pointed to the bottle of brandy.

"So you weren't able to stay with the Trappists, my friend?" inquired the Abbé Merval.

"Good Lord, no! They made me work on the land and when I came in from the field, dripping with sweat, they gave me some filthy home-made wine. A disgusting flat drink and watered down into the bargain. I threw it in their faces. The Abbot gave me a sermon and told me to clear out. So here's old Hodge back again, at least with *this* consolation. I've only got two big glasses. Let's celebrate."

"You're not going to drink that."

"I certainly am. And I'm going to drink it this minute. Why not, since I've nothing to eat?"

"You can eat at the presbytery."

"A black sheep at your table?"

"I'm afraid not at my table. They wouldn't allow that."

"In the kitchen, then? With the girl who's pregnant?"

"No. Certainly not in the kitchen."

"Out in the passage then?"

"In a room that I'll keep specially for you. I'll wait on you myself if necessary."

The drunkard got up, either to fetch a corkscrew or to hide his embarrassment.

"Well, at any rate, Father, there's nothing of the Pharisee about you. You're not afraid of compromising yourself in my company. It's a pity I didn't meet you sooner."

"Why is it a pity?"

"Because you might have been able to make me mend my ways. Now it's too late."

"It's never too late. Please do listen to me. Promise me to come into the church every day about noon and I'll come in and fetch you for lunch."

The suspended priest had taken the bottle of brandy by its neck and was about to insert the corkscrew. The Abbé Merval deftly snatched the bottle out of his hand.

"Don't drink it. I implore you not to."

"*Me* not drink *that*? Hold on, don't throw it away or or I'll throw *you* out of the window."

The two men, both equally tall, were standing face to face. The lips of one were closed and his eyes beseeching; the other's face was suffused and his poisoned breath came in gusts from his open mouth. One was so lean and frail that he seemed no more than a bundle of bones; the other had the torso of a Hercules and the arms of a market porter. Nevertheless the first put his hands behind his back as if voluntarily disarming himself for the struggle which must ensue. He looked like a martyr waiting resignedly for torture. His adversary considered him with an insolent contempt which suddenly gave place to pity.

"That's enough," he said. "Give me back the bottle and don't let's fight about it."

"I'll only give it back on one condition."

"Ah, so you're dictating your terms instead of capitulating. Well, let's hear them, just for fun."

"You'll break it yourself or *I* will."

"Don't you dare smash it or I'll smash you."

"Then it's you who'll be smashed."

"Don't try to be funny."

"Oh no, my friend . . . my poor friend . . . I'm certainly not trying to be funny. I'm thinking of your soul which still carries the seal of God. Remember the day you were ordained. Remember your first Mass. I heard you weeping in my church when I took you into it that first time. Why, your eyes are wet at this moment. Everything in you isn't dead. Our Lady will help you. You don't know how merciful she is. Listen to me, I implore you."

The giant tottered forward. His heavy hand fell like a hawk on a pigeon. He snatched the bottle from his adversary and flung it with a violent gesture through the open window. It hurtled far away to smash in someone's garden. He gave an unpleasant laugh.

"My brandy ought to make the flowers grow."

The Abbé Merval came even closer to him and tried to take him in his arms.

"No sentiment, for goodness' sake," said the other shrinking away. "I've no idea why I did that. Folly. Utter imbecility."

"No no . . . it's the first step towards the Christ who's calling you."

"He stopped calling me a long time ago."

"He never stops calling. And now I'm taking you on."

"Do you mean you're offering me a job?"

"Yes, as gardener."

"Working for *you*?"

"Working for God. All gardeners are special servants of His. Didn't He order them, on the third day, to bring forth grass and flowers and fruit and vegetables?"

"I don't know the first thing about gardening. Still, one's got to live."

Then he added mischievously:

"And earn enough to buy drink. I've got to make up for that broken bottle."

"I'll give you board and lodging."

"Bread and water? Thanks! Anyhow, you know perfectly well you can't take me in."

"I can't actually have you under my roof. You'll stay on here and my housekeeper will come over and clean the place for you. As I've told you already, you'll have your meals in a separate room and I'll wait on you myself."

"What about pocket-money?"

"I'll keep you in clothes and shoes. You need some badly. You must be suitably dressed for your position, ready for when you wear the cassock again."

"Me? Wear the cassock again? D'you mean you've let your mind go as far as that?"

"I've never stopped thinking about it ever since I ran into you in the church porch, trying to get a glimpse of the tabernacle."

The suspended priest took shelter behind his past.

"I saved the Bishop when his carriage nearly went over the precipice. He threw me out. He threw me out for ever. It's all over. Finished."

"He strained his kindness to the limit over you. He's only waiting for you to return."

"Then let him wait. I'll never return."

"No, no, Father Chavord . . . my dear friend . . . don't speak like that. Live simply from now on: work . . . for work makes up for so much. Prayer and repentance will follow. Come with me."

The other followed him meekly. He was conquered by this gentleness for he was weary of everything and longing for affection. The village saw them walk by together and enter the presbytery together. No time, of course, was lost in informing Mme Trabichon of this.

The garden behind the presbytery was not large but it lay on a slope which made the work heavier. As it was almost wild, it needed a great deal of digging up and the gardening apprentice began by attacking this job. At noon his brother-priest came to relieve him of his task.

"Your meal is ready."

He insisted on waiting on him himself in the room they had prepared next to the dining-room. Had not Jesus waited on the poor? He even offered him, with a smile, a glass of red wine.

"It's altar wine. It's pure and it's good . . . only you mustn't drink too much of it."

And the suspended priest lifted his glass and drank his friend's health with a laugh of gratitude. There might even have been a promise in that laugh.

The Abbé Calixte Merval had not wasted his morning. How should he employ his afternoon? He was now provided with a gardener. With the golden stream from his exhibition, might he not acquire the organ he coveted for his church and engage an organist? It was the first thing he wanted to do with his money. He went over to the chalet by the lake to see M. Belarmont whom he found in the act of packing a suitcase.

"As you see, Father, I'm going away."

"Where are you off to?"

"To Belgium and Holland."

"You'll see some wonderful pictures there."

"Wonderful pictures, eh? Talking of pictures, let's have some news of M. Francisque Beauvais. I hear he's launched you on the road to success and done very well for himself in the process. Has he sold the portrait of Mlle Jasmin that I didn't want although I was willing to pay for it? Has he sold the sitter as well?"

"The portrait has been bought by the State."

"By the State? The portrait of that slut?"

"For the Luxembourg Museum. As to the original, I imagine that's been disposed of too."

"Did you meet her in Paris?"

"I met her at my exhibition, surrounded by a court of admirers."

"The bitch! I was absolutely right to throw her out."

Had he really thrown her out? Had he not tried to bring her back? Had she not been bored to tears with too much solitude and too much organ-playing? The priest had no desire to be enlightened on these subjects: he had another end in view. He had only consented to give M. Belarmont some information about the conduct of Mlle Arlette Jasmin in order to mollify him and engage his interest. Now, timidly, he made his proposition. His church was dumb. How easy it would be to give it a magnificent voice; the instrument that was richest of all in harmonies, the favourite of Bach and César Franck. Since M. Belarmont was going away, perhaps for a considerable time, why should he abandon this splendid organ to deathly silence? He argued so persistently, so persuasively that eventually he shook the owner. Very soon M. Belarmont was taking cover behind the question of the actual price.

"But, my dear Curé, have you any idea what such an organ is worth?"

"You won't fleece me and I'm willing to give you proper compensation. Fix the price yourself."

"So you're very well off, then? Your pictures went for fabulous sums, did they?"

"Certainly for sums I never expected."

"Good for you. Because I really don't want to fleece you."

The discussion was soon over. M. Belarmont did not neglect his own interests but he was willing to come to a reasonable agreement. He merely raised one final objection.

"What's the use of an organ without an organist? You don't know how to play it yourself."

"I can play a little. Not very well. I should have to improve a lot."

"You'll need time . . . and a teacher. Where would you find one in Saint-Paul?"

"My organist's found already."

"Really? But who on earth? . . ."

"Mlle Béatrice d'Aimery."

"I congratulate you. She's got music in her bones. She manages the stops and pedals almost as well as I do myself. And she's charming, into the bargain. Most attractive, that smooth white skin and green eyes and fair, fluffy hair. But she'll never accept. She's getting married."

"Getting married?"

"Didn't you know that she's been having an affair for years with the Comte Robert de Cabanel whose wife has just died? So now she's going to marry him. It's a pity. Now we shan't see her any more and I used to enjoy seeing her and discussing our favourite composers. I didn't share her enthusiasm for César Franck."

"It's a pity for my church and for my organ," the priest agreed.

He had said 'my organ' without hesitating, since the bargain was made. Then he added:

"Then I'll have to look elsewhere for an organist. I shall offer a good salary."

He wished M. Belarmont a good journey and took his leave. From thence he made his way towards the Château d'Aimery. On his walk, he sadly observed that everywhere nature bore definite marks of man's imprint. A sawmill was being set up on the edge of the forest. Below him the torrent of the Dranse was going to be put in chains. Did not progress demand that the water power should be used to furnish pipes and reservoirs? Everywhere the civilised aspired to replace the primitive. Yet it was only the primitive who looked at objects as children do, as if no one had ever seen them before. Only the primitive restores to nature her integrity of those first days of Genesis before the appearance of animals and men. In humanity's ruthless march towards the utilisation of matter had not art a vital role to play? Only art could preserve intact that sense of the beauty of things as they had come fresh from their Creator's hand. But where could he still find them in their pristine purity? The mountain kept them still because it defied cultivation. He would seek them higher and higher till he reached the Highest.

Nevertheless he went through the ever-open wooden gate that led into the great overgrown avenue between the oaks and beeches. At the end was the little château where the two women lived. Had they seen him coming, from the window? Béatrice appeared in the doorway and came to meet him. The smooth whiteness which was one of the charms of her face looked yellow and the little wrinkles round her green eyes had deepened. She was at the age where a woman changes from day to day; looking one day young and fresh and the next, almost faded. But is it not circumstances, rather than age, which produce this effect? Does she not bloom or fade according to whether she is happy or suffering?

"Ah, Father. What have you come to see us about?"

"How changeable women are! Yesterday, you wanted to see *me*."

"I'm not asking your help today. Yesterday I was in great distress."

"And today you're not? So much the better."

"I still am. But there's nothing you can do about it."

"Could I have done something when you came yesterday?"

"I was so beside myself that I wanted help . . . no matter where from . . . no matter *who* from. Don't be offended by my saying that."

"I'm delighted that you've got over this temporary blow."

"I haven't got over it. But confidences are only signs of weakness. Like prayers."

"My poor child, you're suffering and your secret's choking you. Won't you confide it to me? A priest can hear everything and won't give anything away."

After her chilly welcome, she suddenly changed her mind. She indicated a bench by a slate table under a clump of trees.

"Let's go and sit over there. I defied you the first time I set eyes on you. I was in my lover's arms."

"Before I went to Paris, you told me yourself that he was free now and was going to marry you. Everything was going to be regularised. I was to bless your marriage which would impose new duties on you."

"Well . . . he's not going to marry me after all."

Her pride broke down. The misery she had hidden from her mother, who knew nothing about her liaison and from everyone else who knew about it only too well, suddenly overflowed. He let her cry, knowing that words were useless to comfort. Suddenly her hair brushed his cassock and her head fell on his black shoulder. Suppose anyone were to see them so close! Luckily, there was no one in the avenue. Was there really no one about? He fancied he heard a movement in the branches. But there were only birds to be seen; birds who continued to sing with no concern for human intimacies. The priest gently withdrew himself from this unconscious familiarity. He ventured to ask:

"Why doesn't M. Cabanel want to marry you now, Mademoiselle?"

"So you know his name! Does that mean everyone knows it? How did you find it out?"

"From M. Belarmont who is regretting your departure from Saint-Paul in advance. He spoke about you with so much admiration and affection."

How could he guess that the wounds of love are only too often poisoned by the wounds of self-esteem and that a girl is always susceptible to another man's admiration?

"All right. You can tell him I'm staying here, worse luck."

"He's leaving tonight for the Low Counties. He sold me his organ and you must be my organist."

"Don't count on me, Father. We've lost my father's pension and my mother and I have only a tiny income. I shall have to earn my living to save the land and the château."

"But I intend to pay my organist."

"Are you telling me you've suddenly become rich? A priest in a mountain parish like this!"

"It's my pictures, Mademoiselle Béatrice. My little sketches, as they call them in the village."

"Ah! I'd forgotten all about your exhibition."

He had momentarily distracted her from her sorrow. But she seemed determined to withdraw into it again.

"No, no, Father. Leave me to my loneliness."

As she had returned to the subject, he asked once more the question they had avoided:

"Why is he taking himself out of your life . . . out of your heart?"

"He's not taking himself out of it."

"I don't understand."

"You will. He can't marry me because I'm almost penniless, because he's in debt, because his son's school fees cost him a lot, because he has expensive tastes. So, for all these various reasons, he's got to have a rich wife. He's found her already."

"So soon after the death of his first wife? Why doesn't he work?"

"Father, he's one of those men who are made for pleasure, not for work."

"But work is the greatest, the most certain of all our pleasures."

"Not for a man who's been idle from the day he was born. Not for the people whose only pleasure is love."

"There's only one love . . . the love of God."

"I'm talking of human loves."

"All human loves do is to hide Him. He lies beyond all their imperfections and all their sorrows. Why doesn't this man come and settle here in Saint-Paul? He could look after your property and you could look after my organ."

Having reverted to his fixed idea, he added:

"It would be so simple."

She smiled, in spite of her misery.

"It would be too simple. Robert would be bored to tears in the country."

"Will you let me ask you a question, Mademoiselle Béatrice?"

"Certainly, Father. And I promise to answer it."

"How can you love him? Why do you go on loving him? You're a musician and contemplative by nature. He sounds so different from you . . . so far away from your real self. He doesn't have the same tastes and interests."

"Does one ever know why one loves?"

"When one's taken the wrong road, the only thing is to retrace one's steps. Listen to me. If one doesn't know why one loves, one ought at least to know why one stops loving. Don't see him ever again. Now you'll be doing wrong if you see him and you'd be more unhappy than ever. You'll find compensations in life. I swear you will."

"What compensations?"

"I offer you one here and now. Come over to the chalet with me. My organ is yours from now on."

He induced her to come to the house by the lake which M. Belarmont had just left in his car. She was so uncertain and irresolute that she followed him with hardly any demur. But, once installed before the magic instrument, she gave herself up to her musical memories and began to improvise variations. Soon the great composers took possession of her: Bach, Widor, Saint-Saëns and, above all, César Franck. She even adapted the famous cantata: *Dieu s'avance à travers les champs*. The Abbé Calixte Merval knew well that God comes as soon as we call Him. The God of beauty draws our hearts and souls to Him through art and teaches them the sweetness of love which only He can satisfy. He teaches them, too, the suffering of love which only He can comfort.

Béatrice had lifted her tired, sensitive hands; those hands which were not yet willing to be clasped in prayer. But had not the Abbé de Servières once said that music led to prayer? She turned towards the listening priest and smiled at him. She looked refreshed and calm; almost young again.

"Father, your organist gives her consent."

Once again, art had consoled sorrow and triumphed over despair.

XI

MARRIAGE *IN EXTREMIS*

THE ORGAN HAD been dismantled and transported, with infinite precautions, from the chalet to the church by a team of experts sent out from Bellerive. Already, under the touch of Béatrice d'Aimery, its great voice summoned the recalcitrant or indifferent villagers to the services. Did music really lead to prayer? Young girls crowded into the sacristy to put themselves down for the choir; some from curiosity, some from coquetry, some from a general desire to please. They clung to each other and then backed out at the last moment, protesting that they hadn't any voice. But Rosette continued to weep in her kitchen. She had no news of Pierre Loriot who no longer wanted to marry her. Nevertheless he had returned from Italy with a whole load of contraband. But he had gone back to the mountains to hunt a herd of chamois which he had tracked down among the bushes of the Reclus. Such was the news which the Abbé Merval had gathered when he went to look for him. He had even braved the hospitality of Pierre's mother. He had tried to make an ally of her but she had answered that she would never let this immoral young woman cross her threshold. Why do women not become merciful as they grow older? Why do they preserve themselves in vinegar, like gherkins, and not in sugar, like fruit? In vain he had tried to soften this harsh old woman who wanted to keep her son to herself, who lived by poaching and smuggling and who remained hostile to God because her husband had died of a stroke while carrying too heavy a load of contraband.

How was he to find the fugitive? He had not responded to Rosette's appeals but he might to those of Marie Bernex.

But would it be right to use the latter to bring him back? The first time, she had obtained his promise on behalf of the poor girl who was going to have a child. Was it not too much to ask her to intervene once more? Yet she and she alone could work this miracle.

The Abbé Merval asked the advice of the Curé at Arvillard who was wise and discreet. The Abbé Rameau had no hesitation in sending him the young girl with the heavenly face. It was as if she were above all human passions and spread peace wherever she went. Her arrival at the presbytery quite overwhelmed the jealous Rosette.

"Why have you come, Marie?"

"I've come for your wedding. It's high time. The child will soon be born."

"Pierre doesn't want me any more. You've bewitched him. My potion isn't as good as yours."

"What potion?"

"The one the midwife . . . the witch . . gave me. He drank it and now he's run away."

"Where is he? I'll go and find him."

"To take him away from me?"

"No, to give him back to you."

"He's up in the mountains. You'll never find him."

"One of the hunters in the village will show me the way. He'll know where the chamois are to be found."

"Marie is right," put in the Curé, who knew the ways of animals. The habits of the chamois bring them back to the same places before the open hunting season starts. Their favourite haunts are clefts in high parts of the rocks where they can pasture on their favourite watercress whose vivid green can be seen at a distance. There, too, they find those flat stones they like to lick and on which the poachers put salt to attract them. The Curé, who knew the mountains almost as well as a hunter, promised to go with Marie himself.

Rosette placed her last hope on the two or them. This

girl Marie had the gift of pacifying her. She had only to use her eyes and her voice to obtain what she wanted. She had renounced Pierre but Pierre had not renounced her. Perhaps he might consent for her sake. Provided he did consent, Rosette was not going to trouble about the reason.

The expedition was put off to the next day. Rosette shared her bed with Marie. But the next day, very early in the morning a shepherd boy came to the presbytery with an urgent message for the priest. Pierre Loriot had returned from the Reclus where he had been hunting, with an eighty-pound chamois buck on his shoulders. After the long descent, he had had to climb up a slope to reach the spur on which his chalet was built. On this slope his heart had given out. He was dying. He might even be dead already.

"Who sent you, my boy?" asked the Abbé Merval. "Was it Pierre? Or was it his mother?"

"No, Father. It was my father."

"Who is your father?"

"Manilier. The neighbour who carried him into his house."

"Be sure and thank your father. I'll come at once."

He called his acolyte, took the Holy Oils and, wearing an alb and a surplice, set out to climb up the mountain path. The boy went before him ringing the bell at irregular intervals to warn people that God was passing. But there was no one on the road; no one to kneel down or to say a prayer for the dying man. For the dying man or the dead? Was it too late to bring this sinner the Last Sacraments and how would he receive them? Had he already closed his eyes to the splendour of this summer day? Even in the course of his sacred mission the painter could not be indifferent to the colours of the plain and the mountains, to the torrent which swept through the valley carrying the sunbeams on its flood. On either bank the golden harvest was ripening. Waterfalls tumbled from the rocks as he climbed and rhododendrons made patches of purple among the briars.

The grassy banks were covered with flowers of every colour and the impalpable mist of a fine day veiled the rocks and peaks and softened their contours.

He remembered the César Franck cantata, *Dieu s'avance à travers les champs*. The voice of the organ was replaced by the orchestra of the river, the streams, the birds and the humming insects. All round him, the whole of nature sang the glory of God.

He did not know that he was followed at a distance by two women, one of whom leant on the other because walking had become a terrible effort for her. Marie, who had got up first, had heard the shepherd's summons. She had woken up the other girl and told her part of the truth. Pierre was ill—very ill—perhaps even dying. She must be with him as soon as possible while he was still in possession of his will and his reason. He must recognise the child even if he could no longer marry the mother. He must atone for his sin before appearing at the throne of God. Rosette, weeping and overwrought, allowed herself to be convinced and escorted away.

"What's the good, Marie? I'm lost."

"No, no . . . don't give up hope yet. Can you climb up as far as Pierre's chalet?"

"I must, somehow."

"I'll help you, Rosette."

They followed in the track of the Abbé Merval and the little acolyte with the bell but they lost ground at every step. One had to support the other and make her rest at intervals.

The Curé had already arrived at the house of the dying man.

"Is he still alive?" he asked the mother, bowed and broken under the weight of this second disaster. First her husband; now her son. Smuggling and poaching had killed each of them in turn. Was there a secret justice, a heavenly police more inexorable than the earthly one? She stood stiffly on her threshold, like an enemy. But she was an enemy disarmed and capitulating in advance, giving herself up without defence but not without hatred. She did not kneel down before the Viaticum.

"May I come in, Madame?"

"What for?"

"I am bringing your son the greatest Help of all and the Holy Oils for Extreme Unction."

"No, no. There's nothing more he wants now. Can't you leave us in peace?"

"Is he conscious?"

"Yes."

"Good. I'll go and see him."

"He's got nothing to say to you. Go away."

"But I have something to say to him."

She went before him into the house, grumbling yet submitting all the same to the priest's authority. Reverently, he laid out the Holy Oils and left them in charge of the acolyte and then went over to the bed where the young man lay in his last agony. His heart was beating wildly and there were moments when he could not breathe. He would die in a sudden spasm or suffocate to death. But his mind remained lucid: he would watch himself die. Youth opposes all its vital powers to the destruction of the living being. Pierre looked unfavourably at the priest, the sight of whom made him realise what danger he must be in. But he must endure his presence since his mother had not forbidden it or rather had not succeeded in forbidding it.

"Pierre," the priest began. "Listen to me. If talking tires you, answer me by signs and I shall understand. You collapsed up on the mountain. In spite of the harm it has done you, you love the mountain, don't you?"

What a question! Of course a hunter loves the scene of his exploits and his victories. He acquiesced with a movement of his eyes. The priest continued his strange interrogation:

"Have you never met God up in the mountains?"

Astonished, the poacher asked, in his weakening but still audible voice:

"Who?"

"God, my friend. God Himself."

"Never."

He even added contemptuously:

"Don't know him."

"You're wrong, dear boy. I assure you you've met Him. Only you've never recognised Him because you've never called Him by His name. On fine days . . . like today . . . when you went off at dawn and the dew was on the plants . . . when the fields were full of flowers and the sky was blue overhead. Or in the evening, when you climbed down again with your face to the setting sun and the waterfall looked all golden, didn't you ever feel anything *here*?" He laid his hand on his breast. "Didn't your heart swell with love and joy as if everything was singing, not only all round you but inside you?"

"Yes, of course," muttered the dying man.

"Well . . . all that splendour of created things you saw about you was the visible splendour of the invisible God. You felt God without realising it. You were breathing God and you refused to recognise Him."

"D'you believe that, Father?"

"I'm as sure of it as I'm sure that you are alive and listening to me."

"It's true that I was happy."

"God visited you and you offended Him. Repeat after me very quietly: 'My God, I adore you for all the beauty of the mountains and the fields; for Yourself, for all my joy in living. My God, I belong to you. My God, take me. Strike me down as I struck my chamois. Carry me as I carried my contraband. Open the gate of Your paradise to me. Receive me because of Your greatness and Your infinite kindness. Forgive me, oh my God, for all my offences . . .' "

The dying man obediently repeated this canticle of adoration, silently shaping the words with his lips. It was true that up there on the mountain, especially when he reached the summit and could look down on four horizons, he felt a strange interior joy. It was like the delight that Marie's face gave him; something entirely different from carnal love and Rosette's embraces; something that was at the same time sweet and strong. It was like the exaltation of mountain air; an impulse towards a happiness keener than anything he could find in earthly pleasures such as making love to a girl or bringing off a good shot. What was this mysterious reaching-out after some immense and inaccessible good? Why not, therefore, give himself up to the priest's words which were sweet as honey and assuaged this strange, burning thirst?

The priest continued to pray. He began the "Our Father" and stopped at the words: "Thy will be done."

"You accept that Will, don't you? Even if it asks for your life?"

"Yes . . . yes."

"And wouldn't you offer even your life to make reparation for your faults?"

Pierre meekly repeated his "Yes . . . yes."

It was strange. He felt a kind of contentment in letting himself be guided like this. He was aware of a peace which would have been blissful had it not been for his fits of gasping for breath and the violent hammering of his heart.

"Your Rosette," went on the Abbé Merval, seeing that he had won Pierre Loriot's complete submission, "is going to have a child. Do you look on it as your child? You can no longer recognise it openly. You can no longer marry Rosette. But you can still express a wish in the presence of your mother here . . . a wish that she must take into consideration in the future."

Between two fits of coughing, the dying man answered: "Yes."

His mother had not uttered a word. Was she expected to admit the usurper? Deeply offended, she left the room. Up till then, she had followed the Curé's proceedings with interest. They were only concerned with the spiritual and all her preoccupations were with the temporal. But there would be nothing in writing and mere words could be ignored. All the same, her departure was a protest against the intrusion of a stranger, even if he wore an alb and a surplice.

She left the room, only to find herself threatened with another intrusion. What were these two women, one supporting the other who was white and trembling, doing here? She recognised Marie Bernex, the girl who had been engaged to her son and broken it off. Was she returning to him at the last moment? Her son had always hoped that she would change her mind. The other must be the wicked girl who had corrupted her son. The girl was carrying his child and Pierre had run away from her; first into Italy, then up into the mountains. Never, never would she allow that shameless creature into her house.

"Let us pass," Marie ordered her with that gentle yet firm assurance of hers. Something . . . perhaps it was the radiance of her face and the purity of her voice . . . conferred a strange gift of persuasive authority on this girl.

"You, yes. But not *her*."

"*She* is the one who must go in."

The old woman did not dare oppose her. The next moment, Marie had pushed Rosette into Pierre's room and closed the door on her.

"I won't have it," said the mother rebelliously. She was on the point of bursting into the room after Rosette. But Marie Bernex remained on guard before the door. Putting a finger to her lips, she said:

"Don't make a noise, Madame. Death must not be disturbed."

"We've had more than enough of the priest, as it is. I'm going to throw that slut out."

"No, Madame. You mustn't drive her away. She's your daughter and she's carrying your grandchild-to-be."

"My son wanted none of her and she's nothing but a loose woman."

"You are lying, Madame. And you know it."

"Let me get by so as I can throw her out."

"I shan't let you get by."

The old woman advanced, screeching and clawing at her with her nails. She looked like a crow croaking over a dead body. How dared this Marie Bernex defy her in her own house?

"Be quiet, Madame. Your son is face to face with God."

She was not afraid of the son who had wanted to take her in his arms with all the fierceness of his desire and whose arms had dropped and let her go of their own accord. Neither was she afraid of the frantic mother who wanted to push her aside so that she could prevent her son's reparation and endanger his immortal soul. Once again, the same mysterious grace operated. The mother of the dying man stopped clawing her. She no longer dared even to touch her, as if Marie were something verminous or sacred. She retired into her kitchen like a whipped dog and contented herself with muttering.

"*That* won't count. *That* won't count."

What was it that had no meaning for her and couldn't count? Could she not guess what was happening in the room next door? Was she so utterly oblivious of the power of the sacraments? Were her eyes blind to everything that could not be assessed in terms of business and profit? Marie Bernex, still keeping guard at the door, made the sign of the Cross and began to pray.

"Madame . . . won't you say a decade of the rosary with me?"

"*That* won't count," came the muttered refrain.

"Very well. I'll say it alone. When he's no longer here, Madame, you must take in his son or daughter."

"Never to my dying day. I swear it."

"Don't swear. Promise me to take the child in . . . and its young mother as well."

"My Pierre never wanted none of her."

"Don't you realise that he's accepting her this very moment?"

"He's going to die. He can't marry her now. You've got to have the Mayor to get married."

"You forget God, Madame."

"God comes after the Mayor. I know that much."

"God always comes first. God must be first served."

Did Marie Bernex know that she was repeating the very answer Jeanne d'Arc had made to her judges? . . . "God must be first served."

"No, no. *That* won't count," the other repeated obstinately.

The door, against which Marie was leaning, opened and the priest appeared on the threshold with the acolyte. How is it that an ordinary man, with no pretension to good looks . . . a lean, angular, even slightly ridiculous figure . . . can suddenly change and assume a kind of majesty? The old woman was almost frightened. She stood before him open-mouthed and gasping. She would even have knelt down if he had ordered her to do so. Instead, he came slowly towards her and said:

"You may come in again, Madame. God, in His goodness, has helped him. He has received the sacrament of marriage and I have given him Extreme Unction."

The sacrament of marriage? Was it possible? But the Curé was not entitled to marry them. He was going beyond his rights. She was dumbfounded and stupid. God had come before the Mayor, as Marie Bernex had declared. Marie Bernex tried to soften her and even tried to put her arms round her.

"Be good to Rosette. She's his wife now."

"She's not his wife."

"She is in the eyes of God."

Once again, this menacing God loomed before her. But this was all a trick. She would go and complain to the Mayor.

In one sense, it was indeed a trick. The Abbé Merval had acted without hesitation. Death is above all laws. When Rosette had been pushed into the room where the dying man had just made his submission, Pierre had looked at her quite kindly.

"It's you, Rosette. You've come."

She had wept to see him so pale and hardly able to speak for his laboured breathing.

"Oh Pierre . . . Pierre, don't leave me!"

The priest, seeing them reconciled, had joined their hands. Then he had asked the man if he took Rosette Billois, here present, for his wife and the girl if she took Pierre Loriot for her husband. They had exchanged the sacramental "Yes" and he had blessed them.

"Kiss your wife, Pierre. She is going to give her solemn promise to bring up your child in the Christian faith."

"I promise you before God," Rosette had murmured, taking her husband's deathly pale face between her hands.

Pierre had let her do as she wished. He seemed content. So many things had happened since the priest's arrival and there was still more to come. The priest had taken the Holy Oils from the case and anointed the hands and feet and lips of the dying man.

"Goodbye till we meet again, Pierre," he had said when the ceremony was over.

Seeing the young man's enquiring look, he had added:

"Till we meet in heaven. You will be there before me. You'll be waiting for me there."

Then, turning to Rosette, he had addressed her for the first time as a married woman.

"You may stay with your husband, Madame."

She wanted to stay but would the mother tolerate her presence? As soon as the priest and Marie Bernex had left, she would become mistress of her house once more. She would drive out the intruder and the dying man would be too weak to prevent it. Marie foresaw the danger and held the mother back by one arm:

"Leave the newly-married couple together."

"They're not married. I don't want them to be married. My son belongs to me . . . to no one but me."

"Haven't you any pity, then?"

"I've lost everything. First, my husband. Now my son."

"You still have God."

But she was deaf to the appeal. What was that sigh or that groan? Rosette herself threw open the door.

"Madame . . . Come at once. He's going."

The three women rushed into the room but Pierre Loriot was already dead. The mother gave a fearful animal moan and Rosette burst into sobs. Marie gave one last look at the face of the man she had loved and renounced. His face was so calm that it reassured her. He had died in the peace of God and it was she who closed his eyes.

"Go away . . . both of you," commanded the old woman. "Now that he's dead, he belongs to me."

The two women walked slowly down the path back to the presbytery, leaning on each other as they had done when they climbed the steep slope an hour before.

"Courage, Rosette. We're not far now."

"Oh," groaned Rosette. "I've got such pains. I'm sure it's beginning. Am I going to have it out here on the road?"

"Just a few more steps and we'll be there."

"But I can't have it in the priest's house."

"There's nowhere else for you to go. And you couldn't get a step beyond it."

They reached their refuge at last.

"Don't worry," said Marie Bernex. "The Abbé Merval will take us in. And I'll be your baby's godmother, just as I always promised you."

XII

THE LIGHT IS DARKENED

BELOW THE CHURCH and the presbytery, among the group of houses which made up the lower hamlet of Saint-Paul-en-Forêt, stood Mme Trabichon's chalet. The clematis had long since stopped flowering over the balcony, but the last roses on the wall and the willow which hung over the well in the courtyard took on a special charm in this golden month of September. It was altogether a pleasant, friendly-looking little house. In the time of the doctor who looked after the whole of this valley whose inhabitants were equally recalcitrant to drugs and disease, it had been open to all comers. His patients had not regretted this man whose devotion to them had resulted in his death. The peasants had considered this devotion a costly and unnecessary luxury. Nevertheless they had been glad enough to drop in at his house and drink at his expense. But, after the doctor's death, his widow had put an end to these invasions. She was one of those active women to whom the presence of even the most easy-going man is an irritating brake on their activity. Widowhood suited her, as it suits so many women, a great deal better than marriage. No doubt this explains the number and the longevity of so many sprightly widows who retain their energy to extreme old age. They cannot tolerate any authority in their homes since they prefer to monopolise it themselves. Mme Trabichon liked to think of herself as the power behind both the Curé and the Mayor. She wished to keep both municipal and ecclesiastical affairs under her efficient and even benevolent yoke. The municipality had seceded, little by little, under certain anti-clerical influences, so she had to fall back on the presbytery. Here she had been the uncontested ruler of an amiable, semi-invalid old priest, the Abbé Perdriset, who had let her act as a kind of administrative curate. He had given her a free hand in the matter of getting rid of drunkards with hard-luck stories and passing tramps who might very well turn out to be thieves. The arrival of Canon Sisteron, who had succeeded this mild and submissive incumbent, had at first annoyed her. He was too much of a great personage for a place like Saint-Paul. Permanent Secretary of the Academy of Letters, Arts and Sciences at Bellerive, an eminent scholar and a mine of erudition, he had abandoned his position and his honours out of humility. He had implored the Bishop to send him to a remote mountain parish where he might bury his pride. But he had not been able to abandon overnight his habit of almost despotic authority, having been too long accustomed to combating intellectual dishonesty and historical errors with fierce energy and unassailable competence. The relaxed morals of Saint-Paul, that haven of smugglers and poachers whose shepherds' chalets were the scene of rustic debauchery, had roused his anger. He had vehemently denounced this immorality from the pulpit with the result that his church was soon almost empty. Like Doctor Trabichon, he had died in harness, sadly conscious that he had failed in the mission which cost so much to his self-esteem. Nevertheless, the widow had profited by his zeal—a zeal which had been strongly tinged with Jansenism—to acquire a firm grasp on the material side of the ministry. Together with Perpétue, she reigned over the soup-kitchen and the presbytery door. She saw to it that that door was only open to the people they knew and of whom they approved. Too many young priests who are not thoroughly broken in or whose presbyteries are not guarded by sentinels like Mme Trabichon, open that door to all comers. Above all, she enthroned herself in the church and the sacristy which became her drawing-room, her boudoir and her linen-cupboard. Never was God more effectively honoured in the meticulous cleanliness of the holy edifice and in its impressive decoration for feast-days. Never were the altar linen, the albs and the surplices so constantly washed and ironed and kept so dazzlingly white; never were the priest's vestments so scrupulously tended and mended.

She had counted on Canon Sisteron's successor to increase her influence still further. She had hoped to take over the direction of the parish which badly needed to be awakened from its religious indifference and thoroughly put in order. Had she not been told that the new parish priest, fresh from being a mere Assistant at Fontaine-Couverte, was a scatterbrained creature—an artist who lived in the moon and whom it would be easy to lead by the nose? Instead, from the very beginning, the Abbé Calixte Merval had displayed a rebellious audacity. For six months now she had remained patient in the unavailing hope that he would become more amenable. She had too much respect for religious authority to want to enter into open conflict with her parish priest. But now her patience was exhausted. Duty took precedence over every other consideration and overrode all her scruples.

This was why, on that fine September day when the roses were still in bloom and the pears were beginning to ripen in the orchard, Mme Trabichon was busy at her writing-desk. For the third time, she was revising, or rather re-copying, a letter destined for Mgr. Hélouard, the Bishop of Bellerive. This letter represented her decision to inform him, at last, of the extraordinary behaviour of the Curé of Saint-Paul. She had taken immense pains with this letter, constantly changing and correcting it. Sometimes she softened her expressions, sometimes she made them stronger out of regard for the truth. This time she felt she had arrived at her final version but, before sealing up and despatching such an important document, she wanted to try it on a select audience. This audience was to be composed exclusively of Perpétue the cook who, though she was uneducated, had plenty of sense. Moreover, having worked for both of the Abbé Merval's predecessors, she was well up in ecclesiastical affairs. It was possible, of course, that, having been rudely dismissed by the present Curé, some lingering resentment might prevent her from judging with complete impartiality. Her mistress would bear this in mind and, if necessary, calm down her over-aggressive zeal. Mme Trabichon was perfectly convinced that she herself had scrupulously weighed up her complaints and had set them down with the most objective fairness.

"Perpétue," she called. "Leave your cooking for a minute or two and let me read you something. When you've heard it, I want you to give me your opinion."

The servant obeyed her order. Her face was flushed from the stove and her apron spotted with grease.

"Sit over there in that armchair."

"Do you really mean me to sit *there*?"

"Of course, since I've asked you to. Now listen carefully, so as not to miss a word."

"I've got my ears skinned. But what's it all about, Madame?"

"It's a letter I'm sending to the Bishop of Bellerive on the subject of our parish priest."

"Ah, Madame! There's no end to what you could say on *that* subject."

"Forget your personal grievances, Perpétue, and be absolutely impartial."

"Oh, I will be, Madame."

She had not the least idea what impartiality meant. She only knew that she had received an order and there was no point in arguing about it.

"Please shut the window."

"Why, Madame? It's warmer outside than in."

"Because someone might pass along the road. No one

must hear what I'm going to read to you. Otherwise we might be betrayed."

"That's true. No one must hear. I'll shut it."

In the closed room, Mme Trabichon put on her glasses and took up the final copy of her letter. It was written in her most careful hand and ran into several pages. She glanced at it for a moment with affectionate admiration and then began her long reading.

"*Saint-Paul-en-Forêt, this 23rd day of September, feast of St. Thecla, virgin and martyr, converted by St. Paul and who, for this reason, should be specially honoured in our parish.*

"MONSEIGNEUR,

"I have hesitated for many months before composing and addressing this letter to Your Lordship. An imperative duty constrains me to this course before the scandal becomes too painfully evident and provokes such widespread publicity that it will give countenance to the enemies of our holy religion. Formerly I have had to warn Your Lordship of the intemperate zeal of His Reverence, Canon Sisteron, who disturbed souls by his continuous threats of hell fire and, in consequence, alienated almost the whole of the parish and prevented their coming to church. But what are the errors of a holy man compared with the systematic violation of divine and human laws practised by our new incumbent?

"His Reverence, the Abbé Merval, before being appointed to this parish had left a somewhat doubtful reputation at Fontaine-Couverte where he was formerly Curate. I cannot ignore the fact that his superior had complained of him to Your Lordship. One might have hoped that the sense of his new responsibility might have produced a favourable effect and have inspired him to discretion in the exercise of his priestly duties. On the very day of his arrival (he was escorted by a whole menagerie of birds, a cat, a dog, a squirrel and even a monkey) he rudely dismissed the old housekeeper . . ."

"I'm not old," Perpétue interrupted. "I'm only fifty-eight."

"You're quite right. I'll put 'former' instead. But don't interrupt again."

"... He rudely dismissed the former housekeeper, Mlle Perpétue Monet, who, for thirty years, had enjoyed the confidence and esteem of the two preceding incumbents of Saint-Paul. By whom did he replace her? By a pregnant girl whom her father had turned out of his house for her immoral conduct. I leave Your Lordship to imagine the scandalous spectacle offered to all who visited the presbytery where the servant openly flaunted her pregnancy which was only too obviously approaching its term.

"It appeared that our parish priest was only interested in illicit couples. On the pretext of being interested in music, he took to frequenting a certain M. Belarmont who was living at that time in open sin with a music-hall singer named Arlette Jasmin. He also paid several visits to the Château d'Aimery. The daughter of the house, Mlle Béatrice d'Aimery, has been conducting an immoral liaison with a certain Comte de Cabanel. Everyone is perfectly aware of this except, possibly, her mother, who keeps her eyes shut, whether voluntarily or involuntarily.

"Had he not been warned by his ecclesiastical superiors against the presence in this village of that priest suspended by Your Lordship, the Abbé Chavord, an inveterate idler and drunkard? I myself had advised Your Lordship of this danger when I reported to you in the case of Canon Sisteron whose conduct in the matter was far more prudent and discreet. Our present Curé, however, far from heeding such warnings, has taken no precautions to avoid him and has outraged all decent feeling. Not only has he opened the church to this unworthy member of the priesthood who can only defile it by his presence but he has even invited him into the presbytery. Now, on the pretext of making him look after his garden, he has installed him in his house and shamelessly takes his meals with him to everyone's certain knowledge. He is openly compromising himself by this intimate association. One might almost suppose that he is defying the episcopal ban and taking it upon himself to criticise the suspension of M. Chavord.

"This is not all, Monseigneur. I am sorry to have to prolong this list of distressing events which are a permanent topic of conversation in the public conveyance between Saint-Paul and Bellerive and in the market-place of Arvillard. Last June, the Abbé Merval was summoned to Paris by some Hebrew dealers who were anxious to make a profit out of the little pictures he is always painting of the countryside instead of devoting himself to his parishioners. These sketches aroused not the faintest attention among art-lovers before the organisation of this affair. He returned from this exhibition with considerable sums of money. Instead of distributing these to the poor, he has employed them in a manner of which it is impossible to approve. Without consulting anyone, he has bought, at great expense, an organ formerly belonging to M. Bel[illegible]rmont and installed it in the church. A harmonium would have been quite adequate instead of this enormous instrument which is far too noisy and entirely out of place in a little rural parish. Even worse, he has engaged an organist to whom he pays a handsome monthly salary. This organist is none other than a woman . . . Mlle Béatrice d'Aimery . . . whose immoral conduct he has recompensed thus. Malicious tongues have even suggested that she has obtained this situation by illicit means and by arousing the carnal desires of the Abbé. Personally, I should be loth to suspect the latter of any immoral conduct. But a photograph, taken by the son of the gardener at the château who had come over from the town and was walking along a path, shows M. Merval and Mlle d'Aimery sitting side by side on a bench and the young woman's head is resting on the priest's shoulder. Your Lordship will find a copy of this photograph among the attached papers.

"Over and above all this, our parish priest has lost all sense of shame and goes so far as to give concerts in our church. Tourists flock to these from a distance. A female opera singer has performed at these and I am assured that some kind of symphony or concerto entitled 'L'Après-midi d'un Faune' has actually been played on the organ.

"I now come to the principal point which I have not touched on hitherto and which has let loose a storm in the municipal offices of Saint-Paul where a complaint has been formally lodged. The young man, probably one of many, who had seduced the priest's servant, a girl named Rosette Billois, was a notorious poacher and smuggler for whom the police and the customs officials had long been searching in vain. This Pierre Loriot lived at the last house above the village, on a spur of the mountain at the foot of the Reclus. This young man caught a fever or had some sort of attack while hunting chamois and returned in a dying condition. Our Curé went and took him the Last Sacraments although this Loriot never went to church. I cannot, of course, blame him for this possibly imprudent zeal which might have resulted in an embarrassing refusal. But he took two young girls along with him: one, the unmarried mother who was on the verge of her confinement; the other, a girl from Arvillard, Marie Bernex, who had once been engaged to the young man and had given him up on account of his deplorable conduct. This young person had formerly enjoyed a good reputation and one wonders how she could have let herself be led astray into such company. In spite of the recriminations and the opposition of the dying man's mother, the Abbé Merval committed the grave fault of marrying this Pierre Loriot to this Rosette Billois. He did this at the last moment, when the civil marriage had not been celebrated and he even had the audacity to inscribe this illegally performed religious marriage in the parish register where the mother of the deceased discovered it. The latter wished to lodge an immediate protest but a neighbour, Michel Monilier, threatened to denounce her for having sold the hide and the flesh of the chamois her son had killed just before he died. This was an illegal transaction as the animal had been shot during the forbidden season. However, in the end, she decided to inform the Mayor of this breach of trust on the part of the parish priest and the Commune is taking legal proceedings. I also attach to this letter a copy of the complaint which will be handed to the police in the near future.

"It was on her return from this ill-fated expedition that Rosette Billois, with unheard-of indiscretion, returned to the presbytery and there produced her child. Her cries might well have aroused the entire neighbourhood. The midwife, who passes for a witch and distributes poisons and love philtres, hastened there to deliver her. Everyone invaded the presbytery—a place which ought to be respected and worthy of respect. It must be the first time it has served as a maternity clinic. The child has been called Pierre in order that it shall be publicly associated with its alleged father. Marie Bernex insisted on being the godmother and Michel Manilier was brought in to be godfather because he is at daggers drawn with the dead man's mother. Mlle d'Aimery even played the organ at the baptism which ought to have been celebrated in strict privacy and without any display.

"With the money he has extracted from the Hebrew merchants, the Curé has now bought a large house on the outskirts of Saint-Paul where it adjoins Arvillard. Here he has set up a hostel for unmarried mothers, as if to encourage the loose morals of the parish. Marie Bernex directs it and Rosette Billois does the cooking and the washing. Her own offspring was the first inmate but others quickly followed; some have even come from neighbouring parishes. The Abbé Merval, after having done his own housework for a time (thus depriving himself of what little remained of his dignity), has now engaged the services of one of Rosette's sisters. No doubt she will lose no time in following in her elder sister's footsteps. This girl is noticeably pretty and well-developed, which gives the presbytery a very dubious atmosphere. All the more dubious since our Curé has been rather too frequently observed in the company of showy-looking women such as this Béatrice d'Aimery, this Arlette Jasmin, this opera singer and even this Marie Bernex who easily deceives people by an innocent face and affectations of piety.

"Finally, I must inform Your Lordship of the last use to which our Curé has put the sums he has managed to extort in Paris for paintings which no one in this part of the world considers as having the faintest merit: he has bought himself a most luxurious motor bicycle so that he can get as far away from his parish as possible. Did he not even rejoice in my presence over the fact that our villagers so seldom came to church because this left him more free time? The moment his Mass (at which I myself and Mlle Perpétue make up the whole congregation) is over, one sees him depart at full speed, making a noise which sets all the dogs in the village barking. He wears a little béret, black glasses, a kind of mask over his face and a cassock split in half for ease in the saddle. He looks like some kind of monster from another planet rather than a priest. He returns late in the evening: often not till nightfall. No one knows where he has been but I am told that often his face is very red and his eyes bloodshot as if he had developed a taste for the bottle along with his taste for the society of that repulsive renegade, the Abbé Chavord.

"No doubt what encourages him in these evil ways is the fact that, on the Fourteenth of July last, he received the Legion of Honour. This decoration was bestowed on him by a Minister openly opposed to religious instruction. He has thus been officially pointed out as a supporter of lay instruction by our worst enemies.

"Would it not be desirable therefore, Monseigneur, to put a stop to such abuses by recalling such an eccentric—not to use a harsher and more accurate term—priest? Might the parish of Saint-Paul-en-Forêt, which has been so sorely tried, be given an incumbent more submissive to the laws of our Holy Mother Church and more edifying to his flock?

"I enclose herewith my usual cheque for the precious work of furthering priestly vocations. This year I have doubled the amount and I humbly beseech you to use it for the benefit of some seminarist who is neither a painter nor a musician, whose piety is calm and of sterling quality, and who has already given proof of a solid character and respect for established custom.

"I beg Your Lordship to pardon me for this overlong statement whose truth can be attested by the entire parish. I also beg you to accept the homage of my religious devotion and of my respectful attachment.

"Véronique Trabichon (*née* Porasset)."

When she had finished, the widow Trabichon took off her glasses which she only used for reading and writing and looked at her audience of one. She was watching and waiting for some sign of approval and the continued silence began to disquiet her.

"Well, Perpétue, what do you think of it?"

"Isn't there any more of it, Madame?"

"Haven't I said everything that ought to be said?"

"It was so splendid, I could have gone on listening till tomorrow."

"One must never repeat oneself, my dear. A Bishop is very quick in the uptake."

"One could go on for ever about it, Madame."

"Don't you think that after this . . . this report, our Curé can start packing his bags?"

"Oh, Madame, won't it be a pleasure to see the last of him? I'll go back to the presbytery that very same day."

"Are you going to leave *me*, Perpétue? I took you in when you were thrown out in the street."

"Yes . . . but only while I was waiting for a new Curé to come."

"Well, you'll have to wait till he's appointed. I hope this time they'll choose carefully. We don't want any more scholars or painters. There! I've sealed up my letter and I'm going to take it down to the post-office myself and register it. Tomorrow everyone in Saint-Paul will know from the postman that I've written to the Bishop."

Yes, everyone would know. Everyone, that is, except the Abbé Calixte Merval.

XIII

THE TAX-PAYER

THE OFFICES OF the Registrar and the Tax-Collector were almost next-door to each other on the second floor of the town hall of Bellerive. This was a vast rectangular building overlooking the beautiful blue lake, half-hidden by great trees which gave considerable shade in summer. On this particular September morning, M. Briare, the head of the registry office who was nearing the age of retirement, saw the young Controller of Taxes entering his office. M. Grimard had recently been promoted to this delicate and important function and was still palpitating with pleasure. Although M. Briare had no particular affection for the new-comer, he received him with an affable politeness not always common among civil servants.

"How well you look! Anyone can see you've been on holiday."

"That's not my only reason for looking well."

"What's the other, then."

"*Teneo lupum auribus.*"

"Now you're talking Latin."

"Indeed I am. I've got a defaulting tax-payer by the ears."

"What sort of tax-payer?"

"The kind that are cleverest at dodging our investigations. The sort that pretend to be poor and get people to make wills in their favour. In other words . . . a priest. A village Curé."

"Oh, those poor devils usually leave nothing but debts behind them."

"Well, this one's earning quite staggering sums."

"Really? How's he done it? Certainly not by saying Masses."

"By selling pictures."

"Whose pictures?"

"His own."

"A painter! What a very odd thing. There used to be an Abbé Guétal at Grenoble who used to paint mountain lakes. But he didn't make much out of them."

"Mine makes a fortune out of his."

"Are you certain? And what's the name of this unknown artist?"

"He's not unknown any more. He's famous. He was even decorated on the Fourteenth of July. Actually decorated . . . think of that! You haven't been decorated after thirty or forty years of loyal service in the Ministry. The Government doesn't protect its officials. It's completely given over to the intrigues of society people and journalists."

"His name, my dear sir?"

"The Abbé Merval, Curé of Saint-Paul-en-Forêt."

"Quite true. There was an article in the *Fine Arts Review* . . . I subscribe to it . . . on his exhibition at a gallery in the Rue de Sèze. He has considerable talent . . . or rather a kind of genius. He puts on his colours with a trowel or a knife and you mustn't stand too near his pictures. If you do, they just look a confused mass. He's after effects of light on empty landscape . . . mainly mountain landscapes where there's no trace of man."

"Ah . . . so you're interested in painting, then?"

"In painting and in literature. One needs a hobby as Ingres needed his violin when one's job is nothing but figures."

"Figures are all I need to satisfy *me*."

"You're lucky. I've never found them enough to occupy my whole mind."

"That's why I feel intense joy when I can catch a taxpayer *flagrante delicto* in a fraud or making a false return."

"You're not going to hound down this Curé?"

"I can hardly deny myself such a pleasure."

"But what crime has he committed? Suppose he has made some money out of his exhibition, he needn't declare it till next year's income-tax returns. You won't have the right to put the pressure on him till then."

"I certainly don't want to wait all that time."

"But you've no weapon against him till then."

"When one wants a weapon, one can always find one."

"Well, what have you found? I should be interested to know. You're very ingenious, Monsieur Grimard. You're dangerous."

"Consider the case, my dear Registrar, and you'll agree with me when you've heard it. How can you admit that a painter can get together a hundred pictures, suddenly exhibit them and become famous overnight? No art gallery would have given an unknown painter a show. Art critics and picture-dealers . . . particularly the dealers . . . don't grope in the dark. They spy out the ground beforehand. They're not going to risk everything all at one go . . . public derision or a total failure. No, no, they know what they're up to, all right. Any artist they've decided to push . . . to turn him into a big success and a big seller . . . must have given proof of his talent. He's already found people who admire his work. He's created the right sort of atmosphere round his name. This Abbé Merval is a cunning chap who's playing at sudden fame and all that while all along he's been carefully paving the way from his obscure corner."

"What are you driving at?"

"Simply this. He hasn't made any income-tax return this year. Now last year he must have made . . . I don't say anything like what he's made out of his exhibition . . . but something quite considerable. So I catch him red-handed defaulting under false pretences."

"It's only a supposition, Monsieur Grimard. My *Review* said that the Abbé Merval was discovered by Francisque Beauvais, the well-known painter of animals, flowers and women."

"The discovery was a put-up job between them. You don't mean you're still taken in by that sort of cock-and-bull story?"

"I assure you you're risking making a grave mistake. Much better wait for the next returns. It would be much wiser . . . and possibly much cleverer."

"How, cleverer?"

"It's obvious. Then you'll be sure of your ground. It will be easy to find out exactly what the pictures sold for and then you can come down on him."

"No, no. I'm all for immediate intervention. Anyway it's too late. I've already sent off my demand note. It asks for explanations of the absence of any declaration made on his last year's income."

"Leave this poor Curé in peace. Don't hound him down to no purpose."

"To no purpose?"

"It really looks as if he never did sell a picture before."

"In any case, as you said, I'll upset him. It does a tax-payer good to spend some sleepless nights thinking up excuses."

"But you're diabolical!"

"I'm an income-tax inspector."

M. Briare gave the excited tax-collector a long and ironical look. Then he smiled and asked him to listen for a few moments.

"I was an income-tax inspector once. I even had a reputation for being outrageously severe . . . the reputation you so justly deserve yourself. One day . . . it was many years ago, but I've never forgotten this incident which was to alter my professional judgment completely, and, I trust, forever . . . a little woman in deep mourning came into my office. She was bothered by her long back veil, though she'd thrown it back so as to see her way better. She shrunk in, terrified, clasping a paper in her gloved hand as if she were terrified of losing it. Actually, I didn't see her at first.

I was perched on a stool in front of my black desk which was piled with files . . . I'd just come back from holiday, as you have. I was busy writing and I called out irritably 'Come in' to those faint, hesitant knocks on my door. I was deep in some urgent work and didn't deign to raise my eyes.—'Are you the gentleman in charge of registrations?' the woman asked.—'Obviously. Who else would you expect in the Registrar's Office?' My manner was far from agreeable and I doubt whether yours is any more so when *you* receive visitors. 'I've come,' went on the terrified little voice, 'to make my declaration of death-duties.'—'What was the date of the decease?'—'It will be six months tomorrow since my poor father died.'—'Certainly taken your time about it, haven't you? Hand it over.'

"This time I had a good look at the lady and I felt triumphantly superior to this sheep which was offering me its fleece for me to shear in the name of the law and to the profit of the State. But she could not bring herself to let go of the paper which she had drawn up, as she confided to me at last, with a little country solicitor.

" 'Hand it over,' I ordered. 'You've arrived on the very last day before it's due: I must make my calculations at once so as to assess the exact amount you have to pay. We have no time to lose. You have the money on you?' I realised that she was summoning up all her strength for the colour came into her pale cheeks as she murmured: 'There's something I must tell you, Monsieur.' Obviously she was hiding something; some fraud she expected me to be sympathetic about. Didn't she know I was ruthless? A tax assessor, as you say, and therefore inaccessible to any arguments but legal ones. Incapable, in fact, of being interested in anything but calculating-machines and the rights of the State, anything outside those innumerable laws that pile up one on top of the other. Goodness knows it's hard enough to find one's way through the tangle, these gentlemen in Paris are so illiterate when it comes to wording their regulations."

"That's going rather far, isn't it?" put in M. Grimard, who had a proper respect for the State legislation. "It's obvious that you'll soon be retiring. All the same, there is the question of a decoration to be considered."

"My dear sir," went on M. Briare, with the same ironic smile, "I haven't waited to arrive at my present age before showing my independence. That dates back to the story I'm telling you and which was enough to make me see the light. I propose to continue my story. The tax-payer makes his declaration and pays up. That's all there is to it . . . isn't that so?"

"Obviously."

"The little lady at last brought herself to hand over her declaration. I hastily read the name and the amount. That name had once been almost illustrious. It was the name of a naturalist who had had his hour of fame and then been forgotten—Vincent Vorey. He left behind an excellent treatise on Alpine flora. I'll lend it you, if you like taking trips to the mountains."

"Thank you, but I'm not interested in flowers."

"I thought as much. Well, she was the only daughter of this botanist who had been a widower for many years. His only daughter and his only heir. The declaration concerned a few stocks and shares and a house in the country with a little land attached to it. The calculation was simple. I was just about to work it out when the little woman made a plaintive sound and stopped me. I thought she was going to confess that she had omitted something and I threatened her with a fine.—'You're sure you haven't forgotten anything?'—'No, no,' Mlle Vorey protested, 'on the contrary . . .'—'On the contrary! Come now, Mademoiselle or Madame, when it's a question of money, even the most honest person has never put down too much!'—'Please, please listen, sir.'—'I am listening. I am devoting my entire attention to listening. But what can you add to this paper?' —'There have been considerable expenses. I've had to run into debt.'—'Expenses of what nature?'—'The expenses of his last illness.'—'Oh, that's quite simple, Mademoiselle. The law does not recognise those. A new law, that of the 27th of April, authorises an allowance for such expenses and for the cost of the funeral up to two thousand francs.'—'Only two thousand francs?'—'Yes, two thousand francs. But wait. The decease occurred on April 25th. Your father died too soon for you to benefit under this new law. Two days too soon. Most unfortunate.' And I ended sharply: 'You have no right to any allowance at all.' Still, she didn't go away and she didn't take the amount due for the death duties out of her bag. What was she waiting for?—'It's an exceptional case,' she sighed, humbly and wretchedly.—'There *are* no exceptional cases.' How tiresome and obstinate women can be. I've no doubt you've observed this more than once yourself, Monsieur Grimard."

"Oh! I'm an expert at getting rid of them."

"She insisted on taking a bundle of papers out of an envelope and handing them to me. 'These are the bills I've had to pay. My father died of cancer. He underwent three operations and two applications of radium. I went to all possible lengths to save him. He was a wonderful man. He never complained. We were so happy together. He was my whole life. I was like his mother.' Believe me or not, Monsieur Grimard, a flood of human feeling suddenly poured into my office. It flowed over my desk, drowned my *dossiers*, swept away all the official figures and tables. But a registry official can no more let himself be carried away by that sort of thing than a tax inspector. He's got to go against the tide."

"He most certainly has."

"I pronounced the usual regrets. The law was the law and so on. But she kept insisting: 'Look at the bills. They're all here. Here's the doctor's. It's very modest—he was a friend of the family. Here's the surgeon's. It's very high. He was risking his reputation and he couldn't save my father. The radium treatment; that was terribly expensive. And the time he spent in the Clinic. And the day and night nurses when, after months and months, I hadn't the strength left to look after him myself. And the chemists' bills: they kept on trying new remedies. I'd had a little legacy from my godfather. It all went on my father's illness. So I thought they might take that into account.'—'Certainly not, Mademoiselle. Nothing is taken into account. Unless the deceased duly acknowledged the debt in the proper form.'—'Oh, I couldn't have asked him *that*,' protested Mlle Vorey. 'Right up to the end, he was able to believe they'd cure him.'—'You have declared these shares. All he had to do was to transfer them to you. That is done every day and not necessarily as a reward for filial devotion.'—'I would have sold my last stick of furniture rather than let him suspect.' The conversation had now become quite pointless. Nevertheless, I took the envelope and added up the figures. They did indeed amount to a small fortune. She saw my surprise and it gave her a gleam of hope.—'Can't I make out a case on them?'—'Certainly not. I'm only looking at them out of pure curiosity. You must pay the full amount here and now.' Obviously, the bills came to far more than the value of the shares. But the law doesn't take operations into account."

"Certainly it doesn't," agreed the other who was getting impatient. He thought M. Briare's story had already gone on far too long and wondered what the point was supposed to be. This boring recollection of a tiresome interview did not raise any interesting point of law.

But suddenly the story-teller went off on an entirely different tack.

"Monsieur Grimard, what do you think of a law which, in this age of surgery, takes no account of the fact that some one might have to have an operation? A law which ignores the necessity of radium treatment, clinics, the progress in medical science? Or which seems to suppose that all these things are to be had for nothing and that doctors are pure philanthropists?"

"I imagine our legislators are concerned simply and solely with seeing that taxes get paid."

"Precisely. But what do *you* think?"

"Aren't we there to execute the law?"

"Execute! You've used the right word. Well, I was going to dismiss the lady in black after having made her pay up the full death duties on the shares and the property. But she collapsed into a chair and burst into tears. Now, I ask you, is a civil service office the proper place for crying in?"

"Certainly not."

"When I called her to order, her face was so appallingly wretched that, suddenly, another scene flashed into my mind. Whom had I ever seen cry like that? It was long, long ago. My father had just died and a creditor came to our house asking for the immediate settlement of a bill. My mother had no money. Her only fortune was her two sons who were still little boys and she would have to work in order to bring them up. My elder brother had been killed in the war and it was a long time before I was able to help her. Her sad face came before my eyes and somehow became mixed up with that of my visitor. A tax-official should have no private life. He only knows human beings as abstract figures."

"Those are axioms which should be inscribed on our office walls, Monsieur Briare."

"Yes, shouldn't they? That is why I got up at that moment and said to Mlle Vorey: 'Sit down over there and write this down from my dictation. Take this statement. Nothing need be changed in the part dealing with the shares; that agrees with the official valuation. I know the village where your house and garden and smallholding are situated. The land is of very poor quality . . .' She was about to object but I went on: 'I assure you this is so. I know the house is very old.'—'Oh, not so very old.'—'I repeat, very old. It needs very considerable repairs.'—'I don't think so.'—'It needs very considerable repairs and the farm buildings need even more repairing. The figures you have brought me need to be modified in the light of these facts. There, now, sign your declaration. You owe . . .' The sum I arrived at for her was just about the same as the little country solicitor's. He'd worked out his, of course, on the basis that they'd allow for the considerable expenses of the terrible illness. The little lady paid the sum, bowed to me humbly and went away with her calm restored. When she'd gone, I rubbed my hands. Believe it or not, Monsieur Grimard, I've seldom had such professional pleasure in my job."

"Frankly, you astound me, Monsieur Briare. I consider this a very serious blot on your reputation. It is my painful duty to say that it lowers my opinion of you."

"I expected you'd reproach me."

"I don't permit myself to reproach you. You belong to Assessment and I belong to Direct Contributions. You're concerned with legacies and I'm concerned with income and tax returns. Therefore it's not my place to judge you. Nevertheless, you have lost the Treasury . . . that is to say, the State . . . a possibly considerable sum. You belong to a sentimental generation which has disappeared today. None of my colleagues would have been guilty of such weakness."

"Are you quite sure of that? I knew your predecessor, M. Vignemale. He was like you, like myself in my youth, burning with zeal for getting in the maximum taxes. When he was appointed to revise the revenues from house property, he wanted to double or treble the tax on the château of La Recluse; a great barrack of a place, very fine architecturally, at one end of the valley of Biolle. He went to the place in person. There he found an old lady in a dilapidated room—one of those octogenarians who have that indefinable distinction which seems to come from generations of ancestors and which compels one's respect. But *your* generation no longer respects anything. She had ruined herself paying her son's gambling debts. That son had died gallantly in the war after a dissipated life and she had taken his wife—she was a workman's daughter—into her home. But the wife had gone mad and spent her days in a locked room, waiting for the dead man to come back. M. Vignemale went all over the château which was three-quarters abandoned. Some rooms were half-furnished and here and there some isolated piece of beautiful old stuff seemed to indicate that the rest had gone off to the antique dealers. Tapestries in rags, traces of damp everywhere, showed the ravages of time and the total neglect of any repairs. M. Vignemale advised the owner to sell the old building and install herself in a small, comfortable, properly heated flat in the town. She replied that they had lived in it for six hundred years and that, in any case, no one would want it. She would gladly leave it to some religious community but any such would refuse the legacy because of the death-duties. And M. Vignemale retired, promising her his help to make it easier for her to leave it to the nuns although his whole object in coming had been to increase the taxable value of the château. Such is the story of your predecessor. And such will be yours too, Monsieur Grimard . . . when you've seen . . . *really* seen . . . with your own eyes."

"But it's not our business to see, my dear Inspector. We are merely servants of the State with no initiative of our own."

"Slaves?"

"No. Executors."

"Executioners?"

"No . . . the instruments of its will."

"All right. Instruments. And will you define the State for me?"

"The sovereign authority."

"An entity—an abstraction—a word devoid of meaning. Once, the State was a man . . . a king. Today, as yesterday, the State is only a ghost. It incarnates itself in one or in several men. At the top of the tree, in a Republic, are there or are there not responsible men? Are they to make themselves hated henceforward by too rigid application of laws which they too often impose in a spirit of equality which does not take time and place, people and circumstances sufficiently into account? Or should they arouse the goodwill of those they govern so that the governed will gain confidence in them and for that reason will work better and be more inclined to pay proportionately higher taxes? The rôle of the State has never been to hinder work but, on the contrary, to encourage it so that the State can take its legitimate share—but no more than its legitimate share. Our interpretation is far less rigid than you appear to believe, Monsieur Grimard. It can be modified in individual cases. It ought not to be pushed to the point of provoking universal discontent, particularly in the matter of taxes where we are bound, in any case, to practise injustice."

"How can you possibly accuse us of that?"

"Very logically. You've only to think. The great international fortunes slip out of our net. The big companies treat us as man to man and force us into all sorts of compromises. The Unions are our masters when it comes to the workers and other employees they represent. You can't get any taxes out of speculators or prostitutes or even waiters. A host of licit and illicit earnings slip through our fingers. We only strike at what we can see and we only attack honest profits and honourable professions. So it's only the finest part of the population that's delivered over to us. Can't we show a little consideration for it? Our very formulas are almost rude and reek of suspicion, if not actual accusation. But we're not forbidden to apply them with a little human feeling."

"We're wasting time, Monsieur Briare. May I remind you, we're snowed under with work?"

"You're certainly wasting time on tormenting a poor

priest about a declaration he's in no position to furnish."

"I'm tormenting him on purpose so that, even if he hasn't cheated over his last income-tax return, he'll be worrying all the time about his next one."

"And by so doing, you upset his work. The result of your machinations will simply be that the State gets less in the end. He'll paint fewer pictures and it will be entirely your fault. This time it's I who am catching you *flagrante delicto.* As you see, the rôle of a civil servant isn't as simple as all that. There is the State, but there are also human beings. And laws are made for human beings. Believe me, my dear Inspector, sooner or later, you'll find *your* road to Damascus!"

"My road to Damascus?"

"Yes. The crossroads where St. Paul was struck blind by the vision of Christ."

"I'm afraid I don't know that story."

"There are a great many other things you don't know. But life will teach them you. Since you need more light, *your* road to Damascus will be the apparition of human reality in that office of yours among all the *dossiers.*"

"Human reality? There's no place for that."

"On the contrary. It will rise up stark naked out of one of those green files of yours in the form of my botanist's daughter or of M. Vignemale's octogenarian."

"Stark naked? No, thanks!"

"Go to Saint-Paul-en-Forêt and see your Curé. Who knows? Perhaps he'll offer you a picture and you'll take back your inopportune declaration form."

"My dear Assessor, I don't accept sweeteners. Nor even free lessons on behaviour. I shall continue my enquiries into this priest's undeclared sales."

On this, M. Grimard retired, with his head in the air and his whole bearing expressing the utmost official indignation. As soon as he found himself alone, M. Briare began to laugh.

XIV

THE CONDEMNATION

THE ABBÉ CALIXTE MERVAL was summoned to the Bishop's palace in Bellerive by a registered letter. It was a typed official letter, brief and categorical, signed by the Bishop's secretary. But the Vicar-General, M. de Servières, had written in his own hand in the margin: *Come and see me before the audience.*

What could this summons mean? Although he was completely ignorant of Mme Trabichon's denunciation, he nevertheless had a guilty conscience. He had already received a demand to present himself before the Mayor of Saint-Paul to give an explanation concerning the religious marriage of Pierre Loriot and Rosette Billois which had not been preceded by a civil marriage. Also, he had been worrying about an income-tax return paper demanding the details of the sales of his pictures. Never in his life had he filled up an income-tax form for the simple reason that he had no income. Not noticing that the form dealt with the preceding year, when his painting was unknown, and not with the current year, he had been anxiously compiling lists of figures, haunted by the dread of omitting one. Instead of pursuing light up in the mountains, he had had to shut himself up in his room. As the Assessor in the Tax Department, who was a sensible man, had foreseen, this had upset his work as an artist and he had been unable to paint. He answered the summons to Bellerive at once, in considerable fear both of the legal and fiscal authorities.

The Bishop's private secretary who received him at the palace saw his discomfited face and chanced to ask him a few questions. The Abbé Merval produced his income-tax form.

"Oh Father, don't make any reply to this. Go and see Canon Rondeau—he's a specialist in these matters. You're early for your appointment. I'll take you over to the Canon's office."

Canon Rondeau was indeed a specialist. He was in charge of the diocesan administration and his competence was formidable. He was dreaded in all the local government offices for he was an expert at playing their own game and had an amazing aptitude for obtaining delays and making affairs drag on for years till they were finally abandoned or forgotten. He promptly seized on the Tax Inspector's claim, sniffed it with his long, sensitive nose, read it first at arm's length and then close to and finally burst into a laugh.

"Aha! I've got M. Grimard this time! *Teneo lupum auribus.*"

How could he know that he was using the same Latin quotation as his adversary?

"My dear Father, just leave this paper to me. I'll answer him myself. He goes beyond anything in his outrageous presumption. You didn't sell any pictures last year?"

"Not one. I gave two or three to some charity bazaars where they weren't in the least appreciated."

"By what right does this fellow ask for your accounts? But once bit, twice shy. Next year, don't you make any declaration without having consulted me. We'll work it out together. Your picture dealers must have a marvellous arrangement among themselves to rig their prices and we'll follow their lead. The income-tax people shan't hamstring you next year either. Set your mind at rest, my dear Curé, you've nothing to fear. I'll take the whole thing off your hands."

He rejoiced in this occasion for an easy victory which would pave the way to a more difficult battle which he would win as well. In the constant war he waged against the State's annexations in order to preserve property in mortmain—gifts made to the clergy and to religious orders and legacies—he found M. Briare human and accommodating in the matter of estate duties. But he did not content himself with being a renowned tactician; he believed himself to be playing, in the material order, a part analogous to that of a Bossuet defending the liberties of the Gallican church.

The Abbé Merval left him, considerably comforted. There remained only the unfortunate affair of the marriage *in extremis* for which he was unable to feel the least remorse.

"His Reverence the Vicar-General is waiting for you in his study."

What a delightful prospect! After six months of separation he was going to see his old friend and well-wisher who had saved him from the episcopal thunderbolts and obtained for him the cure of Saint-Paul where the indifference of his parishioners left him complete freedom to paint. Once again he saw that pale, lean, spiritual face through which the soul seemed to shine like the flame of a sanctuary lamp through alabaster. But why did it look so serious, almost solemn? Was he going to announce some bad news, even some catastrophe?

"What's the matter, my dear Camille?" he asked anxiously.

"My poor Calixte, things look very bad for you. That's why I asked you to come and see me before you went in to His Lordship. I'll come with you, if he'll allow it, to try and temper the storm."

"Good heavens, whatever have I done? Is it this religious marriage?"

"Oh, that could be easily defended."

"My income-tax form?"

"That doesn't figure in your *dossier*."

"I handed it over to Canon Rondeau."

"Then it's in good hands. No, it's nothing to do with that."

"What is it to do with, then?"

"Here, you'd better read your accusation."

The Vicar-General handed him Mme Trabichon's letter. With those eyes accustomed to pursue the light, the Curé of Saint-Paul slowly followed, paragraph by paragraph, this accusation which set out, one after the other, all the events of his ministry. When he had finished reading, his tall body sagged over and he buried his face in his hands.

"Well?" asked his friend.

He raised himself up again but his eyes were full of tears. He had discovered human malice, the depths of which he had never suspected. He had lost that virginity of trust which shines in the eyes of children and dies at the first lie.

"I didn't know," he muttered.

"What didn't you know?"

"That the world was perverse."

"But is all this true or false?"

"It's all true and it's all false."

For some moments M. de Servières remained silent before his shattered friend. His keen intuition, guided by his knowledge of souls, had pierced to the heart of this drama of conscience as a scientist divines the cause of the phenomenon by a brilliant hypothesis. He went up to him and took both his hands.

"I understand," he said simply. "But we've got to explain it to others; to our ecclesiastical chief, His Lordship himself. You must answer all my questions with absolute frankness. I'll begin at the beginning. Before you left for Saint-Paul, didn't I give you some advice on the very subject of this Mme Trabichon who's well known to the Bishop and immensely occupied with good works? Why didn't you take any notice of it?"

"She turned against me from the very first day."

"Who dealt with all the material business of the church and the sacristy? The sacristan?"

"Oh no, Camille. He's never out of the tavern."

"Ah! But were the sacristy and the church always kept clean and the vestments and so on in good condition?"

"Oh yes, perfectly."

"By whom, then? Obviously by this Mme Trabichon. Didn't you ever thank her?"

"Never."

"The Marthas oughtn't to be neglected, Calixte. They need to be encouraged. One oughtn't to humiliate them."

"Yes. I admit I was wrong there."

"If my memory's accurate, there was an old servant in the presbytery who had worked for both of your predecessors. Perpétue was her name. Why did you dismiss her?"

"It was she who threw her apron in my face the moment I arrived at the presbytery."

"Why did she do that?"

"Because of my menagerie, as she called my birds and animals."

"You ought to have smoothed her down with a few tactful remarks. Who did you take on in her place?"

"A poor girl whom I met. Her father had turned her out and she was expecting a baby. She was thinking of throwing herself into the Dranse."

"You saved her—that was as it should be. But why keep her? You ought to have found her a job somewhere else. The Church, in her wisdom, recommends priests not to engage a housekeeper who is not of the canonical age. Is it true that this girl gave birth to her child in your house—actually in the presbytery?"

"It's true, but there was nowhere else for her to have it. I'd just married her to her seducer who was dying. A marriage *in extremis* without a civil one. On the way back, she was taken in labour. How could I not take her in? She was accompanied by a holy young girl, Marie Bernex, who had given up her place to her."

"What place?"

"This girl was the fiancée of this Pierre Loriot who was

dying. When she discovered that he had seduced Rosette Billois, my housekeeper, and that she was going to have a baby, she broke off her engagement so that he could marry Rosette."

"And he refused?"

"He accepted and then he ran away. At the last moment he was reconciled to God and to Rosette. The two of them made their marriage vow in my presence."

"Good. But a presbytery isn't a natal clinic. After the birth of this child, what did you do with the mother?"

"With the money I got for my pictures, I bought a big house at the far end of the village to make a nursery and a kindergarten. Her child was the first inmate. Then other ones came along."

"Is it true that you reserved this place of yours entirely for unmarried mothers?"

"I didn't refuse anyone. But wretched girls without husbands came from Saint-Paul and the neighbouring parishes to have their babies there."

"Good. Now for another ground of complaint. Didn't I warn you, Calixte, of the presence of a suspended priest about whom you would have to be careful in your position as Curé?"

"The Abbé Chavord?"

"Yes, the Abbé Chavord to whom Monseigneur had been very indulgent for a long time because this Hercules had saved his carriage from going over a precipice. He had become a hopeless drunkard. Is it true that you opened your church to him and that you installed him in the presbytery, gave him board and lodging and took your meals with him?"

"In appearance, perhaps, but only in appearance. I surprised him outside the church, waiting for the door to open so that he could see the tabernacle. Wasn't that already a desire to be rehabilitated, an act of faith? I took him by the arm and made him come in. He stayed down at the far end and we prayed together. Then I took him to the statue of Our Lady which is the most beautiful thing in Saint-Paul. He had lunch at the presbytery. He came back there one day. I advised him to go to the Trappist monastery. He went there but he didn't stay."

"Why not?"

"Because they offered him very poor home-made wine after heavy manual work."

The Vicar-General could not suppress a smile and even added:

"Those Trappists showed a want of tact. They ought to have disintoxicated him more slowly. But why give him hospitality? Why compromise yourself by having him in the presbytery?"

"He had absolutely no resources. I found him a job . . . my garden, which was practically waste land. Now it produces potatoes, vegetables and even flowers."

"Couldn't you have given him a job without keeping him in your house?"

"He'd only have got drunk with the money. But he never slept in the presbytery; he kept his room in the village. I pay the rent of it. And I never took a meal with him."

"Where did he eat?"

"In the presbytery. In a separate room where I waited on him."

"Where you waited on him? Good. What about the wine?"

"I rationed it out to him."

"And he accepted that?"

"Sometimes he was angry; sometimes he laughed. But he submitted. He listens to me. He'll be cured. He'll come back."

"Good. And this organ you bought which is apparently bigger than your church?"

"It's true that I bought it. Once again, with this unexpected money from my pictures. Didn't you tell me one day, Camille, that music paves the way to prayer? Music is already a prayer . . . like art . . . like poetry. At least that's how I see them. When they heard the splendid summons of this organ, my parishioners, who hadn't come to services for years, began to come back to church."

"And where did you find this providential instrument? In Paris?"

"No, locally. A certain M. Belarmont who built a chalet by the little lake in Saint-Paul and who is a brilliant musician had installed it in his house. By getting it on the spot, I saved the cost of transport."

"Is it true that this M. Belarmont lived in open sin with an actress?"

"Quite true. But he had turned her out after surprising her with the painter who was doing her portrait."

"An organ calls for an organist. I didn't know you were an organist."

"I'm learning, but I'm not at all expert yet. So I did indeed engage an organist."

"A woman?"

"Mlle Béatrice d'Aimery who plays remarkably well."

"Do you recognise her in this photograph which is attached to Mme Trabichon's report?"

"Where she's leaning her head on my shoulder? Is it possible that wherever you go, even in the woods, there are spies watching you with their cameras? Why didn't this one photograph us at the moment when I drew away? What is the point of snapshots when you don't know what led up to something? That day, Mlle Béatrice d'Aimery was in despair. She had had a liaison which I knew about. Her lover who was married had just become a widower and was to have made her his wife. Then he deserted her because he had no money and and was looking for a rich woman. I comforted her with music. Was I wrong in doing that?"

"No, Calixte. But priests have to observe the most extreme prudence with regard to women. There are rather too many *young* women in your orbit: too much talk of

Rosette and Marie Bernex and Béatrice d'Aimery. Possibly, quite unconsciously, you're a little too concerned with physical beauty. Our model, St. Francis of Sales, said that he never looked at anyone so as to notice whether they were handsome or ugly and when people weren't there he couldn't have said what their faces were like."

"I can't remember them either, Camille. I swear I can't. Except for Marie Bernex."

"Why this exception?"

"Because her face is like yours."

"Now I'm completely reassured," said the Vicar-General with a smile.

"Yes. Marie Bernex's face bears God's reflection in it. One's only to look at her to feel at peace . . . beyond earthly evils . . . purified."

"It's a rare privilege."

"I confess that it is a joy to me to look at her. Beauty is something willed by God."

"Yes. It's like the earthly paradise, in which there were serpents. Now I'll go on with my questions. What about these organ recitals which attracted tourists from a distance?"

"There was only one of them and that came about by chance. M. Belarmont came back from travelling in Holland and invited some of his friends from Paris to stay in the chalet. Among them was Mlle Marguerite Aubier of the Opera. He brought them to see me at the presbytery and asked my permission to let them hear the organ. I could hardly refuse, could I, seeing that it was entirely due to him that I had this wonderful instrument? He himself played Bach's G Minor Fantasia and Fugue and Mlle Béatrice d'Aimery played César Franck's 'Prayer'."

"And the singer?"

"She sang 'O Star of Eve' from *Tannhäuser*, the 'Spring Song' from the *Valkyrie* and Elsa's 'Invocation' from *Lohengrin*."

"And 'L'Après-midi d'un Faune'?"

"That's a symphonic poem by Claude Debussy. M. Belarmont played it."

"Not quite suitable in a church, perhaps."

"No one made any objection."

"Good. Now for the motor bicycle."

"Surely that's not forbidden."

"It's even recommended, if it's to be used for parish duties. Was it so in this case?"

"No, Camille, it wasn't. I used it to take me beyond the parish. It took me up to the passes in the Alps, as far as the roads went. From there I could get right up to the glaciers. You see, I stop at the fourth day of Creation."

"The day of the light . . . of the sun. And of the earth and the stars."

"Exactly. Before the coming of animals . . . and men."

"Why not honour God in all his creatures?"

"Because I don't know how to. Because I daren't. Whereas I feel at home in unpeopled landscapes. I've made a wonderful new discovery about the whiteness of snow White is the queen of all colours. But I'm only at the first tentative stage."

"And you return from these expeditions at nightfall, red in the face and staggering on your feet?"

"Because I'm drunk with light."

Was the long interrogation over? Had the accused made a good defence? The Vicar-General fell silent, as if he really had come to the end of his questions. He thought for a few moments and then declared:

"That's how the truth can be distorted. Was it done in good faith or bad faith?"

"Probably in good faith," admitted the Abbé Merval, forgiving his enemy.

"It's a mixture of the two, as these calumnies and denunciations so often are. People see the possibility of scandal; they get alarmed; they begin to believe the scandal actually exists. Facts can so easily be distorted or, at least, be interpreted in two different ways; one favourable, one reprehensible. That, my dear Calixte, is why the Church never ceases to recommend, indeed to command, prudence in the case of her priests. She is as strict with them as she is with monks and nuns. They must take into account those weak souls, with narrow outlooks, who are so easily alarmed. They must be on guard against the forces of fear, scrupulosity, envy, hatred, unreasonableness. There are always people ready to spy out one's least failing and ignore one's good motives and exaggerate anything that looks at all dubious or even merely unconventional."

"In that case, all priests would be quite paralysed."

"No. They retain their freedom but it must be subjected to that sane, upright judgment which should result from their theological studies . . . especially from studying St. Thomas Aquinas. Too often, this judgment is falsified by excessive self-confidence and by a certain undisciplined pride. Saints can defy human laws. Saints can behave in a way the world thinks extravagant. Sometimes saints can even be, momentarily, targets for scandal. But sooner or later it will be seen that their apparent excesses were necessary for the reform of their time when people needed to be jolted out of their tepidity or indifference."

Then the Vicar-General added, with that smile which could be so enchantingly gracious:

"You're not a saint yet, Calixte, but sometimes you behave as if you were one. That's the cause of all the trouble."

"Oh!" protested the Curé of Saint-Paul. "I'm only a poor devil of a painter who's strayed in among the clergy."

M. de Servières corrected him, not without a certain gravity:

"*Tu es sacerdos in æternum.*"

What was the importance of art compared with that of the sacraments?

But, of his own accord, he tempered the severity of his lesson:

"God can confer genius on a priest for His own glory. Fra Angelico served the Lord in his cell in Florence as much as his brother Dominicans served Him. Do you want to resemble him by substituting your painting for your ministry?"

"How could I possible presume to do that, Camille, when I'm terrified of faces and bodies?"

"Haven't success and the Legion of Honour and so on puffed you up with vanity and pride?"

"I don't think so."

"Mme Trabichon's report isn't the only thing in your *dossier*. I also find in it a bundle of papers and press-cuttings dealing with the triumph of your exhibition in Paris. Some malicious paragraphs are even underlined in red ink at the behest of the celebrated poetess, Mme de Bréhat-Latour. They deal with your meeting with an actress named Arlette Jasmin whom you are supposed to have known before at Saint-Paul."

"I knew her back."

"Her back?"

"Yes. M. Belarmont had surprised her on the knees of her painter and she was running away. All I ever saw of her was her backview on that occasion."

"Ah! Then what's the meaning of this photograph where she seems to be making you a very deep bow?"

"She came up to me at the gallery during the show. Is there always a photographer lurking in ambush waiting to compromise one? I didn't speak to her for more than two minutes."

"That's easily disposed of, then. The most serious document is a long interview you seem to have given to a well-known art critic, M. Charles Dagnaux. It appeared in an important review and an English magazine reprinted it. In it, you give the Impressionists short shrift and, in discussing the Flemish Primitives, you give vent to some audacious opinions. Opinions on feminine beauty . . . which is, after all, God's creation . . . and on the suppression of the human body in painting where you suggest it would be better replaced simply by clothing. Don't forget, God made the body and it has a right to be respected, like the soul. Finally, you appear to have blamed the Lord for not being content on the fourth day of Creation instead of using the fifth and sixth to create the animals, then man and, finally, woman."

"Woman!" burst out the Abbé Merval. "He might well have abstained from that to avoid producing ones like Mme Trabichon. But there *are* the Marie Bernexes."

"Let's forget the Trabichons and the Bernexes. Did you really make these propositions or anything resembling them?"

"That's exactly it. I did say something of the kind and it's been distorted in just the same way. Distortion isn't confined to pious people because here is a great writer using it too. I merely told this Charles Dagnaux, who had written the preface to the catalogue of my exhibition, that I would never dare paint faces, even though God might be present in them, and, still less, whole bodies. He was advising me to paint human beings when we were looking at the Flemish Primitives whom I admired. And I quoted that tapestry at Beaune where the angel escorting the Virgin into the Temple has his transparent robe rippled by the step of the staircase as it would be by water because he hasn't a body. That's all."

"That's all," repeated the Vicar-General. "Just as I thought. Just what I guessed."

At last he was in possession of all the elements of the case. The accused had answered all the questions. The case was clear enough now but how could he state it himself to His Lordship? He was perfectly frank with his friend and old schoolfellow of seminary days. Would he not be intimidated in the presence of the Bishop of Bellerive whose icy reception froze one's words on one's lips? He would falter at every step and get bogged down in muddled explanations. He would have no idea how to justify his leniency towards the suspended priest, the unmarried mothers and the illicit love-affairs. The mere fact of his having allowed Rosette to give birth to her baby in the presbytery would be enough to secure his condemnation. It would be far better if, by some means, he could avoid confronting the Bishop.

But was it not already too late? The Bishop's secretary was knocking at the door.

"His Lordship is ready to see the Curé of Saint-Paul-en-Forêt."

The poor Abbé stood up and was about to follow the messenger. He looked so contrite and humiliated that his expression almost invited the condemnation he so evidently expected. M. de Servières caught him by the arm and stopped him.

"Wait for me here. I'll appear in your place."

The audience went on for a long time. The Vicar-General did not return. The Abbé Merval did not know which saint to invoke. He tried to think of one among the artists but there is none, except the Blessed Fra Angelico who has not been canonised. At last, M. de Servières reappeared, his face radiant.

"Well, Camille? Am I absolved, thanks to you?"

"Oh, you couldn't be let off. I'm bringing you your sentence."

"My sentence? Then why are you looking so pleased?"

"You'll soon know. For one thing, it depends on you and me. Monseigneur, in his mildness, and because it was charity that inspired your most reprehensible acts, is removing you from your parish, but only for a month. During that month, you're to think things over. That month would allow you to make a retreat, either at Solesmes or at the Abbey of Hautecombe on the banks of Lake Bourget. But, during that month, you're to give up painting and to examine your conscience as to whether, in the future, you will find it possible to devote yourself to your parish without giving up your art."

"Giving up my art!" repeated the Abbé Merval, completely crushed.

"But I've got a better idea and I'm authorised to suggest it to you. Have you enough money left over from the sale of your pictures to do some travelling?"

"I've never been good at accounts but, yes, I think so."

"Instead of shutting you up in a monastery, we're sending you to Italy."

"To Italy?"

"Wait. With rigid restrictions. You're not to stop at Florence, in spite of the convent of San Marco. You're not to go as far as Rome. You're to resist those temptations. We're imposing three pilgrimages on you. Siena, for St. Catherine. Foligno, for St. Angela. Assisi, for St. Francis. When you come back, you may return to your parish, but after having told us the result of your meditations."

"But that's a reward, not a penance."

"That's something you'll only know when you've returned."

"I don't understand that reservation."

"You'll understand it later on."

"What about my parish while I'm away?"

"Ah, so you've remembered it at last! I'll take charge of it myself."

"You, Camille?"

"The doctor's ordered me fresh air. Monseigneur wanted to send me on holiday in the mountains. I've asked him for this favour . . . I'm going to replace you."

"What luck for Saint-Paul! But such a post isn't worthy of you."

"Calixte, no religious duty is unworthy of a priest."

"Forgive me. But whenever I think of you, I see you in

a purple cassock and, later on, with a purple cloak, a long train and a red biretta on your head."

"No, no, Calixte. It's quite enough for me to be a priest. The priesthood is only given us for the glory of God. Remember the words of Angela of Foligno whose tomb you're going to visit. 'Angels and men fell because they thought they possessed something. Neither angel nor man possesses anything. Everything belongs to God and God only.' "

Then, having made the Curé of Saint-Paul promise to begin his journey as soon as possible, he added:

"Pray for me in Siena and Foligno and Assisi. Pray for your parishioners who are going to be mine during this coming month. Before you leave, before this separation, shall we say a prayer together?"

The two priests knelt down and recited the rosary.

"Now, goodbye and happy journey, my dear pilgrim," said the Vicar-General, embracing his friend. "One day, you'll know where you're going."

Why this last enigmatical remark? Where was he going? The Abbé Merval could hardly not be aware of that. He was going to Italy, the land of art and beauty.

XV

THE PILGRIM

THE CAMPAGNA STRETCHES to the foot of Siena which looks down on it from the height on which it stands. The plain flows like a river between Siena's two hills, one crowned by the flower-like cathedral with its slender black and white marble campanile and the other by the church of St. Dominic. The latter is like a citadel of brick or one of those sturdy Flemish churches in Ghent or Bruges, by no means equal in splendour to St. Cecilia's in Albi. Certain towns have a perfection of their own because they are in harmony with their own setting and their own past. Siena is one of them.

The typical Italian charm does not preclude strength. It is true that it owes much to the picturesque; to decorative art; to something delightful in the atmosphere and in the faces one sees. But nature itself and men of other days, such as those who endured the famous Spanish siege, have added their own robustness to it. Siena, standing on its two hills, is a maze of streets which climb like scaling-ladders to assault it. These streets, or rather lanes, have no pavements and through the widest of them meanders a tram with no rails. It sways and tacks this way and that at the end of its cable, like a boat, obliging people to walk in file for safety.

The happiest of all pilgrims to Siena had several times just missed being the victim of an accident for he paid no attention to these hazards. The drivers had even cursed him copiously with an astonishing fluency of scalding epithets. He laughed aloud all by himself in the October sunshine which was warm and radiant by day but did not prevent the mornings and evenings from being cool. As a priest, he was certainly interested in the churches, notably in the Metropolitan which was built on the site of an ancient temple of Minerva. But he spent more time in Santa Maria della Scala, now transformed into a hospital, on account of the frescoes by Bartoli and Vechietta in the vaulted ward. They were lit by a great glass bay-window which looked out over the Campagna. Yet his eyes kept straying from Vechietta's slightly faded fresco to the young man in the clean white bed who lay beneath it. His chiselled face, in which the magnificent eyes seemed enormous, was burning with fever. Was it dangerous for works of art to be near human wretchedness or pain? He could not choose between the two sights and therefore he combined them in his mind to make one whole with the view of the Sienese countryside so like those landscapes the primitive painters use as the background of a scene.

He pursued the Primitives almost all over the town. He was coming to prefer them to the Flemish for their manifest delight in painting; that spontaneous joy he felt himself. By chance, he discovered Nartolo di Fredi, Taddeo Gaddi, Taddeo Bartoli and Giovano de Paolo; not to mention unknown painters no less good. He discovered Beccafumi whose "Jesus in Limbo" enchanted him, though he was embarrassed by a female figure, wearing a transparent shift, whose body had nothing of the angel about it.

The Pinturicchio frescoes fascinated him by their colour, their grace and freshness; by the natural pose of the figures and the details of their dress. He was amused by this minute, ingenuous art which never omitted a nail or a shoelace yet remained astonished and delighted by everything—by the beauty of heaven and earth and the grace of the human countenance. What a feast they offered to his eyes, these Sienese painters; each so different in his own way. Duccio di Buoninsegna excelled in painting the Jews of the Old Testament; Sano di Pietro in creating colour harmonies;

Pietro di Domenico in realistic charm. Matteo di Giovani had two characteristic types of the Virgin; one with a little round nose, the other with a grave face and long lashes. But the prince of Siena was not a primitive but the redoubtable, ambiguous pupil of Leonardo da Vinci—Sodoma. Why had Camille de Servières sent the Abbé Merval in search of St. Catherine when her painter occupied the throne of Siena?

The Abbé Calixte Merval was no better informed on the subject of St. Catherine of Siena than the average Catholic. Nevertheless he knew that she was so beautiful and so intelligent that she had been known as Euphrosyne, a name which means 'lovable' and which is that of one of the Graces. Her precocious wisdom was only equalled by her piety and her taste for mortification. She wore a hair-shirt and a spiked iron belt; slept little and then only on the bare ground. At twenty, she took the habit of the Third Order of Saint Dominic. She cared for the most abandoned, the most repulsive and the most contagious of the sick. Neither cancer nor leprosy nor the plague repelled her: on the contrary, she eagerly sought out and cherished those with the most hideous sores. But her skill as a nurse was surpassed by the extraordinary influence of her spirit and her words. So many sinners were converted by what she said that two Dominicans, sent by the Pope to Siena, spent day and night hearing their Confessions and still had more penitents than they could deal with. Her fellow-citizens, realising her astonishing power of attraction, decided to use it for their own ends. They sent her as Ambassador to conclude a peace treaty with the Florentines. Later she went to Avignon to see Pope Gregory XI in order to bring him back to Rome. When his successor Urban VI had displeased the Cardinals by his harshness to such an extent that an anti-Pope, Clement VII, was elected and fled to Avignon, it was Catherine again who attempted to bring about the reunion of Christendom. Exhausted by these religious disputes, she died at Rome when she was thirty-three, leaving a treatise on perfection, a commentary on the Annunciation and some admirable letters. This flower of the Quattrocento combined political sense with mystical fervour and reason with faith.

How did the voluptuous and dangerous Sodoma come to be so deeply devoted to this saint? Art, too, has its mysteries. His three St. Catherines show three gradations of mystical love. In the first, she is praying for the condemned man who is being beheaded and obtaining the salvation of his soul. While the other people in this crowded and amazingly intense fresco are watching the execution, the saint stands looking up to heaven, intent only on her prayer. In the second, she has just received the stigmata. Overwhelmed by pain and love, she is almost fainting. She is supported by two sisters of whom the younger holds her up with a gesture of infinite tenderness; her eyes are closed and her face is radiant in its suffering. In the third, at the right of the altar, she is about to receive Holy Communion from the hand of an angel. Above her the whole of heaven seems to have come to greet her. The angel holds out the Host and the Virgin offers her Child. The saint, almost breathless, raises both her arms. Her half-opened lips seem to be imploring: "Hasten, hasten, O my God." Her face is ecstatic and one can see that her whole being is shaken to its foundations.

Yet wonderfully as the painter has expressed the creature overwhelmed by divine love, there was a picture which moved the Abbé Merval even more profoundly. This was the "Coronation of the Virgin" in the Oratory of San Bernardino. In that he discovered the object of his latest researches and preoccupations as a painter. The Virgin is kneeling before Jesus who is crowning her with filial authority. Her face, which is that of both woman and child, is so pure, so lily-like, so perfect with its half-closed eyes, that it immediately inspires one to pray.

"Holy Mary, Mother of God . . ." the priest murmured.

But the painter added: "Oh those whites! That colour as immaculate as herself! White must be the queen of all colours. It is as dazzling as gold. But gold has not its marvellous blend of all colours, its subtlety, its luminosity."

He decided not to see any other picture in Siena. He would leave with that last vision of Our Lady.

Perugia is on the way to Assisi so he could not avoid it. Perugia was not forbidden territory like Florence and Rome. He therefore stopped at Perugia although there was no particularly saint to be venerated there.

The weather had changed. The sun still shone but a fiendish wind was blowing; a wind worse than the Mistral at Avignon. The Abbé Merval began by losing his hat. He ran after it and finally recaptured it, covered with dust. After that, he kept it in his hand, like a beggar. Perugia is an inhospitable town. It stands even higher than Siena, perched on a hill, and commands a panoramic view as far as the Tiber and the Appenines. He took refuge, first in the Collegio dei Cambio where Perugino's frescoes are; then in the Town Hall which houses the Pinacotheca on its third floor. The antique personages who represented the cardinal and theological virtues in the Cambio left him as cold as he found himself in the presence of the Bishop. But he was interested in studying the various Virgins of Perugino in the picture gallery. They all resembled each other and all sought and attained an ideal of feminine grace. But he found them all insipid and lacking in conviction.

"He never met Marie Bernex," thought the Abbé Merval. "These faces belong to earth, not to heaven."

But what pleasure he found in the Pinacotheca quite apart from that of escaping from the wind and not having to keep running after his hat! There were the Gentile da Fabrianos, the Bonfiglis with their rose-crowned angels, and the brilliantly coloured Firenze di Lorenzos. There were also the Piero della Francescas. A self-appointed companion who spoke French explained to him that della Francesca was the master of Signorelli who was himself the master of Michelangelo. Nevertheless he preferred to avoid these considerations, however erudite, so he shook off his obliging guide and continued his tour alone. He was in ecstasy before a certain Giovanni Boccati who represents Our Lady surrounded by angelic musicians. There were two of these pictures but the one he preferred showed groups of child angels playing cymbals with great concentration or picking flowers while the Virgin, with joined hands, adores the Son balanced on her knees. A little robin is gently pecking the Child's mouth and the Virgin is a girl of fifteen, joyous and pure. It was as if the angels' music had passed into the forms and colours; everything on the canvas seemed to be singing.

The priest thought: "She is like the Virgin of Saint-Paul-en-Forêt whose Child is putting a finger in its mouth. Here the robin takes the place of the finger. Prettier, but not so true."

The next day the wind fell and he was able to stand quietly in front of the famous doors of the Oratory of Saint Bernardino. A Florentine sculptor, Agostino d'Antonio de Duccio has adorned it like an altar with marble and coloured stones. He too had put angels everywhere; surrounding Christ, before Our Lady and all about the saint. He had launched them boldly into the air, flying horizontally with the light folds of their robes streaming. This doorway is unique in the world; it is ineffably gay, glowing and light-hearted. The Abbé Merval smiled and even laughed with sheer pleasure. This example of sacred art was like a flight of birds in the sun. Ought not art to be all happiness and joy?

The pilgrim left the charms of Perugia to make his pilgrimage to Assisi. But suddenly, the cold weather arrived and the sun was veiled. From the station he could see the church of St. Francis up on the height; the church of Giotto's frescoes. Should he not wait till the sun returned to climb up to it? He contented himself for the moment with visiting Saint Mary of the Angels at the foot of the hill. But this vast monument in the form of a Latin cross, with its heavy dome, was only a disillusion to him, in spite of Perugino's "Crucifixion" and della Robbia's terracotta altar. Should he visit Foligno before Assisi? Then Assisi would be the crowning point of his travels in Umbria. After Assisi, his holiday over—or rather his penance accomplished—he would return to Saint-Paul-en-Forêt. "One day you'll know where you're going," Camille de Servières had told him when he had left him to go and take his place in his parish. How could he not know where he was going? He was going to look for perfection in art. He was going to receive from the lesson of the Masters a new enthusiasm for his eternal pursuit of light shining on landscapes unchanged since the advent of man.

Foligno can be seen without the sun. Foligno offers no interest beyond a little old church, Santa Maria infra Portas, built in the fourth or fifth century over a temple of Diana. It has a venerable portico and inside are a Byzantine fresco and the remains of some columns. As the Abbé Merval's eyes grew accustomed to the darkness, he could see some mutilated frescoes which showed some traces of the Umbrian Masters. There was even a Perugino angel with fresh cheeks and enormous eyes.

Why then had Camille de Servières insisted on including Foligno in his friend's itinerary? Why had he added this third unnecessary panel to the perfect diptych of Siena and Assisi? He had done so on account of a tomb. The pilgrim, therefore, went and knelt at the tomb of the Blessed Angela. It was a mausoleum in the Franciscan church which had been somewhat embellished. The saint herself would not have wished this; this saint who had been only an obscure little bourgeoise, so like other bourgeoises that there seemed nothing about her to attract the attention of the Catholic world. After losing her husband and her children, she had distributed her goods to the poor and become a Franciscan Tertiary. She had spent the rest of her life under this Rule in obedience, humility, work and prayer. Nevertheless, people round her began to feel that there was something extraordinary about this woman. They believed that she received special graces, that perhaps she had direct intercourse with God, Incarnate in the person of Christ. She dictated to Brother Arnold those dialogues or meditations which have come down through the centuries and retain their power of exaltation.

The priest therefore went and sat in front of the tomb, as naturally as if he were at home. He had brought with him the *Ways of Redemption* in which the saint reveals her conversations with Jesus. She is plunged in despair because she believes that she can never atone for her sins; He shows her that He has borne them all on Calvary and that, therefore, man must never despair. He goes over them one by one; they have been expiated by the very variety of the torments he endured for men . . . for all men. As He proceeds to give details and comparisons, the tone becomes more pathetic and moving:

". . . For the sins of thy shoulders mine carried the Cross. For the sins of thy hands and thy arms, my hands were pierced with great nails and were fastened to the Cross. And for the sins of thy heart, that heart from which sprang hatred and envy, from that heart which was filled with guilty desire and sinful love, my heart was transfixed with a lance and from this wound blood and water flowed to redeem thee from the domination of anger and sorrow. For the sins of thy feet, for their idle dancing and delicate movements, my feet too were fastened to the Cross by nails. And the blood ran from their wounds while all the blood of my body bedewed them.

"For all the sins of thy body, for the sensuality of thy days and nights, I was struck on the Cross. The sweat of blood covered me from head to foot; the hard wood of the

Cross bruised and flayed me; I suffered fearful pains; I sighed, I cried out and I died groaning. In expiation of thy proud ornaments, I hung quite naked on the Cross. Naked as I came forth from the Virgin's womb, exposed to the cold and the wind, to the stares of men and women; raised up on a high Cross so that I might be better seen, better jeered at and insulted . . ."

Through the saint does He not speak to all men and women guilty of so many overt and secret sins which He assumed on the road to Calvary? And He ends His conversation with her by adding: "In truth, thou wilt find no sin, no malady of thy soul for which I have not been chastised and which therefore I cannot heal. It is on account of the terrible sufferings which your poor souls would have had to endure in Hell that I myself desired to live only in suffering. Therefore, my daughter, do not afflict thyself but only follow Me in suffering, humiliation and poverty . . ."

All the divine poem of the Incarnation and the Redemption is in this supreme consolation of Christ to the desolate soul. No artist has been able to express it so poignantly in his painting. Nevertheless the Abbé Merval thought he could remember a Flemish picture . . . was it by Jerome Bosch whose " Christ before Pilate " had impressed him in the exhibition at the Orangerie because of the concentrated expression of the Christ resolved not to defend Himself? This picture represented Jesus on the way to Calvary, falling, but ready to rise up again, under the weight of the sins of the world, symbolised by a hideous crowd in which every face bore the mark of a vice. But, here, the simple words of the little bourgeoise of Foligno carried the tragic vision even further. What was this obscure woman compared with a Catherine of Siena who had been publicly deputed to negotiate with Florence; who had gone to Avignon to bring back the Pope to Rome, wearing herself out to preserve Christendom from schism? Yet all the same, she equalled her in love. Was it possible for human creatures to return love for love to

God Incarnate? Must they not always be immeasurably surpassed? Surpassed they must be, yet these women had made the attempt. They had offered themselves in sacrifice; they had thrown themselves into the fiery furnace. Sodoma had painted the ecstasy of the one. The other, with no beauty and no grace, yet transfigured nevertheless, lay there in this little Oratory, ignored by art. The priest murmured:

"Saint Angela, pray for me. Saint Angela of Foligno, guide me. For I still do not know which way to go . . ."

The sun had returned but, during the night, snow had fallen on Mount Subasio. Its twelve hundred metres seemed paltry compared to the chain of the Alps which dominated Saint-Paul-en-Forêt. That fresh, immaculate snow, that white which is the queen of colours was what the Abbé Merval dreamed of capturing one day.

Assisi summoned him at last. He responded to the call of Francis the saint and Giotto the painter. There had been nothing extraordinary in the appearance of either of these men. This is how Thomas of Celano describes the saint: "A round head; a small forehead; black eyes with no malice in them; straight eyebrows; a straight, fine nose; small outstanding ears; a gentle yet vehement voice; white, even teeth; thin lips; sparse beard; slender neck; short arms; long fingers and nails; thin legs; small feet; hardly any flesh."

Hardly any flesh . . . perhaps that was the characteristic to remember; the soul had devoured it all. In the *Little Flowers*, his disciple Masseo does not hide from his master his surprise at seeing him so much sought after: "Why does everyone run after you? Why does everyone seem to want to see you and hear you and obey you? You are not handsome; you are neither very learned nor very intelligent; you are not of noble birth. Why then does everyone run after you?" Was it to test his humility that he spoke to him in such terms? Was it out of humility that the saint answered that he had been chosen by God to accomplish this marvellous work of His precisely because he was the simplest of creatures so that the nobility and strength and beauty and learning of the world might be confounded?

And Giotto? Petrarch assures us that he was ugly. He was a good Florentine bourgeois, the father of eight children, with solid property in land which he administered shrewdly. He liked to laugh and had a reputation for witty epigrams. He had a keen sense of the ridiculous; he was realistic and practical; he judged men shrewdly and was no more than moderately religious. He was, in fact, the painter who might have been least expected to be capable of expressing the peculiar Franciscan quality. How did they come to choose him after Cimabue for the frescoes of the two superimposed churches which rise above the tomb of St. Francis? These twenty-eight frescoes are not all by his own hand. But he kept a watchful eye on the ones he entrusted to his pupils. No doubt he was chosen for his humanity and for his taste for truth in art. But that humanity was widened and, as it were, divinised by its contact with this other, spiritual reality.

The Abbé Merval had been content with these few preliminary ideas before he made his pilgrimage to the paintings. When he entered the church, the high altar was lit up by the sun and the four most beautiful of Giotto's frescoes which adorn the four intersecting vaults could be seen in all their glory. They cannot always be seen thus for they depend on the way the light falls. The pilgrim thought there could be no lovelier sight in the world than these frescoes. Three of them represent St. Francis's three vows of poverty, chastity and obedience and the fourth shows his apotheosis.

He contemplated them one by one, came back to the first again and decided that poverty, symbolised by a woman dressed in rags, but white and fair, was his favourite. Once again he found that white which so passionately preoccupied him; Sodoma's white and Giotto's white both shone as brilliantly as gold. This woman with the thin, transparent face did not hold out her hand. It was Jesus who took it and placed it in that of Francis. The saint's face is grave and concentrated as he looks at his bride. He accepts her not only with love but with deliberate will. The wings of the angels who surround them are of a thousand delicate shades of rose and green. The whole makes up a harmony in which white and gold predominate. And the angle of the vault contributes to the devout impression of this work, seeming to draw it upwards and spiritualise it till it becomes a living prayer.

"When art is understood like that," the Abbé Merval asked himself, "doesn't it border on sanctity? Isn't it capable of bringing about conversions?"

Obedience is an elderly woman, dressed in a coarse serge robe. She has the same gravity, the same interior fire as the old women of the Flemish painters. She makes one realise that obedience is something arduous and painful. And she, too, is surrounded by angels.

Chastity is a beautiful woman in a tower. The Abbé wondered whether this tower were necessary. If the tower meant the impossibility of occasions of sin what became of victory over temptation? He himself hardly suffered from such temptations. Nevertheless it seemed that he had been accused of being attracted by beautiful faces. Who had thus accused him? Mme Trabichon whose features he could not even remember and whom he would be incapable of recognising. Beauty comes from God; it is a symbol of God and should not be despised. He called up the face of Marie Bernex which Perugino had not seen when he painted his Virgins. An angel in pink, leaning over a monk who was being baptised, must symbolise purity, so ignorant did he seem of all passions and desires. Passion and desire were words which had no meaning for Calixte Merval. He had been protected by that exclusive love of art which had entirely possessed him.

Lastly, there was the Apotheosis. The saint is enthroned among the blessed and escorted by all the angels. One of these angels, dressed in white—that marvellous white of Giotto—is walking forward as if he wanted to invite the visitor to follow him. "Oh beautiful angel, take me by the hand and lead me to God by the way of beauty!"

To crown that first, unique day in Assisi, the sun set in a cloudless sky over the gentle yet austere Umbrian landscape.

The Abbé Merval stayed more than a week on the hill of St. Francis. A Franciscan who had made friends with him, because he had surprised him in ecstasy before the Giotto frescoes, had given him the following advice: "We must pray very hard because the world is sad and God does not want us to be sad . . ."

God does not want us to be sad. How right this Franciscan was! Happily, art has been given to man to drive away sadness; that is its sacred mission.

The priest had no temptation to be sad as he walked about Assisi and its surrounding country. The whole neighbourhood was so beautiful that a smile of pleasure was constantly on his lips. Once he heard a peasant who was ploughing talking to his oxen—great white oxen with lyre-shaped horns. He spoke to them so gently that spontaneously and without realising it, he was obeying St. Francis's precepts to be kind even to animals.

"*Piano*, *pianissimo*," chanted the ploughman.

It was an exquisite morning, like that sunset over Umbria which had closed the wonderful day when he had first seen the frescoes of Giotto.

But the Abbé Merval went further that day. He climbed up the side of Mount Subasio to the Carceri. The path was flowery and easy. Why, with his quick mountaineer's step, did he successively overtake a monk on a donkey, a monk on a mule, and a monk in a cart drawn by two cows—cows that should not have been used for such a purpose? What would Francis of Assisi think of his successors? The saint could be vehement at times. Nevertheless the priest was not at all inclined to be scandalised. He was too happy and too gay not to feel indulgent.

"The poor wretches have probably got rheumatism or corns," he thought and he felt a certain satisfaction in the superiority of his own legs.

He arrived at a three-cornered forest which makes a sombre patch on the bare, rough mountain. Some of those green oaks are very old and were possibly there in the time of St. Francis. An urchin, stationed there to extract money from the few pilgrims who venture so far, showed him the tree where the birds to whom Francis preached had nested. Up there are the two caves of which one served as the saint's oratory and the other as his bedroom. He used to seek out this bleak solitude far from the fertile plain where life was too easy.

Even that did not satisfy him. He discovered a still more austere retreat on Mount Alverno. It was there that, on the 14th September, 1224, he saw, in his sleep, a crucified angel bearing down on him from the sky. When he awoke, he found on his body the stigmata corresponding to the wounds which the nails and the lance had made in the body of Christ. Immediately he gave thanks to God for the great honour accorded to him by this likeness to the Passion.

But why this avidity for suffering; this running-ahead of destiny which only too often will bring us pain enough? Why delight in this painful intercession as Catherine of Siena and Angela of Foligno had also done? The Abbé Merval had brought St. Francis's immortal "Canticle of the Sun" to reread on the way. Was it not a hymn of joy? As if to accompany its music, he heard the bells of the Franciscan basilica ringing in the distance. To praise the Lord, Francis invokes the sun, the moon and stars, the wind and clouds;

our sister water "who is very useful and humble and chaste"; the fire, "which is beautiful and joyous and strong and robust"; and lastly the Earth, "who sustains and supports us and produces the various fruits and the trees and the coloured flowers." But he even invokes death; "our sister, bodily death, whom no living being can escape." Bodily death, for the other can do no ill to those who have accomplished the divine Will. It is a hymn of happiness and peace. Why then this appetite for suffering?

Giotto has not dared to paint Francis crucified in the place left warm by Christ. He felt that the saint of the stigmata was beyond the scope of his painting; even beyond the scope of art. But what was the Abbé Merval doing in Assisi; why had he made this journey to Italy if not to further his artistic vocation and to strengthen his impulse towards the light? Had he not already found it in the gold and white light of these frescoes—in the gold and white light on the mountains?

He had tasted the joy of living in the pure air of beauty and freedom. Why should he desire anything else? Had he not read in one chapter of the *Little Flowers*, that one day Brother James of Fallerone had asked Brother Masseo why he did not change his manner of rejoicing and sing a new song. Masseo had answered gaily: "Because anyone who finds his happiness in one thing should only sing about that one thing." He himself had no desire to venture into some other unknown, or almost unknown, way.

Before leaving Assisi—for this delightful month of holidays was drawing to an end—he decided, one day, to climb up from the Carceri to Subasio. He wanted to find some fresh snow, the first snow of the season, and take it in his hands to try and surprise the secret of its colour. His only privation during his Italian pilgrimage had been this temporary ban on painting. The Umbrian landscape had been almost irresistible. It would take him nearly three hours for the climb from the Carceri and almost as much for the return to Assisi. He would take some food with him and spend the entire day in the solitude and peace of the mountain.

But the snow had already gone from the slopes. The thin grass which grew on the summit was still powdered with a light covering of it which melted in the sun. Mingling with the gold of the sunshine, it might have served for Our Lady's cloak. What little he scraped up soon turned to water in his hands, hardly chilling them. As he climbed down again, the whiteness vanished. Where would he find it again, that changing, elusive whiteness which attracted and discouraged him by its indefinable tint, almost impossible to catch under the play of light?

The day had come for him to leave Assisi. He would go straight back to his village; avoiding, for the second time, the temptation of Florence and of the Convent of San Marco. He would resist the appeal of Fra Angelico, as he had promised. But why had his comrade and friend, Camille de Servières, who was so intelligent and understanding, banned this visit to the Florentine master? Was it because Fra Angelico had been authorised by his superiors to paint in complete freedom without the rigid strictness of the Franciscan Rule? Had he been afraid that, on his return, the Curé of Saint-Paul would try to avoid his parish duties? Why had he said to him, when they parted: "One day you'll know where you're going"? He had spoken as if he did not know or as if he were at a crossroads and had to choose one road or the other.

The pilgrims were now pouring into the basilica of Assisi. At his Mass, which he had celebrated very early so as to get to the station in time, he had given Communion to a large crowd of the faithful. All these open mouths waited hungrily for the heavenly Bread. All these faces lit up as the Host approached. There were beautiful and ugly ones; old and young; healthy and sick; but, to the celebrant, they were only so many mouths waiting to receive God. God refused Himself to no-one. He did not even choose anyone; they chose Him. His infinite, inexhaustible love surpassed all other loves.

And yet, here and there through the centuries, among that vast flock of human beings, there had been men and women who, ravished by so much love, had attempted to return it. To return it, they had had to be willing to resemble Christ and therefore to share His torments, His sorrows and His redeeming death. They had asked to be made like Him. Catherine of Siena, Angela of Foligno, Francis of Assisi, had all asked for this and Jesus had heard them. Why this desire, why this appeal, why this ardour—almost this delight—in suffering? Because it was the only means of collaborating with Christ in the redemption of souls sunk in sin; souls corrupted and contaminated and in danger of being lost forever. Because Christ had accepted the Communion of Saints; the interchange of merits and sins; the compensation of the saint for the sinner. Perhaps the world only endured through the mystery of those unknown prayers.

But had there not been a class of men specially designated for this work of perpetual redemption? *Tu es sacerdos in aeternum*, the Abbé de Servières had reminded the Abbé Merval. Once his Mass was over, the latter could not bring himself to leave the basilica without kneeling down to say a final prayer. Little by little, he became so immersed and so lost in his own thoughts that he forgot the Giotto frescoes which surrounded him. The priest, in receiving Ordination, becomes the auxiliary of the living God; His representative on earth, answerable to Him for his parish. Certainly the artist prays in his own way by praising the Lord in His works; in the wonders of the earth; in the Light which he has separated from darkness; in the human face, in all that human splendour which crowned creation on the sixth day. Cannot the good and the beautiful be reconciled? Does each jealously exact its own ministry? Is there an order of precedence between them and must one choose which one will serve?

One day you'll know where you're going. Why had he had to wait till this very last day to understand the meaning of this warning which had been given with no solemnity but in a friendly, almost familiar tone? Only the day before, he had been quite certain where he was going; now he no longer knew. Must he make a renunciation? But what must he renounce? This art which was his joy—which had become as necessary to him as breathing? The question could be put in no other way. He had been consecrated forever. He belonged to God before belonging to men; before belonging even to himself. But there are many ways of serving God. God is indulgent; God is good; God accepts this diversity of service. How could He exact such a renunciation? So many artists, especially among the Primitives, had served Him in their own way. There was Giotto, an excellent family man, though somewhat grasping; there was Perugino who was said to be miserly and debauched; there was even Sodoma whose morals were equivocal—they had all served him in their own manner. But they were all free; they were not under orders. Had not God Himself given him at birth that love of the light which he had never ceased to pursue? Why should He withdraw it now; now that his talent was recognised and could exert a happy influence in art? Did not this joy of human creation, the humble reflection of his own, redound to God's glory? No, no, He was not asking for such a sacrifice. But the joy which had overflowed all during his pilgrimage, particularly during those days in Umbria, had given place to a new disquiet which accompanied him during the whole of his return journey.

XVI

LUX PERPETUA

THE ABBÉ CALIXTE MERVAL did not stop at Bellerive on the way back. He was in haste to return to his parish and to take up his old work and his old life again. The work and way of life of a priest or of a painter? Both, since one did not preclude the other. Médor, the black dog, welcomed him with joyful barks. He jumped up on him, leaving dusty paw-marks on the cassock already much the worse for his travels. The white cat purred with pleasure on the window-sill where she had installed herself. The caged birds sang as if they would burst their throats: were they welcoming his return or that of the morning sun? And the parrot repeated his incessant "It's the will of God." Suddenly the door opened and the housekeeper appeared. But it was Perpétue, who had returned to the presbytery, who received him with an affable though slightly anxious smile.

"Ah, Your Reverence! We didn't expect you so soon."

Who could have recalled her? No doubt his friend Camille de Servières had brought her back during his brief suspension. But, in re-engaging the old maid, he had inspired her with a new spirit. She had lost that dictatorial temper which his two predecessors had encouraged; one by his laziness, the other by forgetfulness or contempt of material details. She said deferentially:

"His Reverence the Vicar-General will be pleased. I'll go and tell him you're here."

The presbytery was undoubtedly far better kept than in the days of Rosette whose broom swept far from clean. The change was obvious at first glance. He only hoped

Perpétue would not be followed by Mme Trabichon. The mere sight of that lady would spoil the joy of his home-coming although he had forgiven her and even owed her a debt of gratitude since her denunciation had been the cause of his journey to Italy. But already the Abbé de Servières was coming to meet him with a hurried step which could not diminish his natural dignity; a dignity which came from an aristocracy of mind and spirit even more than from his ancient lineage.

"Ah, my dear Calixte! You're ahead of our programme. You had the right to two more days of freedom."

"I know, Camille. And I ask you to wait till tomorrow evening."

"To wait for what?"

"For my answer. For my final, definite choice."

"But I'm not in all that hurry to submit it to His Lordship. Whatever you decide, welcome home! This is your house and I'm only your tenant just for one month."

The two priests embraced like brothers.

"Now will you tell me about your pilgrimages to the tombs of St. Catherine and St. Francis and Blessed Angela of Foligno?"

Was he only interested, then, in the devotional side of his pilgrimage? Were the Sienese Primitives and Sodoma and the doorway of San Bernardino, Perugino's Virgins and Giotto's frescoes nothing to him compared with the stigmata of Catherine and Francis and the dialogues of Angela with Christ? The pilgrim was distressed by this one-sided demand for information. He was afraid of displeasing his friend by a recital which would be such a poor answer to what he obviously wanted to know. He avoided the dilemma by taking the initiative himself:

"Oughtn't you first to bring me up to date about what's been happening in my parish while I've been away?"

"You're perfectly right. I'm delighted that it's been on your mind all this time."

The Abbé Merval hated lies as much as he hated flattery. He could not accept praise, even by implication, when he knew he did not deserve it.

"To tell you the truth," he confessed. "I forgot all about it. I gave myself up to the infinite delights of Italy."

"Only God is infinite, Calixte. And it was God who absorbed you so completely. Very well, then. While you were away, God completed your works in Saint-Paul-en-Forêt?"

"My works?"

The Curé's mind flew at once to his painting. But the Vicar-General hastened to be more precise.

"I've only reaped what you have sown. And the harvest has been rich."

"But I don't understand, Camille. I thought His Lordship had censured me for my inefficiency in the parish. Yes . . . and even for my scandals, on the report of that lady whose very name I wish to forget."

"Mme Trabichon? She'll be coming to the presbytery as soon as she knows you're back."

"I forgive her . . . I do forgive her . . . but I implore you . . . don't let me set eyes on her! My eyes are still full of the exquisite things I've seen. She would ruin all my memories."

"Camille, I don't believe you've changed in the least! At the Communion rail, do you refuse the ugly? God is the same for all of us. He is the hope of all the disinherited, the refuge of all the unhappy, the shelter of all the repentant. This woman realises the appalling thing she has done. She wants to expiate it by working herself in your unmarried mothers' home. You can't drive her away."

"Was it you who converted her?"

"No, no. I wasn't the person. It was one of your clients. A woman."

"One of my clients?"

"Yes. You've quite a number of them and they've replaced you better than I could. All I did was to encourage them and benefit by their work."

"I understand you less and less, Camille. And, listening to you, I get an impression that's . . . well . . . rather painful."

"What sort of impression?"

"Look here. I'm too simple to understand irony. Irony's a superior game, all very well for highly educated people. Don't play it with your old friend who knew you in the seminary."

"But I'm as incapable of irony as you are."

"Well then, who are these 'clients' of mine you're talking about?"

"The parishioners whom you drew to you and who have gone on obeying you from a distance. They have followed the path you marked out for them and they've ended by leading the entire parish into it. It's a miniature Golden Legend—an almost miraculous story."

"Don't talk nonsense! It's your authority and your goodness . . . and nothing else . . . which have produced this miracle. I've had nothing whatever to do with it."

"How little people know about themselves! Would you like me to give you a list of causes and effects?"

"I'm certainly curious to hear them."

"Let's begin with the most serious . . . the case of the Abbé Chavord."

"Ah, yes. What did become of that unfortunate drunkard?"

"He's working in the garden. You'll see him in a moment. He was waiting for your return to say goodbye and thank you."

"Goodbye and thank you?"

"Yes. He's going back to the Trappists. But this time for good."

"Then you've cured him of his vice?"

"I haven't . . . *you* have. When I came here and took your place, I waited on him at table, just as you did. But, when

I offered him a glass of wine on your behalf, he refused it. He said, 'No. I'm giving up drink.' And he kept his word. Monseigneur is going to pardon him . . . very soon now. As soon as he's convinced his cure is really established, the ban will be lifted and he will be reinstated. The day that you invited him into the church when he no longer dared to cross its threshold, you touched him to the heart. Everything followed from that. Sometimes a gesture is all that is needed."

"But such a feeble gesture of charity!"

"There's no question of feebleness when it comes to charity. Bossuet said that it covered sins. Now which of your other parishioners do you want to know about?"

"I'd like to know what happened to Rosette Billois who had her baby in the presbytery. I admit that did give cause for scandal."

"She lives in the last house in the village, up at the foot of the Reclus."

"But the last house in the village is Pierre Loriot's—or rather his mother's. And his mother was a tartar and denounced me to the Mayor for marrying Rosette and Pierre *in extremis* without a civil marriage."

"She withdrew her complaint. I went to the Town Hall and now the whole thing's in order."

"What! She actually withdrew her complaint?"

"Naturally. Since she's taken this girl who—thanks to you—is her son's lawful wife, under her roof. And the grandchild too."

"Is it possible? That spiteful old woman? Now that really is a miracle, if you like. And no one could have worked it but you."

"No, Calixte, it wasn't me. It was the young girl whom you asked to come to Saint-Paul and who's stayed here ever since."

"What young girl?"

"Why, have you forgotten Marie Bernex?"

"Oh! Marie Bernex with the seraphic face. I've been regretting that she didn't live in Perugino's time to inspire him for his Virgin. Not one painter nowadays knows how to paint the Virgin-Mother. Saint Sulpice inundates our country churches with atrocious statues of Our Lady of Lourdes. The human face is lost. Human beauty is lost because art has lost the taste for God. But what's become of Marie Bernex?"

"She also wants to say goodbye to you."

"Why is she going away?"

"To enter the noviceship of the Little Sisters of the Poor."

"Isn't she already a little sister of the poor here in the village?"

"She'll be able to hide her beauty in an Order and under a nuns' coif."

"But she mustn't hide it. In any case, she won't be able to hide it. That beauty is part of her extraordinary influence. It acts on people before she does. It drives out jealousy and purifies their hearts. But when did Marie Bernex meet Pierre Loriot's mother?"

"She went up to her house with the baby who's astonishingly like his father. The grandmother began by threatening her but, when she saw this likeness, she took the child in her arms and said: 'I'll keep him.'—'Only with Rosette,' Marie answered. The old woman refused and as the argument looked like being endless, Marie took back the baby. She was just going to carry him off when the grandmother changed her mind and accepted, saying: 'Very well. Bring him back with the mother.' "

"That's typical of Marie Bernex. She has that intrepid faith which breaks down barriers and which even the bad can't resist. But who'll take her place in my home?"

"Mme Trabichon."

"Mme Trabichon! What an appalling idea!"

"Don't be so prejudiced, Calixte. The Church knows how to use all people of good will. After the innovators and the pioneers, don't we need the organisers and the administrators? Mme Trabichon has never stopped looking after your church and your sacristy. Now, overcome by the example of Marie Bernex, she is putting that overflowing energy of hers into the running of your Home. The trouble was she didn't know how to use it . . . that was how she came to turn it to such shocking ends when she made that report against you. The nursery needed linen, blankets, baby-clothes and so on. She provided everything that was wanted. The unmarried mothers began to get a little above themselves as soon as they found themselves so well looked after and felt themselves secure. She inspired them with a certain salutary fear which is tightening up their morals. Marie Bernex attracted them and calmed and comforted them. Mme Trabichon inspires them with respect for order, teaches them to look after their babies and imposes some sort of physical and moral discipline."

"All right, Camille. I'll thank Mme Trabichon. But listen . . . isn't that the organ I hear? What joy to hear it again!"

"Your organ. That organ they reproached you for installing in your church has worked miracles too. At this very moment, Mlle Béatrice d'Aimery, with Marie Bernex and the choir of Saint-Paul, is rehearsing a canticle to celebrate your return. Now I've given away their secret."

"The choir of Saint-Paul? When I left, it was reduced to two or three falsettos."

"Practically all the young girls in the parish have joined it now. They can't resist the organ. The organ even brings about marriages."

"Marriages?"

"It's brought about the marriage of Mlle Béatrice d'Aimery and M. André Belarmont. Their taste for music brought them together. They've forgiven each other's respective faults."

"That's another splendid piece of news. Didn't you teach

me that music paved the way to prayer? May God in His mercy bless them! What about Béatrice's mother?"

"The Baronne d'Aimery? She wears white as her widow's mourning although the autumn's come. She's never without her butterfly-net and is immensely proud of having caught two rather rare specimens. But she comes to church now to thank God for these triumphs."

"The poor woman has found God in happiness as others have found Him in suffering. I rejoice with you about that."

"But all the news I've told you has been good. Your parish has meant an immense amount to me. During this month which has taken me away from my diocesan duties and put me in direct contact with souls, it has been a great consolation, a great inspiration. Confessions and Communions are frequent nowadays. I did not think one would find one's ministry so absorbing in a tiny mountain community like this."

Was this an allusion to the future? Was it a thorn stuck carelessly yet adroitly in the painter's flesh?

"No one's more surprised to hear it than its parish priest," smiled the Abbé Merval, shaking his head incredulously.

Privately, he considered the humility of the Vicar-General, his old friend from the seminary, in attributing the change in the parish to him, Calixte Merval, and ignoring his own part in it. Perhaps there had been no need to go as far as Siena and Foligno and Assisi to discover the virtues which make saints. But people do not know how to discover them close at hand; they have to wait for death to fix them in their truth. Life moves too fast and changes too rapidly for us to catch them on the wing.

It was time for lunch and the new housekeeper knocked on the door and announced that His reverence the Vicar-General was served.

"No, no," the latter corrected her. "His Reverence the Curé is the host."

Then he turned to the Abbé Merval:

"Will you allow me to invite someone to your table?"

"Of course. But who?"

"The Abbé Chavord."

"There's nothing I'd like better. But I shouldn't have dared."

The next day was his last day of freedom or rather the last day of the episcopal punishment. The Abbé Calixte Merval said his Mass very early while the church was still dark. When he entered, the little sanctuary lamp was the only spot of brightness in the dusky nave. He did not switch on the electric lights but was content to have only the two altar candles which he lit himself. Never before, except the first few times he had said Mass, had he performed the sacred actions more slowly and attentively. He lingered reverently over each from the Offertory, in which he avowed his sins and prepared his spirit and offered his heart, to the Elevation which called God down to earth at his summons. God was always ready to answer that summons from one invested with a priest's authority and to give Himself, at the Communion, to the creature who was permitted to distribute Him also to others.

Then, since the housekeeper was not yet up, he warmed his coffee, cut his bread and breakfasted alone in the kitchen. After that, he donned the outfit he wore for his long drives into the Alps; a pair of dungarees and a leather cap with goggles. Then he went off on his motorcycle. He had strapped his painting gear on to it the night before, along with his mountaineer's knapsack containing a little ham, two hard-boiled eggs, some bread and a water-bottle. At the top of the pass whose further slope led down into the Italian valley, he hid his bicycle in the bushes and set off with his baggage to climb the Reclus.

It was the 30th of October but, as on Subasio, above Assisi, the snow had made its premature appearance. When the snow appears on the summits of the Alps, it comes to stay. Their altitude of nine or ten thousand feet retains it all through the spring. The sun which had returned with that ineffable golden splendour of autumn attacks it in vain and only succeeds in transforming it into a sparkling carpet of diamonds. That was what the painter had climbed so far to seek. He wanted to capture that unique, unrivalled whiteness; the whiteness Giotto had found for the robe of Poverty wedding St. Francis and which Sodoma had found for the spotless mantle of the Virgin crowned by her Son. Could it not add the divine touch to the landscapes of Poussin and Claude and Corot?

All day long he waited for the favourable moment which never seemed to come. The marvellous vision for which he was waiting, as one waits for one's beloved at a tryst, eluded him. Would he have to wait three hundred years for it like the monk of Heisterbach who was looking for the secret of eternity? The sun's too brilliant reflection made the snowy mass too uniform and opposed it too crudely to a blue sky as dense and solid as itself. There was only a monotonous duet of two equal colours; hard blue and hard white. Little by little, the sun declined towards the horizon and its rays, less ardent now, fell slantingly. They were no longer hard and sharp like lances but soft and flexible as flowers. Then, little by little, these flowers took on all the hues of the most exquisite hanging gardens; gold and violet, lilac and purple, lemon and orange, indigo and rose. Every colour in the rainbow . . . but where was the white? The whiteness of the snow had vanished under this avalanche of colours as brilliant as some festive illumination. Was white, then, the absence of colour as so many painters had supposed? Was it no more than that, this white which signified purity, which symbolised the Immaculate Virgin herself? But, suddenly, the painter, standing under this rain of jewelled light which turned the mountain into a vast, variegated flower-bed, perceived something else. Far up on the highest peak of the Alps, the one which was the last to be lit up when all its train had fallen back into shadow was one untouched dome which the setting sun softened without transforming. There the snow kept its whiteness: it seemed only to be animated like alabaster through which a flame glows. It was like the faces of Marie Bernex and the Abbé de Servières in which the flesh bore the imprint of the soul.

"Ah!" cried the Abbé Merval in ecstasy. "There . . . there it is at last!"

He seized his palette-knife. In front of him the long-prepared canvas awaited him, inviting his eager hand. With the lightning speed which was his special gift, since he had always fought his fierce duels with light on the spot, he flung himself into this supreme struggle. When he had asked the dying chamois hunter whether he had not met God on the mountain, how could the unbeliever, struck down by reality like St. Paul on the road to Damascus, not have recognised that presence? It was there before him, invisible perhaps but how clearly betrayed by the splendour of visible things marked with its eternal imprint. He was keenly aware of it there on the mountain, the natural throne of the Most-High, the footstool of His omnipotence.

The artist could not wrestle fast enough against the encroaching darkness. Already it had invaded the plain and the shadows were advancing like a fantastic squadron of aeroplanes, flying wing-tip to wing-tip. The lower slopes vanished in darkness, then the upper ones; lastly, the peaks themselves were, one by one, engulfed. For a while the king of them all clung vainly to his white crown; then he, in turn, was dispossessed.

Discouraged by his defeat, Calixte Merval had not noticed that the shadows had a companion—the cold which gripped and threatened to overwhelm him. Hurriedly, he rolled up his unfinished canvas and climbed down as fast as he could. He found his motorcycle, but the wind, as he rode back, froze him almost stiff. Why did he not go straight back to the presbytery and have a hot drink in front of a blazing fire? Perpétue, now thoroughly softened and repentant, would have been only too delighted to wait on him. Why did he do something so imprudent that it might well prove fatal?

Before returning home, he wanted first to go into the church, as if his day would not be properly finished till he had done so. The church, too, had long been in darkness. He went straight to the little side-chapel where stood the stone statue of Our Lady holding the Child with its fingers in its mouth. In the faint glow from the sanctuary lamp, he could barely make out the pure face of the fifteen-year-old Virgin and the gesture of the Child Jesus which reminded him of Boccati's robin and made him smile at the recollection.

Then he did a strange thing. With the knife he used as a paint brush, he slit the canvas he had just begun to paint and all the other sketches which would have been the joy of art-lovers. Then he put all his tools, his box of paints and the pile of his mutilated canvases in front of the statue as an offering and a homage. Did he remember, at that moment, the Tumbler who had dedicated his best somersaults to Our Lady and whose forehead she had wiped with her cloak? But now that cloak was not blue. It was white and gold like that of the "Coronation" in the Oratory of St. Bernardino of Siena. It was the colour which had just been shown to him like a vision on the mountain; that white which seemed alive because the snow seemed on fire from within. And then all these colours blurred together before his eyes which had so loved the unattainable light and so passionately pursued it. He collapsed on the stone flags before the Madonna, but far enough away from his painting gear to leave no doubt, when they found him, what he had done. He had deliberately laid them there before he fell, like a vanquished soldier laying down his arms before his conqueror. Was it the intervention of Our Lady which caused him to be struck down? She had not descended from her pedestal to warm his frozen body. But had she not called him so as to put an end to his inner conflict and to accept and crown that renunciation which must have cost him so much?

She had never broken the thread which bound her to her servant, to the man who worshipped her Son through her. Sometimes that thread had stretched so fine that the wind might almost have blown it away like a strand of gossamer, but it had never snapped. And was it not now already turning to gold in the light of the setting sun?

At the very moment the priest fell forward on his face, the church was suddenly flooded with light. Was it that light which he had always invoked? By that chance which St. Francis of Sales calls the God of strange encounters, Béatrice d'Aimery and Marie Bernex had just come in to go up to the organ-loft and rehearse César Franck's *Dieu s'avance à travers les champs.* Struck by the same sudden anxiety, they asked each other:

"Didn't you hear something, Marie?"

"Yes. Something fell down. Something . . . or *someone* . . . Yes . . . there's someone there . . ."

They went round the church; then, in the little chapel, they saw their parish priest lying on the ground.

"Oh, my God!" they cried out.

Marie, who had nursed so many sick people, bent over him first. She felt the pulse which had stopped beating and listened to the silent heart.

"Quick . . . Call M. de Servières," she said to her companion, still making all the tests she knew. "Perhaps he's still alive."

But he gave no sign of life. If he had awakened from that last sleep, he would have seen those two beautiful faces bending over him like Our Lady and St. Mary Magdalene in some picture of the Descent from the Cross. One was delivered from the unrest of a guilty love: the other shone with a heavenly light.

A few minutes later, Béatrice, breathless with running, returned with the Abbé de Servières. He, in turn, bent over the dead man. But what is bodily death in the eyes of a priest? Another care preoccupied his mind. This soul had flown but in what state had it taken flight? Suddenly he gave a cry so joyous that the two weeping women were startled, almost shocked.

"Look!" he said. "Look there . . . in front of Our Lady. All his painting things . . . everything his artist's eye and heart loved most. He'd given up art . . . he'd given up beauty for the same of souls. He wanted to be a priest and only a priest. He had made his sacrifice . . . he had made it in honour of the Mother of God. And she spared him the fulfilment of it. She dried the sweat of agony on his brow as she did the poor tumbler's in the Golden Legend. God be praised!"

They did not altogether understand the drama to which he referred but they grasped the rare beauty of its *dénouement*. The three of them reverently carried the body back to the presbytery and laid it in his own room. Then they put flowers and candles round it while the terrified parrot kept screaming hoarsely: "It's the will of God." It was, indeed, the will of God.

The whole parish, in deep mourning, passed in procession beside his coffin in the church. Mme Trabichon wept because she had not personally heard him say the words of forgiveness. Pierre Loriot's mother came with Rosette who carried the child she was suckling. The baby kept its finger in its mouth, repeating the gesture of the sculptured Child. The Abbé Chavord knelt by the bier of the man who had led him to the feet of Our Lady. As the funeral took place on All Souls' Day, the chrysanthemums and the golden leaves to be put on the family graves had been collected together in the church. The nave and the aisles were strewn with flowers and branches. The colours of the chrysanthemums seemed to reproduce those of the setting sun on the mountain snow: violet and mauve, gold and purple, lemon and orange, indigo and rose. But everywhere white predominated as if by the dead man's choice. Béatrice d'Aimery played César Franck's beautiful and moving "Prayer" and Marie Bernex, in that voice as sweet as her face and pure as a woodland spring, sang a "Pie Jesu" which brought tears to everyone's eyes. And, last of all, the Abbé Camille de Servières pronounced from the pulpit the funeral oration of his friend, Calixte Merval. He took his text from the Requiem Mass itself: *Lux perpetua luceat ei* . . . .